AUTILIZATION CHRONICLES

glitch in the system

book one

TROUBLESHOOTING

Troubleshooting

BOOK ONE, GLITCH IN THE SYSTEM

Selene dePackh

Reclamation Press

Reclamation Press
E-mail: RecLaPress@gmail.com
Online: RecLaPress.com

Reclamation Press is a fiscally sponsored project of Independent Arts and Media in San Francisco, California.

Disclaimer: This is a work of fiction. Names, characters, places, and incidents are a product of the author's imagination. Locales and public names are sometimes used for atmospheric purposes. Any resemblance to actual people, living or dead, or to businesses, companies, events, institutions, or locales is completely coincidental.

Illustration & design: Selene dePackh/Asp in the Garden

Troubleshooting/ Selene dePackh — 1st ed.
ISBN: 978-1-947647-00-8
Library of Congress Control Number: 2017954621

A Reclamation Press First Edition

For my fraternal twin of another mother,
                              P. Polus,
           for always being there.

"Be careful when fighting monsters that you don't turn into one yourself. When you stare too long into the void, the void starts staring back."
Friedrich Nietzsche

I'VE ALWAYS BEEN DRAWN to crossroads and the edges of things. Maybe it's the out-of-synch way I'm wired that means I need to be up against limits and caught in webs to understand what I am. It wasn't my choice, but I found many of those perilous intersections hiding below the surface of Wyandot County. Underneath the logging-scarred blanket of birch and conifers and the snow that some years didn't melt from the deep shadows until May, that place was the crux of countless conjunctions. Things joined up there, and they pulled apart. What bound it together were the echoes of rifle fire across the hills, the hardness of cold, oiled gunmetal, and the deep red stickiness of half-dried deer blood whose warm smell faded slowly in the sharp chill. What destroyed it was another story...

I WASN'T GOING TO BE CATEGORIZED without a fight. "Autistics aren't supposed to be able to do this, either."

I drilled my gaze into Angela Dark's brother's light gray eyes just to make it clear I could parse the bulk of his irony, and I could look him in the eye just fine. He'd been testing me playfully, but I didn't intend to let him get much further with it.

Chill laughed more easily than people usually did on the receiving end of that stare. "So you're The Void that Looks Back, huh? Betcha can't tell me where that's from without digging for a web search, smart-girl."

"You lose. Nietzsche, Aphorism 146."

"Nicely done—no hesitation. I like losing sometimes."

...

That was a couple of decades ago, back when we first met in the drilled-out, logging-stripped, mining-gouged backcountry of Wyandot County, before Chill became probably the best friend I'll ever have. I was at Thunderbird Mountain, the "calming, wilderness-based life-skills development center for troubled teens" his half-sister Angela and I were compelled to attend in lieu of hardcore juvenile detention. The calming wilderness part was a joke; the vast grounds were leased to a natural gas extraction company and the inescapable pounding subsonic scream from the well-pumps would have given anyone the will to homicide.

Angela was local. I was from the decaying city on the far side of the highlands. I'd made an idiot of myself drooling over her, and I latched onto her brother when he visited to learn more about her, even though, or because, he was said to be Very Bad News. He was a Known Prostitute, half-seriously calling himself Gabrielle D'Arc at the time. He'd feminized his given name, and he said the French spelling of his family name was the correct one, from before it was butchered by ignorant record-keepers when they entered it into the local registries generations ago.

Angela called him Runt. Everyone else called him Chill, for his reputation as a wicked shot. Supposedly, whatever he got in his rifle sights was cold dead, the more challenging the target the better. He might have been in trouble a few times, but he was a subsistence hunter like most of the locals, and you didn't take away people's guns around there.

The Dark family was originally Métis from north of the Canadian border. They'd probably mixed with Haudenosaunee and Anishinaabe Nations, but the lines were blurry. None in Chill and Angela's line had the provable blood quantum to merit official membership in any tribe. A more recent carnal contribution from generic Whites of unknown origin predominated in many of them. However shadowy, their roots ran deeper under the landscape than frack drills could ever reach. They were a notorious irritant to the flesh of the Wyandot County body politic.

I was Scope Archer back then. My given name Sophia never felt like it belonged to me. The nickname was supposed to be an insult to the way I used my eyes, analyzing people as if they were things under a microscope or in a rifle sight, but it fit. I'm autistic, but I don't look down and away like a good autistic; I stare. That complicated my diagnosis for the early years of my life. I first got into fights because I looked at people like any other object in my field of vision. When I started grade school I learned fast that they didn't like that.

Kids on the autistic spectrum draw bullies like flies to roadkill, but I fought back. I was beaten up harder for it, but I could look at myself in the mirror without shame. I didn't let anyone pick on me without consequences; I didn't let the fire eat me out from the inside to the point I might be driven to wipe out half the school in a glorious bloodbath, either. If I hadn't left a few bruises of my own I could have built up enough rage in me to do something like that, and the System smelled it on me. It took a while to determine I'd get the blue jigsaw puzzle piece tattooed inside my left wrist, but one way or another I was doomed to be branded.

The blue puzzle piece tattoo tied me like not-quite-human chattel to the "charitable" money-sucking machine it represented; the entity behind it had built an empire by creating and sustaining panic about autism. An entire industry, encompassing everything from education to pharmaceuticals to incarceration, was ready to cater to those made miserable by my existence.

Angela's brother thought that was interesting enough to bother talking with a 15-year-old "special needs" dyke in baggy institutional chartreuse coveralls, there in the dusty late August heat of the inner yard, despite his being all fashioned-up vintage-industrial bishonen-style and old enough to buy liquor legally even before the vice laws were changed. He'd brought contraband for Angela past one of the guards open to appeals based on sexual favors; what Angela had to offer was worth extensive co-operation. I had nothing to share with him but my scowl; he was huge and disgusting and I'd told him that with my eyes. He was ex-military, like most senior staff there, and it amused him that I had what he called a "first lieutenant's glare." He'd joked with Chill over it, pointing me out as he pretended to pat him down. Then he'd slid his hand down the back of Chill's snug little black women's-cut t-shirt and given him a pinch on the butt inside his stud-belted jeans out of range of the security cameras.

I went up and introduced myself even though making social is usually something I'd rather scrub a free public toilet than do; stomach-twisting lust is a powerful motivator. I needed to know about Angela, and her brother had given me what felt like a friendly look. It was a bit hard to parse, but his made-up face reminded me of a husky dog deciding if it wants to roughhouse.

Chill took my stiffly-offered handshake with a raised multiple-pierced eyebrow and suggested we wander the grounds together. Angela ignored him after the handoff. Once we were out of ear-shot of the guard station, I made dubious noises about brothers bringing sisters controlled substances and whether that was actually a favor.

Chill walked beside me, scuffing his heavy boots in the gravel. His soft, unfamiliar, slightly singsong inflection was even harder for me to follow than most strangers' voices; he'd been talking for a few seconds before the first information made it to the appropriate parts of my brain.

I realized he'd turned to check whether he was getting through. His sounds and expressions were coming into focus. He'd begun rephrasing what he'd probably already said. "Better she gets safe shit from me than the poisonous crap she'd sell herself for in here. Gives her something to bargain with other than her body, even if she doesn't mind doing that with Massa Sam Champetty."

I didn't say anything.

He filled in, speaking more slowly: "She's probably moving in with him when she gets out. No accounting for taste... The Champettys think they own us from way back—our clans have loitered on each other's battlements for the last hundred years. Not what we would've liked for her, but she has her reasons for telling the whole family to shove it and leave her alone."

I still didn't say anything, and he raised the pierced eyebrow at me. "Yer not angling for a delivery for yourself, or are ya?"

I said I had enough crap in my system from chemicals that didn't belong there; I had no interest in adding more. He smiled and said I was a smart kid. I didn't feel smart just then; I was still struggling with getting the words in his voice to line up with the expressions on his face.

He pointed to my left wrist. "What's the deal on the tat? Not familiar with the specs on that one."

I told him the spiel I'd heard when I was a newly diagnosed little autistic and the doctor in charge of testing at the University Hospital had suggested my mother enter me in the tattoo program "for my own protection and my mother's peace of mind." He'd handed her a blandly slick pamphlet showing how authorities would know not to use potentially deadly force to compel me to comply with their orders if I had a panicked meltdown and couldn't process what they were demanding. They'd check my tattoo and understand I needed a quiet place to calm down when the feral rage caught fire in me. They'd look up my mental disability in their manuals and see what laws governed my treatment, since I was no longer a citizen with the usual rights and responsibilities.

They could also forcibly medicate me, administer neuro-electric treatments to my brain, perform "adaptive" or "preventative" surgical procedures or send me to "therapeutic facilities" indefinitely; tattooed, I was no longer entitled to due process. There would be no presumption of innocence. I didn't understand that part until later.

Chill chuckled sardonically. "Yep, they never put the really fine print in the client copy."

I was starting to get him synchronized; the laugh came through clean and hard-edged. As we walked toward the tall wire fence just beyond the stunted pines struggling out of cracks in the ledge rock, Chill showed me where he'd had the circle-with-a-line-across-it tattoo that the various breeds of sociopaths got. The scarred ghost of it showed after laser treatment. He'd had that done the day he turned twenty-one. He had the start of a covering tat that looked like a snake sketched over it. His arms were criss-crossed with cutting scars worse than mine, and his neckline showed more. He had enough surgical steel in his piercings to add a percentage to his meager body weight. He had a nice smile though—easy and sweet, but a bit fierce and wicked too—with big, straight white teeth and a chiseled fullness of the lips; when he showed it, the sibling resemblance made me ache for Angela.

We walked along the cinderblock boys' wing in the shade of the low shed roof, crossed a few yards of granite slope and looked through the chain-link down to the cool, tantalizing shadows of the hemlock grove at the base of the jagged 40-foot drop on the other side. When I told Chill which Nietzsche aphorism he took his "Void" joke from after he bet I couldn't, he seemed to decide I was worth more extensive conversation. He motioned me to sit, told me to pull up a rock out of sight of the lookout, pushed his fingers through his retro yaoi-manga haircut and told me not to let Angela get under my skin or I'd regret it. I said it was too late on both counts.

Angela Dark was the most hormone-addlingly gorgeous female I'd ever been within touching distance of. She knew I had it bad and she played it. I was too easy a mark. At 16 she was already taller than her brother. Where he looked like he ate once every day or two if he remembered, she wore her appetites on her thick, strong body like the firm curvature of willful craving. She was mixed race like a lot of the local kids at the center, but they were mostly dark- haired, sallow-skinned mutts who appeared to be Indigenous and Caucasian mixed-breeds like her half-brother, or me for that matter, even though my family had never talked about ancestry so I didn't know where I got the look. Angela was different; she was part Black. Chill's eyes were light hazel-gray, as if all the color had been washed out in the collision of bloodlines, but hers were green as spring sunlight through new leaves, sparkling against a complexion like warm caramel.

She loved to set things on fire. Arson was in her blood, and that's what got her incarcerated in a place she couldn't jimmy her way out of. She'd set off a tanker parked at a gas well and pissed off an extraction contractor unattached to any of the strings her family could pull.

The Great Gray Authority of the Court sent her to Thunderbird Mountain to be purged of her sins. There was irony in that, as Chill noted; the land had been looted from the Darks' butchered First Nations ancestors and then used as a prison camp for their maladjusted young, named in a cheesy echo of their obliterated faith. In spite of that, Angela seemed immune to the internalized humiliations of the invisible American Holocaust.

Chill was embedded in everything Angela swept over, using the fortress windows of the occupation for target practice. He was smart and interesting, if hard to follow. I liked hearing him talk, there under the scrub growth, but the cold granite was wearing a bruise in my backside. He'd read most of my favorite culture-crit books, and then plowed into some I'd barely heard of. I helped deconstruct colonialism until I couldn't keep up with the reading requirements. I stimmed as unobtrusively as I could, soothing my nerves by rolling glacier-rounded pebbles between my hands. The stress of wondering how long it'd be before the staff decided to look for us was building in my body. I began rocking myself after a few minutes of listening for footsteps in the underbrush.

Chill wasn't talking about Angela much after saying her diagnosis was Borderline Personality Disorder. That fit with the dash-outlined square on her wrist marking her for "intensive therapy." Chill said he'd been tagged Narcissistic PD/Oppositional Defiant, so his sociopath tat had been black rather than the red that kids who couldn't/wouldn't control their anger got. After that, he wanted to talk more about autism and staring. My incentive to stay sitting on the rock was devaluing fast.

I was exhausted trying to listen to him. I have an "auditory processing lag," which means I hear words with one part of my brain before I hear them with the part that makes sense of them. Words get routed through my visual cortex. Non-verbal sounds are easier to decipher. Visual information gets funneled through fast; words have to take the literal "scenic route." I see someone speaking, I know they're speaking, but the words take a while to reach me. Familiar voices are easier; I calibrate to them eventually. Chill wasn't familiar, and other than the chafing intelligence in his voice, not much was getting through anymore. I felt a soft humming noise coming out of my throat and turned away from him, trying to find something in the sky to look at.

He laid a weirdly long hand on my knee and focused his thickly eye-linered, too-pale eyes hard on my face. "Dunno what you might know about the Dark clan already. You'll hear about us, and you can believe most of it. Me likes ya much, little girl—not many I can talk theory with around here, even if I bored you to death—please not to sell me out for it. Don't know what you did or how they conned your family into sending you here, but watch the shadows, small-stuff... a lot of kids don't make it out except on paper. They get declared 'escapees' and get laid to rest in the cold, shallow loam. I was careful not to be one, even though security gave me opportunities. Some in the sheriff's department put a stop to the worst of it, but that won't last... never does."

He paused a moment and scratched the scars on his stringy arm. "FYI, and *do not tell anyone* you know this: the pills they give you that everyone ditches are fake. Your real meds are in the desserts. You may have noticed they come down hard on sharing. Frostings, fillings, gummy swirls, artificial-flavored gunk they can stir your personalized compounding pharma syrups into. The cake parts are probably safe—cooking doesn't do good things for the junk. Took me a few months to figure it out and then a couple years pretending to be in a stupor. Let them see you eat it a few times after they've seen you talking to me, then tail off the dosage so you don't kick up a reaction, and ditch the sweets wherever you can."

I stared into his dishwater-colored eyes and tried to dissect what he was saying.

He looked down. "Don't hold it against me if I act like I'm ignoring you sometimes. It's not personal, just best you don't look like you belong to any of the packs around here. You know your theory enough to get that this place is a business, and you're just livestock product for profit. They get as much reimbursement for you dead as alive if they don't report it, and you're less expensive if you don't eat. They've quit the 'outward bound' wilderness course drills for now—casualties started drawing attention. It's easy to get picked off that way, trying to 'escape'. If they start up again, be too valuable in production to spare for their next human behavior experiment. Hope whatever it was that got you in here, you enjoyed it—you're gonna need the memories."

He told me about an office in the administrative wing that was usually unlocked and had a Federal Web-connected landline that actually worked, and wrote something for me on a sheet from his memo book: "Gabe D." in a clean, left-handed slant, with a phone number. He put down another name that he said was someone from the sheriff's department. If I needed law, that deputy was the only person I should talk to. I was to memorize what was on the paper and then flush it.

A staffer's voice carried through the scrub. I looked toward it, and when I looked back, my new friend had evaporated into the foliage, leaving me with a vacant sense of faint industrial irritants buried in the still, dry, pine-needle scented air, and a lot of new things to think about.

CHAPTER TWO

Travelers planning to visit our neighboring Regions in the Heartlands or New Confederacy will have to be aware of uncertain and changing border-crossing requirements. Union citizens must understand that conditions in our surrounding areas are fluid and potentially risky. All travelers are advised to carry the names and contact information of the parties they intend to visit within those regions. The NorthEast Union has attempted to establish temporary consulates in all adjacent regions, however, only Atlanta has offered a clear set of instructions. The Heartlands have not yet named regional capitals.

The Unionist Free Press, 9/25/2031

IT WAS ABOUT A MONTH into my stay at Thunderbird. Chill's tiny, graying fairy Uncle Gabriel was braiding Angela's hair into a thick cascade down her back. Juvenile Corrections Officer Samuel Champetty watched approvingly. The late September sun glistened on the sable whips falling into place under Gabriel's slender hands. The three of them sat at the bolted-down institutional gray plastic picnic table in the middle of the camp yard, where Champetty could keep an eye on Chill and me standing about four feet apart with our fingers laced through the fence as we looked down into the hemlock grove. It wasn't anything we'd been ordered to do; it just kept the attention at bay when everyone could see we weren't passing anything to each other.

The breeze had an edge, coming up the cliff from the black grove. Pale birch leaves swirled in it. Chill's split upper lip and bruised eye were healing from a week ago. The stud through his lower lip was gone; reddish-black dots from stitches closing the tear it left still showed. He said he was lucky the sucker punch hadn't broken any teeth. He wasn't hiding that three of his nominal cousins had done damage to his looks. He'd brought his uncle along for his regular visit to the camp this time. They'd paid off Champetty to take care of arena duties and settled the score.

The yard had cleared. Champetty accepted bets as the pair of little half-breed queers made it a fair fight against the big, slow boys who no longer had the advantage of a concealed attack. Once they were flushed out, not allowed out of the ring of spectators until they folded, they'd barely made a match of it. Dainty Uncle Gabriel might have done the occasional drag show in his city-living days, but he had potent martial-arts skills, and he'd passed them along to his nephew. When Champetty collected his winnings, he joked that the professional risks the Dark fags took in their line of work weren't as dangerous as they might appear.

I asked Chill what the bad blood was over.

He tightened his scraped-up knuckles through the chain-link, leaned back to hang from it with his throat exposed to the sky, and closed his eyes. "That batch of relatives identifies as full-bloods, even if their Iroquois and Algonquin ancestors, to use the schoolbook names, flayed each other alive in the pre-colonial wars they never bothered to learn about, and they couldn't find their way through these woods if you dropped them a hundred yards in—but full-bloods with tribal papers hate half-bloods without them, and half-bloods from one side of the border hate the ones from the other side, and Red River Métis say we eastern half-breeds can't even call ourselves mongrels with a capital M because we can't trace back to Louis Riel in 1870—but whatever—the ones around here that don't speak French hate the ones that talk farog to each other..."

He raised his head and clicked his teeth together: "...And my half-blood farog drug-smuggling whore granny bought up most of the land in this county that Laithbourn Cap and Champetty don't own—bought what was left from their grandpas for the price of a good time and the fairy dust that rotted their brains... And, it turns out, there's gas under it, so even now the coal's run out, the Darks, specifically me once I inherit the land out of Gram's trust, might still be collecting royalties they think should be theirs if I decide to look for a driller willing to risk quakes on the fault-line. So, yeah, bad blood."

He pulled himself up and rested his forehead against the fence with his eyes still closed like he was done talking. I sat down under the scrubby trees.

A meager colony of feral cats sheltered behind the gas company commissary on the far side of the ravine. The mothers would take the kittens hunting in the grove. I'd spent hours chirping and cooing at them, my face stuck against the fence until I had the pattern of the wire pressed into it. I'd been making friends with an adventurous half-grown tabby whose sex I didn't know because I couldn't get close enough. A few days before, it had finally slipped in to take bits of cardboard Salisbury steak I'd left near a gap under the fence. As I sat there, it slithered under, greeted me with a wave of its tail, rubbed against a contorted pine trunk and thought about sniffing my hand.

The lanky kitten suddenly popped a couple of feet in the air and screamed as something hit it in the side with a fleshy smack. It took off for the tiny gap in the fence where it came in. I whirled around as Chill launched another wickedly accurate stone at its bony flank. I was in his face snarling before I knew I was standing up. He had the fist I'd aimed at his discolored face cupped firmly in his hand.

I pulled back to hit him with my other one and he pushed me away. "Don't make me hold you, Scope—I know it freaks you."

I stared at him. His unpainted eyes were moistening. I was too pissed to register it, and he had to block the left cross I sent at the side of his nose. I heard Champetty guffaw about taking more fight bets. The expression on Chill's face finally got through as he maneuvered us out of range of the laughter.

He nodded to the place the cat had been. "You never, *ever* want them to see you getting attached to an animal. If you have to know why, ask Uncle Gabe what happened to the cat I tried to take care of here, but believe me, you'll sleep better if you don't know the details."

He swallowed hard, and as fast as I'd been trying to hit him, I tried to hug him.

He pushed me back with a wincing wink. "Better they think you're angry at me."

I watched him walk up the slope, shrugging and making the yard laugh. I let the staff find me there in the scrub with tears running down my face. They let me shower even though it wasn't my day to have one. Angela watched as a staffer guided me through the unheated locker area while I held the rare treasure of a fresh blanket around my shoulders, and gave me a slow, sly grin. Chill was right, it was better.

...

I'd been pulled out of the work room where I'd been assembling a case lot of the useless Regional Net tablets. I was nowhere near done with what I had to do before I could head for bed, but when Champetty brought me to Angela's room he'd said I could save it for tomorrow and left without elaborating. It was the best job at the camp, and my fingers were small enough for it. The alternative was heavy refrigerant equipment assembly work that generated quite a few injuries, so I didn't want to lose my spot by not getting my quota finished. I had more things in my head than I could process when I went in and sat stiffly on the bed where I was told to.

Angela laid her beautiful long fingers over mine. Her nails were perfectly almond-shaped and still had chipped flecks of deep emerald sparkles left on them from the manicure she'd gotten from her Uncle Gabriel. "So how come you and Runt had issues? I thought he'd *finally* found someone he could talk to—and not just over the price of a blow. Mostly he creeps people out except for the guys that want to fuck him, and he creeps most of them out too."

I'd given my word to Chill never to share what we spoke about. I understood so little of what was going on, I wasn't going to second-guess him over it. I gave his sister a genuine enough baffled shrug and what I hoped was a pleasant smile.

She leaned against the wall with her arms around her knees. Her room was one of the ones featured in the camp brochure the hospital neuropsychiatrist had shown my mother, with real beds and sheets, papered walls, and a linoleum floor. Mine had metal bunks with inch-thick vinyl-covered foam mats on them, with a raw-cinderblock decorating scheme.

She noticed me looking at the other bed, with her sweaters and makeup case and earbuds thrown on it. "Yep, finally ditched the roomie. Probably won't get another one for at least a couple of months. You get along OK with yours?"

I said mine stole my things, and she had too many friends for me to get them back.

Angela's face looked lovely and sweet when she said she'd see what she could do about getting my property returned, but there was always a bit of slyness in her I couldn't parse. I blurted for her not to get in any deeper with Champetty over some noise-canceling headphones, a music player, and an e-reader; they were just objects, and objects come and go. She had to know where I got the information on how deep she was in already.

She asked why her brother was my only visitor. I didn't have much to say about that.

She reached for my hand again, running her fingers along the marks on my arm. "You're all messed up like he is. How come you do that?"

I shrugged, not so pleasantly this time, and kept my mouth shut.

"OK, tell me about the first time you did it. What made you start?"

I said it was a long story. She said she was listening.

...

I had an autistic cousin who didn't talk, but I'd always understood him. For eighth grade, I was sent to his "special needs" school, but I was put on the "high functioning" track. There wasn't much autistic-friendly there, from blaring colors to grating happy-music to loud, fake-cheerful voices talking to us like we were morons, but it was supposed to be one of the best for pounding kids into shapes pleasing to their parents. It was more expensive than a public freak warehouse, but the "personal attention" we got made straightforward neglect appealing.

Schools like that were designed to teach us "social skills." It was essentially making us learn to keep from blinking while they threw sand in our faces. "High functioning" autistics are more compliant than "low functioning" ones with grit being sprayed in our eyes, even though it generally hurts us as much. The school encouraged those of us they labeled HFs to consider ourselves superior to the Low Functions. I wished I had the integrity of the kids who were able to stay inside themselves instead of being one of the pathetic collaborators trying to dance on our hind legs until we dropped.

The HF kids called me the Retard Whisperer for the way I'd get called in to deal with Cousin Archer when he'd start going into a meltdown. I could usually calm him, but eventually I got so angry with the staff for riling him up that I started getting into trouble myself.

There was no need to withhold his lunch to force him raise his eyes to people and shake hands before he could eat. There was no need to bully him into sitting perfectly still with the threat of getting shut in a pitch-black isolation room for being "disruptive" if he tried to shift his legs. They kept trying to make him "use his words" because he'd once stammered a couple out, and he wasn't allowed to use typing to communicate.

As it is for most of us, being touched was alarmingly intense for him. He couldn't reduce people's eyes to colored camera lenses the way I did. When he was forced to connect with someone's gaze, the intimacy seared, and he reacted to the pain. They were "autism experts"; they should have known, but they didn't care. The web-based autistic rights movement had tried for decades to explain how we think and feel to anyone who'd listen. Autistic activists who could use a computer weren't considered defective enough to be allowed to speak for Archer against "expert-mandated" treatments, so their opinions could be discarded by those experts and their followers. Archer was never given the opportunity to learn a way to express his own opinions, or he would have been one more on a computer, with no standing to advocate for himself or other autistics. His pain wasn't important. He wasn't really human, and the experts were doing their best to make him as close to it as they could, whatever it cost him. Cut a piece off here, jam something in there—Frankenstein's monster, maybe, but less autistic to outward appearances.

If they'd let him rock quietly with his spin-toys, he could've learned something useful, like how to use a communication tablet. If they couldn't do that, then leaving him in peace wouldn't have hurt anyone, but they had to keep gouging away at him.

Before he got sent to the school, he'd worn noise-canceling headphones to prevent sensory overload. He wasn't allowed to wear them there because it was embarrassing to his family. Before then, he could perceive sounds so accurately he knew the temperature from listening to crickets. We had a game where we'd bet on it—he'd hold up fingers to name the number, and I'd look it up on my tablet. I always lost, and knew I was going to, but I was the only one who'd play with him. After a few months without protection, his beautiful, delicate sound processing was as broken as a speaker with a cracked cone. His circuits got as fried as mine; the subtle shadings of the world-music couldn't get through, but at least it couldn't blast so loud anymore.

I used to wish I'd go deaf even before I got sent to that school, and in some ways I did. I sometimes wonder if I could've matched Archer and his cricket songs if I'd been able to protect myself. I wasn't allowed to put my hands over my ears when I was little; it was rude, and my mother would slap them down. I learned to stand still while her screaming broke the exquisite connections in my brain like glass spider-webs shattering from an opera singer's shriek. By the time I got to that school, I was already half-broken. It was supposed to finish the job with a professional touch.

The school used things like oversized swaddling boards and padded closets. They were always getting some new design of straightjacket in mismatched cheery colors for that "calming" effect. The object was to immobilize you to the point barely this side of suffocation and contusion; sometimes that line was crossed, but schools had the right to do it. The legal term was "restraint and seclusion," part of the approved menu of "therapeutic techniques" for managing autistics. Eventually, you were confined so completely your fight died. You fell down as deep inside yourself as you could. You killed off the animal inside you so you didn't have to feel anymore. Then when you were broken enough, you watched yourself puppet what your owners wanted, got your unwelcome pat on the head, and treasured the moments you were left alone.

Something began falling apart in me after a few months. The fluorescent lights buzzed in my head, and the teacher's grating voice tangled into the shrieking colors on her clothes. When I was called on, I stammered and looked around or closed my eyes, searching my vocabulary of sounds and where they fit together. The staff was to lift my chin and make me look them in the eyes when that happened. I surely did give them that, and they weren't used to it. I'd always had a lag between forming the intent to speak and making it happen, even under the best conditions. Being forced to stare into the face of someone whose breath smelled of fast food chemicals while I was trying to think was more than I could achieve. When I was told for the thousandth time "look at the bridge of the nose if the eyes are too much to take in," it took more and more of my energy not to bite like Archer did. When I felt the world trying to reach down my throat to pull out something I didn't want to say, I felt a violence inside me growing like part of someone I didn't know.

I had a set of three ring-race ball bearings my dad gave me; they were surplus from his work as a power plant engineer. They were about my only connection to him after he left. They were smoothly spinning parts from the machinery that kept the city lit, and we both thought they were beautiful. When he'd tossed them to me, he'd said, "Now don't say I never gave you anything," and winked. The inner and outer bearing rings were cool, satin-brushed steel, and the sides were open so I could see the tiny polished balls rotating inside. They were the right size to slide over my fingers and spin with my thumb. The stim was more soothing than the drugs I was supposed to take. My ball bearings never bothered anyone. They spun in elegant silence, perfectly machined, making order and sense of everything. Of course when the school staff found them, they tried to confiscate them.

I fought the teacher's aides trying to yank them off my hand. I kicked like I'd never kicked before. I heard, like it was miles away, the panic alarm go off. I made a rush for the window, using my knuckles with the steel bearings over them to bash at the safety glass. It didn't break out, but a small spray of shards—beautiful, clean, sharp slivers of glass—showered onto the ledge, sprinkling it with tiny diamond knives. I picked one up; it was so exquisite the tips of my fingers bled. I drove it into the blue puzzle piece on my wrist until it vanished in a well of deep red.

...

Angela had a tear running down her face. Those cat-green eyes were crying, over something that had happened to me. Being so close, I smelled the warm, sweet layers of scent breathing off her body, every different place intoxicating.

She wiped her cheek. "I guess objects do come and go, like you said. Did you ever tell Runt about that?"

I hadn't, but I didn't know if answering a negative fell under my agreement. I think my brain freeze told her all she needed.

She slid closer and then stopped short. "Sorry, I didn't know the deal about touching."

I said it depended on the context.

She gave me that wicked grin again. "So—the runty little Gabriels did OK today, huh? 'S generally not such a good idea to pick on Darks. Or their friends."

I didn't know what to say to that.

She put herself to face me. "Are you gonna tell me what you did to earn yourself a spot here or not?"

I said I'd never been convicted of anything, but I'd been arrested once. I'd been labeled "non-compliant" by third grade. My mother had called the cops on me more times than I could remember. She'd had ideas about "curing" my autism, making me go in for "treatments" like chelation injections to precipitate heavy metals from my body. I got pills that caused fevers, vomiting, and bloody diarrhea to "cleanse" the autism out of me, because autistics must be full of parasites, obviously—because, well, "autism." I had sessions of targeted brain stimulation that burned my scalp and left me feeling like I didn't recognize myself for a few hours or days.

There's a quack-cure promo video of me that's still getting swapped around the perv circuits. I do not want to hear about autistics being physically or sexually naive; if there was a moment I was developed enough to have a second of genuine naiveté, that experience depicted in the video destroyed it. I was a pure cynic from the moment I saw it on my mother's guru's website.

I'd seen enough of my father's porn to know the vocabulary and grammar. He made a point to leave it up for my mother to fall to her knees sobbing over. The idea that family members were supposed to love one another seemed as much a fairy tale as the Santa Claus myths they trotted out every winter. I knew one thing when I saw mainstream porn—if that was what being a woman meant, I must be something else. No matter how many disgusting pink dresses my mother tried to keep me in, I never wanted to be the princess; I wanted to be the one who won her.

As Angela listened, she clasped my hand—the princess so close I could smell the sweet, delicate oil that glistened in her sable braids and hear the tiny click of the beads in them as she leaned closer. I asked if I should keep talking; she nodded and bit her lip.

I said the thing I was in was made as mommy-porn instead of daddy-porn, but it had the same denominators. I steeled myself to describe the undying video.

In it, I'm about 10, drug-groggy and restrained, getting an invasive medi-scoping that shows on a monitor how fucked my insides are, as my mother watches with Madonna-like concern. The screen crawl describes the Terrible Plague of Autism sweeping the country, and how I've contracted it through poisonous vaccines. The quack is explaining that the Dreadful Autism Disease has clearly attacked my gut. My mother nods gravely, saying my behavior has been worsening. He tells her they will now do an enema protocol with their special compound, since I've physically resisted taking my medications orally. I knew then the stuff was killing me; I know now it was compounded from industrial bleach. The video ends with a testimonial from my mother that the treatments have given her a glimpse of hope for my recovery.

When I fought going to those appointments, she'd call the police to help her put something "comforting" on me so she could get me into the car.

When they came, they weren't in the mood to play nice. "Hey, the tattooed kid won't go see the doctor again because she's too dumb to understand what's good for her, now we gotta go tase her one more time. Just put her the fuck away already and quit bothering us." My roaring nastiness when I imitated them surprised me.

Angela flinched, but kept her hand on mine. She asked how I ended up at Thunderbird.

I said I started running away. When I was arrested, my mother sent a private truant officer to admit me to an in-patient program at the University Hospital. The psychiatric unit director was another order of charismatic above her small-time quacks. He'd started his ascent as a guest expert on a syndicated daytime show. When its original host was fired for hawking a weight-loss regimen that killed several dozen women, the great doctor had taken over. His prestige made the show a hit in every region—he had enough letters after his name for the Northeast, enough manly discipline for the South, enough sensationalism for the West Coast, and enough judgmental vitriol for the Heartlands.

I'd been shown into his office. The first things I noticed were the fake color in his hair that I wasn't supposed to pick up on because he'd left the temples gray, and the odd, slick texture of his chemically peeled, over-moisturized skin. He'd granted my mother an audience; she was permitted to approach his big, fine desk. When an expert declared from such a height that she had suffered beyond the minimum requirements for martyrdom, she'd swooned in radiance like she'd been assumed up to heaven.

The Great Man pulled up a website for a network of residential facilities that specialized in "cases like your child's." He'd often sent the "troubled teen" family members of his teary guests for treatment to one of them; the saintly mothers would blubber their gratitude for later promotional use in exchange for stays for their children that would have cost more than those families made in a year. Their spawn sat in shell-shocked silence until prodded to give halting statements about how much better they were for the experience; they kept their hands still in their laps, and showed their teeth appropriately while staring into the camera. I may not be able to read expressions well, but I can smell fear sweat, even on a monitor.

The doctor showed my mother the online brochure that had pictures of the rooms like Angela's, and the deep woods, and the cheesy fake Native logo with the small print underneath:

Corrective Applied Behavior Analysis Group (a Laithbourn Capital Investments subsidiary), Wyandot County facility, Thunderbird Mountain Camp.

This is a limited liability institution. Parents and guardians of enrolled students agree to hold Laithbourn, CABA, its agents and subsidiaries harmless for results consequential to any treatment offered. Corporate obligations are exclusively construed under the laws and regulations of the Northern Heartland Regional Confederation of States.

We pledge to do our professional best to help your child become a contributing member of society.

CHAPTER THREE

When our office attempted to learn more about the privileged relationship of Laithbourn Capital and the Wyandot County juvenile justice system, we were met with little cooperation at the local or regional level. Several months ago, a spokesman for the Wyandot Sheriff's Office had warned The Northeastern NewServiceCo-op (our parent organization) that outside reporters might not be viewed kindly. When we tried to contact him more recently, we were told he was unavailable.

Unionist Free Press, Sunday Online, October 26, 2031

S AM CHAMPETTY gave me a smoke-stained leer and waggled my phone from across the steel table. I folded my arms. He pulled out a gaudy cigarette pack and reached over to offer me one, the "Semper Fi" tattoo on his meaty forearm deliberately in my face as he stretched toward me. I didn't move. Tobacco products from New Confederacy states weren't subject to Federal regulations anymore and were notoriously addictive; I wasn't setting myself up for that.

Champetty sighed and leaned back, imitating my folded arms. "You're putting yourself in my business, girly. The Runt keeps trying to run interference for you, but I'm making my last offer before I turn you over to the dogs. It's cute when you follow my Angie around with your tongue hanging out, but you better quit trashing me to her. You should pray she doesn't start listening to you instead of just telling me what you say, but I listen. My check is signed by Laithbourn Capital, and it pays me well to listen. I have to report on your progress, and sad to say, your progress is a backwards thing right now. "

He spun my phone on the table. "I think it's time I told you: I've had this dream, ever since Angie's little breast buds started popping. I've always wanted to watch her play with other girls. She says that's not what she's into, but she'll give me what I want. She likes me to play rough with her, an' it's one of the things I like best about her, but I wanna see some pointy little girly tongue like yours lick her good enough to make her squirm and scream..."

If I told him the truth—that no girl had ever let me give her more than a clumsy caress—my value would hit zero fast. I needed to be worth something to someone with power at Thunderbird Mountain, or I was going to be in the camp's not-so-secret graveyard soon. I'd considered going back to eating the saccharine garbage they put on my food trays just to shut myself down so I wouldn't keep getting in fights with the wrong people. I shifted around and tried to look hard-ass as Champetty shuffled my intake papers.

He laid them on the table. "I see you got prostitution counts you wriggled out of. Precocious little slut—no wonder you get along with Angie's faggot brother. Maybe you can learn something from the Runt. I hear he's good enough at it his johns forget what he looks like, so there might be hope for you. I'm gonna make you an offer: You want Angie? You get to play between her legs—but I watch. Any interest?"

My head swam, but something hard and clean in the back of mind kicked into gear. I had absolutely nothing to lose, and it was almost exhilarating.

I met Champetty's eyes. "Maybe. Depends."

"Depends on what, girly?"

"Depends on you understanding just what it is I do. I'm a stone-cold pure top. I don't need to learn anything about that from Chill Dark—we're in a different line of work. Dom girls are rare enough that I got some lovely training expended on me. I'm an experienced, underage female dom who'll play with girls, boys, or both, and you won't find them too often. If I play your game for you, you make sure I get to stay arrogant. There are pricks here that want to break me of my ways, and if I'm broken, I can't give you your performance."

My heart was flipping like a bird stuck in a chimney. I'd learned a bit of trade practice from a few upscale, kinky boys who'd paid the price of a pair of beautiful handmade shoes for the backhanded pleasure of the game, but I'd never even touched a naked girl.

I had to play the cards I had and bluff. My neck ached from bruises left by the couple of rape-happy trusties who'd trapped me in the administration wing hallway when I'd gone looking for the phone Chill had told me about. Inmate trusties at Thunderbird were handpicked by the staff, and had the run of the facility in exchange for providing another level of enforcement over the rest of us. There was no appealing to authority against them. I'd fought hard enough they'd saved the idea for another day, but that day was coming—and when it came, there'd be interest on what I hadn't paid out. I didn't have much hope I wasn't going to be dead soon, or wishing I was.

Champetty's leer spread across his face with carnivorous laziness. "We'll look into that... Angie does say bad girls like it the hard way. We were considering a consensual game with one of those 'pricks' that gave you those marks on your neck..." He snickered as I put my hand over the bruises. "Yeah, we were spectating on a feed off a new camera the Runt doesn't know about. I bet her they couldn't get you all the way down. Half-pint terriers like you are hard to pin for the count. little dogs with big dog fight—rather get bloodied up than give in—fun to watch. Angie lost the bet, but she was nice and frisky after watching the show.

"Now I'm thinking I like your idea better. You give her something she likes, you'll be giving me something I like. I'm gonna give you a little scene to act out—you deliver on that, and your time here could get downright pleasant. Now—I'm gonna write up a report that says this was stolen from the depository, so you hide it good. I'll give you the juice pack for it when you deliver."

He slid my phone to me across the dinged-up gray-painted steel.

...

Everything from the shopping list I'd given Champetty was laid out on the narrow metal-framed bed. The harness was the same type as the one I'd left buried in November leaves at the end of the overgrown oak avenue on Sterling Island the day I was arrested. The phallic toy Champetty and Angela had chosen to use in it was more gnarly than any I'd used on the Island boys. The long, wicked graphite switch was the one I'd recommended. Sam and Angela already had well-worn restraints; they looked like the ones the camp used, but in businesslike black instead of the real ones' nauseating neon-cheery colors.

As I stripped and set up the harness, I could hear the two of them building up their charade in the other room. She was giving him seriously toxic lip, like she was the boss, until his temper seemed to come up hotter than just play-acting. I heard him slap her hard. I buckled the harness around my hips, snugged it up, and hid in the cramped space behind the dresser. I went over the script in my head again. I was supposed to stay out of sight until Champetty whistled. Angela would never see me; she'd pretend I was a male.

I peeked between the wall and dresser as the door whipped open with a kick. The pig dragged beautiful Angela in by her wrists, and it was a hefty hoist—I smelled his charged-up body. They were naked, and sweat glinted in his buzzcut, blondish hair. The expression on her face was the one I'd ached to put there, but if he could give it, I never could. The best I would ever do was be a part in their act, and that meant carrying off something I'd never exactly done before. The anatomy's different; girls don't have a sweet spot to honey up—and if I couldn't give it up for her the right way, I was likely dead.

He threw her down, bent over the edge of the bed, then twisted a handful of her braids around his fist and spanked her with muscle behind it. I shuffled myself, waiting for my cue. She squirmed and sneered at him. He jerked her up, buckled her wrists into the restraints, lanyarded them to the ring on the head-board, and blindfolded her. She crouched, offering her masterpiece of a bum expectantly. Champetty swished the graph-ite whip in the air a few times and whistled for me. When I emerged from my hiding place, he told Angela he'd called in a well-equipped expert to deal with her since she was such a brat. I knelt behind her on the sagging, dingy little bed. He handed me the switch. Angela had stopped pretending she was being forced into anything.

Champetty pulled up a creaky little metal chair next to the bed. I tried to give him a good viewing angle like in my father's porn. The first part, I knew how to do. Angela made sounds like the boys would when I'd used the switch on them, but so much sweeter that I warmed to what I was doing. I didn't have the luxury of feeling as complicated about that as I wanted; I had to sell that my heart was in it, and it wasn't as hard as I thought it would be. When the sounds got jagged and tight, I stopped. I tried not to look at Champetty stroking himself.

He handed me the jar of cocoa butter. I rubbed a dab of the cream into her blotched and striped backside. She was making her own lubrication abundantly. I blended the lovely salves in the stubbled outer creases of her shaved privates. Champetty nodded as I ringed her bumhole. He'd told me she didn't want me touching her directly on the genitals, and made sure I respected the terms. He stood to lean close and ordered her to take what was coming to her. She made a gasping coo and settled her knees firmly. She opened for my smoothing fingers inside her easily enough to let me take in a relieved breath. Her body knew how to handle what she wanted. She rested her face against her cuffed wrists and whimpered comfortably. Champetty moaned and licked his lips. Angela grinned at the sound.

I entered by the gate assigned to me. Angela's lip curled into that exquisite sneer that tells a top the work is good. She made sounds like it was painful, but they seemed more directed to Champetty than me. I didn't think I was doing damage.

She pulled herself away from me as much as she could. "Too much, too much—hurts, Daddy..."

It was Champetty's turn to grin. He waved me to go after her. I couldn't tell if the thing about her liking it rough more than he liked her getting it that way was another part of their act, but they both seemed to feel the fire. I moved slow and firm, following her harsh, steady breath. Champetty reached between us; she writhed against his hand and he pulled it away. She let out a petulant wail that was the most real sound I'd ever heard from her. She fought the restraints.

I tried to look like I was in control. I reached for her breast; the nipple was as hard as a pebble and she keened and ground herself against my pubic bone when I pinched it. Champetty looked like he was getting what he wanted.

Angela whispered "Daddy... please... I need to..."

Champetty climbed onto the dangerously overloaded bed and released her hands. He grabbed her blindfolded head and penetrated her mouth like he was trying to choke her. She took it like she was starving. She reached back to hold me firmly against herself, and then rubbed her hand greedily between her legs to climax with him.

When they were done, Champetty grinned sloppily and gave me a high, inaccurate handslap. "Get outta here 'fore the bedsprings pop. Compensation's in your room."

...

I stumbled out of the harness and into my jumpsuit in the cramped bathroom of the watchman's suite. Angela's deep, wicked laugh came through the thin wall, lazy and purring; his came alongside it, weaker and teasing. I stepped into the stark anteroom filled with banks of monitors feeding from every corner of the camp. I located the one aimed on the administration wing hall I'd barely escaped from. I pictured the two of them watching me being assaulted for their personal live-action porn, and wondered if the trusties had found me looking for that unlocked office purely by accident. I heard Angela laugh again as I slipped out.

A staffer leaned against the corridor wall opposite the door, and roused himself to accompany me, chuckling under his breath. I hoped to stop at the showers, but that didn't happen. Someone held my door open. It was one of the trusties who'd tried to rape me. His face was swollen and purple with half-dried blood smears and he had a broken nose that hadn't been set. He hissed something as I passed. The staffer made a "tsk-tsk" sound, smacked his fist into his palm, and then made an exaggerated gesture for me to go inside. My cellmate had been moved out. My things she'd stolen were on my bunk, along with the fully charged battery pack for my phone.

...

A seductive purr answered my call, identifying itself as Gabrielle.

When I said "Chill?—it's Scope..." the voice turned matter-of-fact. "Hey—got your fancy FedWeb mobile back. Good. Didn't recognize the number—city area code. Thought it might be a little high-end work coming my way."

Something seemed to distract him; it sounded like he was holding his phone away from his face. "Heyyy, it's an onion... Nice spoof! Number changes every few seconds, but keeps to urban codes. Must give out a random scroll of hacked numbers to identify itself. Sweet feature."

My screen flashed "Detected! External ping test in progress— Terminate connection?"

I couldn't get my words out. Chill muttered reassuringly about needing to trace his calls. He apologized for not warning me in time about the new cameras in the administrative wing. He said Angela mentioned seeing something happen to me, but wouldn't be specific. He asked if everything was OK. I croaked some almost-words about what I'd done and how sick I felt and how I wanted to wash myself inside out. Chill asked if I was banging my head into the wall, because it sounded like it. I settled on the floor next to my bunk and tried to stop. That lasted about fifteen seconds.

Chill let out a harsh sigh. "What my sister wants and what we'd prefer her to want from inside the comfort of our politics aren't likely to match up—but she's got Champetty mainlining her, and that's a good thing for you right now.

I garbled about having ruined the first time I made love to a woman with the filth I did for money with boys and how I'd never get clean. He let me go on until I said I needed to cut myself, and he should understand. He asked if there was anything I was planning to use; when I said no, he told me not to assume we did the same things for the same reasons. There started to be holes in the conversation where I couldn't process what I heard. I asked him to slow down.

He said "Sure, Scope... you set the pace—but tell me... did he touch you?"

"No."

"Did he keep to the script you'd agreed on?"

"Yes."

"Was the client satisfied?"

I said yes again, with a swallow that hurt; some of the gaps in my comprehension were from being pulled into places I didn't want to go.

"And were you paid OK?"

I stared at my stuff on the bed in dim fluorescent light, and forced the words. "More than."

Chill snapped hard enough about quitting the goddamned head-banging that I actually stopped.

He told me he didn't want to see self-injury marks on me and sighed a deep breath. "OK, if he kept his hands and his junk off you, stuck to his side of the bargain, and then gave you more than he promised, I would say the gig went well. You're in the life just like I am. When we work, we swim under the surface in the murk where everyone hides their kinks, and you've got kinks there's a market for. Politics can't breathe down where we do our jobs, so don't try to hold yourself to what you live by up in the air. You're good at what you do—now you know you're damned good at it. Just be careful... when you have big friends, you have big enemies.

"Now, take the juice off that phone—you ain't likely to get another charge on it for a while, so don't waste it. Get some sleep, little girl. You done fine."

CHAPTER FOUR

A stringer for a Northeast Union news organization was found dead in Laithbourn Capital's law enforcement training facility. The property was clearly posted with signs warning would-be trespassers that the only safe way to get on-site was to request permission at the front gate. Laithbourn Security says they have no record of the reporter attempting to check in at the front gate.

Garth Carpetlayer, Heartland Freedom Herald
Weekly Print Edition, 11/2/2031

I SAT IN MY SPOT under the scrub trees. The defoliant applied by the camp's parent company to every growing thing in the inner yard was taking effect; the pine needles had yellowed and started to fall. A few days of rain had cleared the worst of the corrosive smell, but the damp-darkened granite exhaled a trace of it. The contaminated runoff had blighted some hemlocks near the base of the cliff. The empty containers the day-laborers had left around were covered with complicated advisory labels. The stuff was infamous for killing people hired to apply it. Laithbourn generally used workers who couldn't read the English-only cautionary small print allowed by the Regional legislative overlay that superseded Federal regulations.

Chill waved to Champetty at the picnic table, now visible through the shriveling foliage. Champetty returned a mock salute. Chill muttered that it was a damned shame about the trees. The twisted pines no taller than saplings had probably fought for their foothold for a couple of centuries.

Chill leaned back against my knees, examining my phone. "I'm sure you got told to keep this out of sight. Best be extra careful of it around Angie, since she knows you have it."

I made a questioning noise; he sighed. "She don't like it when other people have nice things. It's not that she wants them; she just don't want you to have them. She doesn't know where I keep my hunting stuff anymore. It always... well, whatever.

"Gran died when Angie was eight. She never accepted Angie was kin, but she wasn't in denial so deep she didn't leave her a hundred bucks to make her will cast iron. She willed my mother the few good pieces of jewelry she had—Gran's way of apologizing for making my ma trustee instead of one of her blood sons. My dad was so worthless and my uncle so not around, Luce got left to handle a lot of family shit."

Chill made a little noise in his throat and changed it to a nod as he pointed out the "Product of New Albion" stamped on the phone's polished metal edge. I followed his fingernail tap and saw the words slashed through with a precise line, with some kind of hallmark crest etched next to them. I nodded back like it meant something.

Chill's mouth twitched on one side. "Anyway, Gran's jewelry box disappeared right before my dad took Angie to visit her momma in the big city. Was a good time for them, shitty one for Luce and me waiting for them to come home. Mommy ain't too sweet when she sits in the dark with a bottle of Canadian. So, anyway, Luce thought they'd taken the bling for Angie's momma. When they finally got back, she laid into Angie for truth she wasn't getting from my dad.

"Turned out Pappy never knew Angie had the stuff. He'd pulled into a truck stop—too much good time he needed to sleep off—and Angie dropped the things down a port-a-john. Latrine company truck had come and gone when we drove out there to look for it. Probably the first time they'd been emptied in a year."

I didn't say anything.

Chill inserted the power pack, turned the phone on and waited for it to boot. "So who gave you this sweet piece, girl? Has to be worth double what I paid for my best long gun—and you say you never call anyone but me on it. Don't add up."

He knew his way around the hacked and remanufactured phone. He scrolled through screens, trying different encrypted

FedWeb bands, including a couple of military ones; each gave a decent signal in answer to the emitted code. He slid the hinged keyboard out and snapped it into place with a switchblade click, making a long-text communications device delicate as a spread-winged origami bird. I'd never even gotten it open. He showed me how to slide the release to get it to drop into place. He balanced the folded-out phone on his knees as his fingers flew around the small keys, entering codes into the security windows that popped up. He accessed the ID screen, noted the hacker's mark with approval, and then pulled up the contacts list. There was one number in it, with just the initial "B" to identify it.

He held it up for me to read. "Who dis, Smallstuff?"

I looked at the number. "The guy that gave me the phone."

"And do you think he might be expecting a call? From you? Maybe? After giving you something I personally know people have killed for?"

I said he could afford it.

Chill folded the keyboard, tucked the phone between my knees and rolled over to look up at me in a parody of a flirting pinup—lying on his stomach, propped on his elbows with his crossed ankles in the air and his cocked head resting lightly on the backs of his fingertips.

He batted his mascaraed eyelashes. "Tell me more..."

I muttered about wishing I hadn't said it like that.

"B" had risked quite a bit getting the phone to me while I was in custody. He'd promised he'd always be there for me, and that he'd be around even if I wanted him to stay in the background. If I needed anything, anytime, I was to call him. He'd bribed the "challenged adolescent transport service" driver to pass me the phone before I was put in one of those comforting jackets for my trip back to the mainland from the resort town where I'd been arrested. I'd held it in my sleeve for a day and a half while the hospital intake went through. By that point I'd gotten used to having straws stuck in my mouth for my legally-mandated drink every four hours and getting my ass wiped for me by people who weren't paid enough and acted like it. They weren't going to bother searching my sweat-stinking restraint jacket when it was finally unbuckled.

I'd kept the phone, never turning it on. It was something to remind me of what I used to be when I was free. When my mother tearfully sent me off to Thunderbird with a pink, daisy-patterned duffle, I'd slipped the phone in like she'd given it to me.

I told Chill "B" was my first client. He'd brought me others he thought he knew were safe, and when I'd been arrested I hadn't given him or his friends up. I'd stayed in jail a few nights with my mouth firmly shut; the phone was, I supposed, a thank-you gift.

"So you had a pimp?"

I said I hadn't thought of it that way.

My protector had helped me when I'd taken off after over-hearing my mother make reservations for me for an "intensive detoxification protocol" in Mexico. The words "hyperbaric chamber," "fecal transplant," and "supervised concentrative chelation" were all I'd needed to hear. I'd grabbed a few clothes and been out the door before the call was finished. I'd landed in B's lap and he'd tried to protect me. I'd been the one who'd insisted on paying my own way.

I could pass for older, but I was legal poison since I was under-age. He'd kept me from being sent home for a few blessed months. He'd gotten me a room near his family's place on the off-season on Sterling Island, set me up with my own online account and a fake ID, and helped me earn the money to pay for it with enough left for safety net if I got out of Thunderbird alive.

Chill swung his crossed ankles like a 1950's bikini girl. "Ooo... Ster-ling Eye-land... now you has mah full ah-ten-shun. And what, pray tell, does this "B" stand for? I wishes to hear this story, please."

I said there wasn't much to tell.

My pre-divorce family spent a couple of weeks there every summer. When I ran away, I used the last few Federal dollars my dad had given me for the ferry because I knew the tradition. Kids who made the cut could scrape by on the Island. I didn't have many options. Sterling Islanders had the healthcare to stay clean of STDs, and reputations that would be damaged by dead jailbait. I went to the athletic club because that was where the runaways hustled for money and a shower, sneaking in on someone's card.

I'd been spayed before it was mandatory. Sex questions were always on the menu for us with the puzzle piece tattoo. Whether it was in a hospital, a school, a jail, or a charlatan's shabby storefront, the "experts" had to ask about the juicy bits. Sterilization before our kind reach puberty is a time-honored tradition. I've seen eugenics texts a century old saying what my mother's docs advocated. I'd started menstruating at eleven, and they were ready; the surgery was a profitable sideline. If she'd waited a few more years to conceive me, she could've legally terminated the pregnancy once the insurance-mandated prenatal screening showed those troubling genes, even after the laws reverted and normal angel babies couldn't be aborted if their mother's lives were at risk.

I kept hearing how autistics didn't understand sexual boundaries. I decided to make it work for me. It wasn't a new concept. I couldn't exist around humans without being slathered in it. Some autistics like my cousin Archer identify as asexual, but plenty of us play the hands we're dealt. We can have a kind of root-level radar, even though we might seem cold. Some of us have precocious, ferociously intense, unconventional sexual appetites. It's the bogey in the closet that no one talks about except in trying to discreetly stamp it out.

Even though I was spayed young, my sexual wiring was in place, and the touch of androgyny from the surgery didn't necessarily hurt an edgy attractiveness. My body didn't match my desires—I accepted being a small female without caring for it—but sometimes it matched with other people's hungers. I'd been hit on plenty. I figured I was pretty enough to fake my way through.

My third afternoon on the Island, I caught the interest of four guys out of military college enjoying their late-summer freedom. They invited me onto the Athletic Club grounds to watch them play doubles tennis. They looked like barracudas in their sunglasses, hunkering and swaying, waiting to jump on each other's serves. The lead barracuda slipped me money and told me to take a bath and come back the next day. He didn't ask anything in return, but he set off a prickle on the back of my neck. He joked I'd been paying a lot of attention to them bending over with their stretchy shorts snugged up across their athletic little buns, and I guess I had been.

One of the others stepped in, saying "Hey, Jeffy—you so much of a horndog you're gonna mess up a kid now?"

The one called Jeff said he liked me, and I didn't look or act like any kid he'd ever met. A taller, quieter barracuda asked where I'd spent the night. I said on the beach, camping with a few other kids. He offered to find me something better. He was the one who eventually gave me the phone. Barracuda Jeff snickered and backed off.

The tall, quiet guy invited me into the locker room after the others left. He apologized that he didn't have access to the women's showers. He stood guard by the door and never stared at me. He gave me his robe to wear when I was done showering. We talked, and then he asked if I minded if he showered. I watched, and when he asked if I wanted to touch his bum since I'd been admiring it I went along with the game, and found my calling in the process. "B" was for "barracuda," or "bottom," or whatever Chill's imagination might desire.

Chill cupped his chin in his hands and looked up at me with most of the snark drained out of his expression. "You know, you're growing on me to a scary degree, Smallstuff."

...

It started spitting cold rain. Chill handed me the phone and told me to keep it in my underwear. Champetty motioned us to get under the overhang as Angela came around the corner of the boys' wing and grabbed Chill's arm; I couldn't look at her face. I went where I'd been told to. Angela made tight, fast gestures as Chill set his hands on her shoulders. If I hadn't been so sick over her, it would have been funny, him in his eyeliner, the reassuring big brother, with her standing over him, outweighing him by close to forty pounds.

Champetty yelled for them to get where they'd been told to as a couple of Laithbourn paramilitaries walked toward them. Chill looked at the uniforms, his eyes round and black. He gave me a quick hug, whispering, "Watch. Your. Back." before sprinting to the gate; Champetty waved him through like he was just sending him to off to his truck to get out of the rain.

...

We juveniles sat at long tables in the assembly room. It was a half-hour after we usually lined up to have our so-called food thrown at us, along with those special desserts. Tables were set up on the raised stage where we used to have to parrot whatever the production company wanted us to say when they'd shoot another promotion. There were extra lights, and the backdrop had been lowered.

The staff never bothered with that kind of window-dressing when they announced who hadn't made their quotas for the week and was going to pull double shifts—with a suspiciously sweet house-made energy bar, a bottle of water, and an hour's sleep on the workroom floor—until it was made up. Those announcements were unrecorded and accompanied by dead silence. Groaning got you more hell. I'd been through it once. I'd been too fast to earn the lesson, so one of the trusties knocked everything on my bench to the concrete floor. It never mattered how the quota didn't get met, only that we'd suffer if it wasn't. My stomach was conditioned to knot up once a week when the staff supervisor stepped up to the mike with his list of names, no matter how well I'd thought I'd done.

This was a more special occasion. A half-dozen of the privileged class arranged themselves onstage with their high-end electronics. Four were in professional suits—one of those a female who looked younger than the men. The other two were Laithbourn brass in uniform. One suit was announced as Head of Developmental Disorders Studies at the University Hospital—he was the Great Man responsible for my being at Thunderbird.

Champetty wasn't at his usual spot at the head of the favored table, and his trusted staff had been replaced by strangers who sat in their places. Angela looked like she'd been given heavy meds; her head nodded as she tried to sit upright next to Champetty's empty chair. I was grateful I hadn't been included in that table assignment when my status was secretly upgraded.

...

The Laithbourn officer-in-charge droned about changes in institutional culture and introduced the new staffers. He went on about partnering with the university in upgrading the "quality of care" at Thunderbird, as well as the other CABA Group facilities. He tried for a rabble-rousing team spirit thing that Thunderbird was going to outperform the others. Some kids tried for a half-hearted rah-rah while the rest folded our arms. Angela laid her head on the table. The wise-asses began whispering. That emboldened a few more, and the snickers got louder.

One of the replacement staffers stood up, apologized to the speaker and pointed out the whisperers—several members of the favored table, some at the heads of tables, and the whole banquet arrangement of pricks. The replacements swept up like storm troopers.

The group of whisperers were lined up against the wall. Each was taken up individually, made to apologize to the Laithbourn officer for interrupting him, and marched out in zip-tie handcuffs. The new staffers came back in and rearranged the seating. The rah-rah kids moved to the favored table, Angela was sent back with me at the losers' table, and the pricks' empty table was folded up.

The Laithbourn officer tapped his mike. "All righty then—now that that's sorted out, we can get down to business."

CHAPTER FIVE

*We are no longer able to report from the Northern Heartland, how-
ever seismographic equipment located on the East and West Coast
has picked up significant temblor events in the heavily fracked Wyandot County area. We've heard complaints from border areas and
in New Albion and Free Quebec Sovereign Canadian Provinces that
there may have been disruption to water tables. The Northern Heartland Environmental Protection Agency was disbanded under the
Laithbourn Development Pact signed earlier in the year; there appears to be no existing official agency tracking the water issue at the
source.*
<u>*Unionist Free Press AllMedia FreeAccess live report, 11/28/31*</u>

T HE YOUNG WOMAN in medical regalia who'd been onstage was talking about things we had in common—where
we'd grown up, the city neighborhoods with big trees, the
parks and museums and the seagulls along the lake. She was New
Administration, and working on being my friend. She said we
weren't that far apart, and how I could be in such a different place
if I could get my act together—that I'd had so many advantages
other kids at Thunderbird never had.

I said there was one difference—there was nothing but milky
skin inside her left wrist. She had the blue puzzle piece on an
enameled "Autism Support" pin on her lapel instead, with a red
rhinestone heart stuck on its crudely anthropomorphic outline to
show her noble intentions. She'd be someone I "role-named." It's
one of the rude things we autistics do. We designate people by
how they fit in our lives, because arbitrary personal names
require a lot of brain-space. She'd get a label on her pretty face
when it came up in my head instead of *Ariel,* which the fake

crayon kid's-writing print on her name tag reminded me was the correct way to address her.

She was the Golden-Haired Protégé of the doctor who'd landed me at the camp. The Laithbourn officer who'd neatly sifted out a couple of hundred inmates by troublesome temperament type at the assembly represented the company, but he wasn't in charge of CABA. He'd introduced the Golden One's mentor, Dr. Oliver Asalvo, "The Great Man" in my naming system, as part-owner and managing director of the entire Corrective Applied Behavior Analysis Group. The Great Man said his intern would be interviewing those of us diagnosed with autism. All "client" diagnoses would be re-evaluated, and "treatment plans" revised accordingly.

The distinguished, telegenic Dr. Asalvo hadn't thought it necessary to disclose his relationship with CABA in his paid professional advice on where to send me for my next round of brainwashing. He'd shown my mother his slick presentation for Thunderbird without mentioning he'd profit directly from my parents draining their retirement savings to put me there. He'd only mentioned a "cooperative arrangement." For the fifteen minutes of his time that had cost about what my engineer father would make in a week, he'd extracted every accessible nickel my family had.

When I pointed that out, the Golden One put on her stern, professional, work-toughened face. "I'm sure Dr. Asalvo would have been happy to answer any questions about his interest in any of our facilities. If you had those concerns at the time, why didn't you ask him directly?"

She was going to be one of those "twist it around and throw it back on you" therapists. I mentioned that she hadn't paused to process my remark before she had her comeback. She looked at me, and this time she was definitely processing what I said.

She changed the subject. "You probably have good reasons for not wanting your family to visit, and we'll certainly respect your wishes on that, but is there anyone you miss?"

I said I missed my cousin Archer; she asked about him.

I said he was autistic too, but more inside himself. He was older than me by a few years. He wore diapers until he was five, and never learned to dress himself in anything more complicated than sweats. At one time, he'd started using a little speech, but then he'd gone quiet.

He and my father shared the same old family first name, but he'd ignore anyone using that. He insisted on being called Archer because that was what he'd been called in his first boarding school. He wasn't about to reprogram himself one more time to please another set of humans, and after being turned over to institutions from an early age, he was probably more bonded to me than he was to anyone else.

He and I got along. He sometimes bit when he had a meltdown, but he'd never bitten me. I could usually understand what set him off, and help back him out before it went nuclear. I'd been reading to him since before I started school. He'd want the same book for a month or two, until he got everything he needed from it. I'd run my finger under the line as I read until he could follow, not just the words but the meaning of the story; by that time we were both ready for a harder book. I felt more kin to him than to my other relatives. They'd joke in front of us about how we had our own language, as if we couldn't understand theirs.

The Golden Intern asked how I thought I was different from Archer.

I said I respected his integrity, and I thought in a lot of ways he was happier than I was.

She asked if I thought Archer's silence was a choice, then.

"No... more like a dream that could be bad if you fought it, but could be deep and wide if you went with it. Archer's tagged as retarded, but he sees a lot that gets missed by noisier people."

"Would you like to work with your cousin and other people like him?"

I felt my face open up for a second before I remembered how many times I'd gotten screwed for having that kind of hope. I said it depended on what "work with" meant. If I could spare anyone what I went through, I'd give it a shot.

The intern asked me to tell her how I'd been diagnosed, from my perspective.

I folded my arms and said my unconventional approach to eye contact, particularly with people who thought they had a right to my deference, got me onto the psychologically-labeled track as soon as I started kindergarten. I was always in fights because I wouldn't take getting teased without objection, and I was always the one who got in trouble. When the Authority of the Day expected me to look down in shame, it didn't happen. It took a summer-long ordeal of Trial-by-Neuroprofessional to nail me as "suffering from autism," since the very thing that had attracted the attention was an "atypical manifestation of classic autistic gaze aversion."

The intern typed a few things on her tablet and asked for more detail.

I said she apparently already knew everything she wanted to about me, true or not.

She smiled. "Try me."

I said the school psychologist had made me play creepy games about recognizing people's faces and what they were supposed to be feeling until I got so frustrated I stopped cooperating. My mother never mentioned I could read before I first was in a classroom; that didn't fit her drama. She was happiest when she was martyred. Early in my vivisection the school psychologist mentioned I might be retarded, and my mother latched onto that.

The neurologist had studied the stiff-legged walk that got me laughed at in school. He made me play reaction-time games until I got so stressed I bit my arm. I was brain-scanned, genetically profiled, and physically assessed until I snarled every time a white coat got within ten feet of me.

The neurologist thought he saw abnormal patterns in my brain connections. The three-vial blood test my mother held me down for showed those "troubling" genes. My mother was told to bring me to the Behavioral Sciences Department at the University Hospital for more screenings.

The hospital examiners had new challenges I actually enjoyed, like making increasingly complex patterns from blocks in two colors and a word test about drawing conclusions. The gray-haired woman assigned to play with me would smile and roll her eyes like we both knew the games were silly.

It was those games that exposed my lack of "Theory of Mind." The hospital summoned my mother in triumph. Diagnosis: Autism. My mother wailed and gave the Great Man the go-ahead to ink the puzzle-piece into my wrist. Her friends eyed me like I might be contagious. I got tutored in a room off the library so I wouldn't contaminate my classmates with my disruptive behavior, even though other kids could do the same things without being quarantined for it. I was part of the dreaded ever-widening Autism Epidemic; never mind that my father would have been picked out by the tests they gave me. He was born too early to get caught in the dragnet.

I was just a stupid little kid. I hadn't gotten the point of the game when the gray-haired behavioral studies technician put old black and white photographs of people in front of me and asked about their eyes, or tricked me into showing how slow I was to follow when she pretended to suddenly turn her attention to something off in a corner. She'd showed me dull picture stories and had me say what the people in them were thinking. The cookie-cutter citizens looked like they might be bored or constipated or their feet might hurt while they held up glasses of water or boxes at each other or pointed at things across the street. They weren't doing anything to require much mental activity. I said the lady holding a box missed her sister and the couple at the window didn't like each other anymore. I didn't get that I was supposed to pretend all the blandly-drawn people were so obtuse I had to go step by step to work through their most rudimentary thinking for them.

The hospital report said I was missing a mirror in my brain that would project my thoughts about what I would do into everyone else, which was what people with a healthy Theory of Mind did, and therefore I could never be genuinely compassionate. I might learn some neurological workaround to mimic natural empathy, but I'd never be fully human. My mother bought a book about psychopaths called *The Science of Evil* by the same autism expert who came up with the Theory of Mind concept and the tests. After she read the thing, she never looked at me the same way again.

...

The Golden Intern walked me back to my cell. There was a distant rumble, and then the floor shook. She looked around and gasped. I said it was something at one of the gas wells, and you'll have that in Wyandot County. The ground was seismically unstable; when the drillers set something off, they'd dump cement over the cap and get out fast. That particular well had been shifting for a couple of weeks. She smiled weakly and said it must take some getting used to, and it didn't seem like the best acoustic environment for the autistic "clients." I gave her a crooked look.

She said the administration would review roommate assignments. She asked how I'd feel about sharing quarters with Angela, since we'd both been sexually exploited by a previous staffer and might be some support for each other. I wasn't sure how she knew that. I didn't say anything as I walked in and sat on the bunk. The Golden One gave a little bye-bye wave and closed the door, saying she'd talk with me again tomorrow.

...

I woke up vomiting. The soup at dinner had a harsh, detergenty taste like the bowl hadn't been rinsed. I shouldn't have eaten it, but I was starving; I'd drunk a couple of cups of water that hadn't helped the metallic feeling in my mouth. The tinnitus-on-steroids feel of the fracking pumps made my teeth ache until I was too queasy to keep a straight line of thought in my head. Usually I could ignore sensory triggers if I concentrated enough, but I couldn't make it go away. I was used to "cleansing protocols" that made me feel that way when my mother would take me in for treatments, but I was out of practice for thinking about precautions like sleeping on my side with my face at the edge of the bed. The new staff had watched me take every pill; it made me wonder if they weren't fake anymore.

I wiped up with my blanket and tried to think. A replacement staffer peeked in the door slit, called for assistance and then came in and screamed at me to get on the floor face down. That method of saying "hi" hadn't changed with the new nametags. He yanked my left wrist around to check the tat. The backup gagged about the smell and cursed that they were going to have to get me cleaned up. He talked into the radio on his shoulder.

Two female staffers watched me shower. I overheard one warn the other about not drinking from the camp faucets, that there was a cistern that would be filled from water buffaloes for drinking. The cold water fog off the showerhead smelled like fumes from the gas well pumps. I got a fresh jumpsuit shoved in my hand as I tried to dry off. I had goosebumps so bad the thin, coarse towel scraped more skin than it dried. The wind leaked in around the rusted frames of the cracked windows; the wire mesh embedded in the beaded glass held the main pieces in place, but ice crystals had formed along the fractures. One of the staffers said to hurry up so they could get the fuck out of the dank room. It didn't seem as though there was much transformation at the heart of the beast.

I came back to the same fouled blanket, and felt a queasy triumph for having made the right choice. My phone was still wrapped in it, and probably no one would touch it if I left it under there while the cheap felt ripened for another month, when new blankets were due to be handed out.

When I turned the phone on, there was a text from Chill. "Wht's happening there? Evrthng OK??"

I wrote back "don't know much yet. Am sick. Prbly frac fluid in water. More ltr, low bat. Need 2 save charge. Will txt when I knw anything."

...

I had heavy chills the next morning; my hair was sweat-damp and my feet kept going out from under me when the early shift staff did the regular pre-dawn turnout. Someone showed Angela in. She made such a scene over the disgusting room that the radios started squawking back and forth and they took her away. She would always find a way to get herself treated better; it was just in the glow her skin breathed off. I overheard something about leaving the sick kids in isolation until they could get a doctor in to figure out what was going on. I rolled over, pushed the blanket into a bundle at my feet with the cleanest parts on the outside, and smiled to myself.

...

Sometime the next day, the Golden One came in. She set a couple of bottles of water on the floor next to the bunk. I tried to say something, and she brushed the nasty hair out of my face. I shuddered and reflexively touched her hand. She tried to hide her recoil with her pretty smile, but her reaction was too raw to mistake. She softly said we'd talk later, but she'd brought me a treat to try to tempt me back to solid food.

It was an iced brownie with a jelly filling; I woke up inside fast. She waited for me to start eating. I picked at the cake parts and said it would take a while to get it all down, but it tasted good. I couldn't tell if I'd sold her, but I hoped she believed the crap that autistics can't lie. We don't usually like to, and we aren't usually good at it, but we do what we have to just like anyone else.

There was an odd, bitter overtone to the bit of filling sticking to a bite of the crumbly part I couldn't avoid without calling attention to it. I figured I'd hide the gooey mess in my blanket when the intern left, and the smell from the stained blanket was doing a good job of making her want to do that. As she was closing the door, I saw someone standing at attention with his hands folded behind him in the hall.

It was the trusty with the broken nose. He was wearing a stripped-down, low grade version of a Laithbourn uniform, and he gave me a slow wink behind the intern's back.

CHAPTER SIX

The Franco-Anglian Joint Canadian Science Foundation has con-firmed a series of earthquakes in late November, centered in a sparsely populated part of the Autonomous Northern Heartland Re-gion of the United States. Further, the Science Foundation has confirmed significant drops in the water tables of several New Albion municipalities near the border with the Northern Heartland. Hydro-levels are being monitored in closely adjoining Québec Libre areas. Given the already-alarming draw-down in the lower Great Lakes, ap-parently related not only to climate fluctuations but also to the existence of a frequently-denied pipeline network running from the Northern Heartland to the SouthWest Autonomous Region, further damage to the water resources of the Canadian Alliance may be met with a significant response.

La voix du Québec libre, édition en ligne anglaise
(The Voice of Free Quebec, Online Edition,
for our international audience) 20th January, 2032

T HE AFTERNOON SUN came through the unbarred win-dows of Angela's room. They were reinforced glass, and the sheer curtains hid the net of steel wire embedded in the small panes. The Golden Intern had sent Angela to help care for me after the contaminated water outbreak, and her refusal to be placed with me temporarily had gotten me placed with her permanently, with a warning that if it didn't work out, we'd both find ourselves in worse circumstances. It had taken a few weeks to get my digestion back. My mother's "autism cures" left my in-sides so messed up they took their time recovering.

Uncle Gabriel had brought his magic kit and said he was going to make me handsome. He warned me each time before the dron-ing clippers touched my scalp as he shuffled and danced, shaping my hair into a soot-colored version of his velvety pewter buzzcut. He understood what would look good on an androgynous little punk with decent bones. Angela's earbuds were in; she nodded her head to whatever was in them and stared at her e-reader, pointedly ignoring us.

Chill had stayed away since the Laithbourn crackdown, but he'd asked Gabriel to look after me. I found myself liking him, and it seemed reciprocal. He said I should plan on being treated as a member of the family. I wasn't entirely sure what that meant, but that was nothing unusual.

Gabriel carefully lifted the towel from around my neck and shook it into the paper bag next to him. As he brushed clippings from my shoulder, something small and heavy slipped inside my jumpsuit and caught in my waistband. He leaned forward to sweep his gentleman's clothes brush under my collar.

His voice was barely louder than his breath. "Check that later. It's from Gabie... Chill, as you call him. He says instructions haven't changed. Don't ask me anything—just between us, you might wonder why they're leaving us alone together in this room. Consider internal sight-lines..."

I took the brush and swept my lap, discreetly adjusting whatever was inside my suit so it stayed trapped when I stood up. Gabriel stepped back with his strong, pretty hands on my shoulders and nodded approvingly.

He turned toward Angela. "Much better, don't you think, darling?"

She barely looked up. "Sure that, Uncle Not-Daddy. She looks more like Runt's little sister than I do, thank-ya-jeezuss."

...

Late that night was the first time Angela said more than two words together to me since I'd been rooming with her. I could finally get up without help to use the toilet. She'd leaned in over the privacy half-wall with her back to the small dark spot near the ceiling that didn't quite match up with the wallpaper pattern. She reached over so her hand was hidden, made a quick gesture with her thumb toward the dark spot and rolled her eyes.

I could barely hear her say, "How's your phone working?"

I flushed. Under the plumbing sound, I said, "Useless. Nothing in the battery. Can't exactly ask for the charger clip that came with it even if Sam didn't pocket it when he left."

"Can't you swipe a battery pack from work? Don't they got you on phones now?"

I said the North Korean battery packs were custom fit to Heartland Regional Service phones, and not even New Confederacy equipment could take them.

"I got a charger..."

Angela managed to get around the regs on that too. Chargers were "held for you." You had to kiss up to get yours out of hock every couple of weeks so you could use your electronics, and then you had to come up with another act of contrition to get them to unlock your outlet for an hour to plug it in.

I pulled up my long johns, careful not to dunk the phone, and said I didn't think her little universal power-plate charger would cut it. FedWeb equipment took a lot of current to juice up and she'd need access to a socket for longer than we were allotted.

Angela reached over and snapped her fingers. "Gimme. Let's take a shot. I can jimmy the outlet box—the lock's pathetic. Grab your bedcover around yourself and stand over me like you're pissed. I'll kneel and make like boo-hoo, then I'll yank the cover off you and throw it so they can't see the box is open."

I told her I'd need to take the battery pack out for it to have a chance; the case was shielded so a contact charger like hers wouldn't work. I said I'd do it in the morning at my workstation.

She whispered, "Yeah, we'll get it going." in the same voice we'd been using, and then turned toward the spot near the ceiling and cursed me loudly for being a thankless bitch. She flounced on her bed, rolled over to face the wall and pulled the covers over her head.

...

A few days later I had a counseling session with the Golden One. I'd been told to wait in Angela's room, even though I could've put in most of my shift before my appointment. There'd been a suicide in the girls' wing, and I was to consider what I might have done to help her. I doubted my opinion would be approved. Angela was at her new job in the kitchen. I breathed the solitude like a clean wind off the lake.

The broken-nosed trusty had the appointment before mine. He was in uniform, like most of the fuck-ups who'd been pulled out of the Laithbourn assembly. Apparently they made the best goons, and Laithbourn was making it official, unlike the old system where you had to guess. Broken-nose pushed past me in the office doorway.

The Golden One complimented me on my hair. She reminded me that her first name was Ariel; I could call her Dr. Matthews if I preferred, but she'd like me to address her directly. The way she arched her eyebrow and flattened her voice seemed to imply that if I chose her last name, I was telling her to keep her distance. I said I was more comfortable with that.

She spoke with a snide over-politeness. "Very well then, 'Miss Archer.'"

She spun her RhinePact-made workstation toward me. Onscreen was the view from the spot near the ceiling in Angela's room. Angela and I were sitting on her bed; her sweater and earbuds were spread across the one I was now using. The feed was paused. Angela's eyes looked teary, but she grinned, her pose frozen as she reached to touch my knee.

I tried to sell that I didn't know about the camera. I couldn't fake surprise, so I went for stony anger. The Golden One smiled tightly and started the playback.

Angela had leaned back with a smug look. "So, the runty little Gabriels did OK today, huh? 'S generally not such a good idea to pick on Darks... or their friends."

I watched myself stare at Angela, my expression attractive as cold putty.

Angela's eyes seemed more calculating than I'd remembered. "Are you gonna tell me what you did to earn yourself a spot here or not?"

I listened to my sketchy description of my times in the psych ward.

The Golden One tapped the screen showing my records. "You may not lie, although that tenet doesn't stand up in this place. You do conceal things, such as the contraband communications device

I was just informed, and have confirmed, that you've kept hidden from staff. You certainly withhold things, such as the fact that you were arrested last November, but didn't come here until this summer, after you'd put your mother in the emergency room. At that meeting in Dr. Asalvo's office, she was wearing a neck-brace from your having pushed her down your apartment stairwell. Would you like to offer an explanation for that?"

I'd figured Broken-nose would rat on me about the phone as soon as he could get an ally worth selling me out to, but hearing the war with my mother brought up was a jolt. I couldn't put into language what I'd felt when that white rage had come out of me. I'd just learned my mother had enrolled me in an immersion program Archer's family had found; it combined "alternative healing practices" like chelation protocols and dietary purges with round-the-clock ABA-based supervision and intensive "rehabilitative sessions," as well as mainstream drug interventions and neurostimulation. She'd brought me to my cousin's evening session; a therapist was training him to "dine appropriately" with the family. My mother rhapsodized that Archer's clan dragged in nightly to eat with him even though he'd never be capable of the gratitude he owed them.

Archer had jumped up from the fake dinner table, yowling and flapping his hands when he'd seen me for the first time in years. I was hurried out before I saw what they did to shut him down.

As we'd been walking up that flight of apartment steps, my mother was telling me how superb this program was since it was based in an institutional "home-type environment." She'd come in mornings and evenings to participate in my therapies and "nurse" me through my purges.

There was always going to be some program. When this one didn't work, she'd find another one, even more hellish. I'd never have a moment to re-find my soul or breathe my own air, never have my guts left alone, never have a free day without straitjacket drugs poisoning my body and systematized brainwashing destroying my mind—I'd stared into my mother's gloating face, pushed her away, and watched her fall and curl up on the landing, sobbing triumphantly. I'd proven her point; I was too violent to be free. She'd won. I'd called the police myself.

The Golden One scanned my expression. "We're taught to say that we can't deny the parents hope in these situations, and that their children's lack of empathy toward them shows how deeply in need of treatment they are, but I wonder... Do you think your mother was using some of the more intrusive therapies she put you through to vicariously attack your father, who does sound quite similar to you? She's said she blames him for your autism, albeit because of his insistence on you having your vaccinations rather than any genetic contribution."

I clamped my jaws tight.

The Golden One leaned forward. "Sophia, I see considerable evidence that your mother has some form of schizoid personality disorder. You may have been subjected to Munchhausen's Syndrome by Proxy in her efforts to get attention by projecting a non-existent form of disease onto you. If ever there were an argument for a common genetic basis for some forms of autism, schizophrenia, bipolarity, and whatever associated disorders, it would be your family. We can get all of you screened—confront the issue head on and at the same time further research into understanding this hereditary monster that has molded all of you. We can get this treated."

I didn't bite. There was a time when I might have gone toward that anglerfish lure lighting my way into her maw, but not anymore.

She pulled up another file. "Suppose I told you that after your cousin completed that program, he was able to enter a sheltered employment situation. Suppose I told you he's getting regular behavioral treatments and medication, and now he's earning his own money and contributing to society. He had his savant skills analyzed and was placed where he could accomplish something useful instead of being a parasite on the rest of the world."

She spun the screen around to me again. The file it displayed was my cousin Archer's; there was a still image of him at a monitor with a grip-modified joystick in his clumsy hand. His monitor showed the edge of the lake from the height of the abandoned skyscrapers he was maneuvering the camera drone through. He was wearing his goofy grin, showing off as a uniformed handler watched him navigate the aerial maze. A huge Laithbourn seal dominated the wall above his row of "specials" aligned in their little booths. Another photo showed him in his booth, but turned sideways to study the handler's face for legible signs of approval.

I shook my head and turned the workstation back around.

The intern leaned forward again. "He gets medical care, Sophia, not just palliative. Someday that's going to have meaning for you. Once you leave here, if you're an unemployed autistic, you don't get lifesaving treatments. Do you understand that?"

I said, "Not sure I'd want them."

The Golden One heaved a deep, professional sigh. "So we seem to have settled on an adversarial approach. Very well, Miss Archer. We shall be adversarial."

She cued up Angela's room from the night before. The fisheye lens caught Angela at her tiny desk, holding up the welded plastic mess of melted battery pack after she'd "accidentally" spilled contraband professional-strength nail polish remover on it. Her face was trying for apologetic, but her eyes glistened with laughter.

I'd screamed through real tears of disappointed rage that Chill was right: she couldn't stand anyone else having anything good. "I risked my ass to pull that custom pack out on company time. For you. Now this thing is permanently useless—are ya *happy!*?"

I watched myself take something from inside my jumpsuit and stomp on it until its case cracked and the little screen shattered. I left the pieces on the floor and curled in the corner behind my bed, where the video froze me. I stared at myself, wondering if I'd pulled it off. The jagged pain in my recorded expression was real enough.

The Golden One didn't cover the hiss in her voice this time. "Dr. Asalvo and I agree it's time to get back to basics. We're resuming the wilderness programs this facility was founded on. The whole precociously oversexed, oppositional-defiant lot of you will be fitted for electro-aversive equipment. We'll also be scheduling a tattooist to make adjustments based on additional diagnoses.

"One more exhibit, Miss Archer, this one in real time. When you violate our trust, there are consequences. Your little lovers' tiff has exposed your culpability, and you'll learn the consequences of that shortly. You aren't the only one who's been abusing workplace privileges, however. You may consider yourself lucky to have betrayed yourself already. We'll find where every single missing piece of equipment and minute of misappropriated time has gone.

"Please take a moment to watch that in process. Five minutes, then you may leave."

She set a timer on her desk. The workstation showed the electronics assembly room. Kids lay on the cement floor in rows, face down and barefoot. From their blotched faces and some urine-soiled clothing, they'd been there since the start of the shift—close to eight hours. One pleaded he was going to wet himself, and a uniformed trusty cracked a length of rubber hose across the soles of his feet in response. A Laithbourn staffer screamed they could move once they talked the right way to the right people—starting with the names of anyone who'd stolen from the workroom. When the kid who couldn't hold it soaked his jumpsuit, he got beaten again. Another stood on a chair with a hand-lettered sign around his neck that said "I betrayed my peers" as a group of rah-rah kids jeered. They sounded tired of yelling, but knew it wasn't a good idea to stop. They had the best job in hell.

...

Angela was in counseling. I paced the tiles of her room in patterns. Every time I completed a signifier I stopped at the tile nearest the wall and pivoted five times on each of the five adjacent tiles, counting aloud as I shuffled. It was a soothing stim even if it had another purpose. An eight-pointed star finally completed itself out of range of the fisheye lens.

I pulled my phone out, newly fitted with the battery pack Chill had sent via Gabriel when I got my haircut. While continuing my audible turn-count, I powered it up, silenced the ring and sent him an urgent text. I left the GPS signal on and stuffed it back in under the sanitary pad I didn't need. I paced a few more patterns and then swept the stomped bits of the decoy phone I'd swiped from my workstation into the trash, palming anything with the Regional Net brand-name on it to flush. The little electronic corpse couldn't pass close inspection by anyone looking for my FedWeb phone, but the Professionals had decided what the truth was and hopefully wouldn't look for contradictions.

...

The kids targeted for "aversive technology" passed slowly through the frisk line in the hall leading to the checkpoint in the assembly room. We'd been standing for hours. Close to midnight, the Golden One peeked at the line and disappeared. When I got to the checkpoint, the trusty in charge of it grabbed the wad at my crotch and called the staffer over.

I played up the stammer in my voice, going for the "crude and clueless" stereotype. "They give me nappies... I had the surgery... but I still got a discharge sometimes... see...?"

I opened my jumpsuit and pulled down my long john bottoms in the front to show the pad I'd stained with vegetable soup smuggled from lunch in a small-parts ziploc. The kids who were already in the room snickered.

The staffer spat into the wastebasket full of confiscated items. "Geeeauchh! Autistics! Gimme a nice clean rape-and-battery type any day..." He whirled around and snarled the snickering kids. "Think that's funny? It'll be funny when I make you eat it."

I snapped my jumpsuit closed fast. I wasn't sure if he was serious. Autistics may be literal-minded, but in the new Thunderbird, anything was possible. I sat at the losers' table. Angela was alone there, and rolled her eyes and turned away. In the far spotlight, Dr. Asalvo and his golden acolyte gestured at each other on the stage. Once the room settled, the Great Man raised his hand to shield his eyes from the single glaring stage light. The fake color in his hair and the weave extensions knotted through it over his bald spot caught in the hazy beam and throbbed neon orange, the dingy roots showing above his damp, blotchy forehead.

His booming voice slurred slightly. "It seems an injunction has been issued. The Yanks won't permit us their electroshock harnesses for the moment. The court is hearing arguments that they should be destroyed. They're no longer legal there—thus the CABA system ends up with so many little Yankee wretches. We'll get past this bleeding-heart grandstanding." He stalked offstage.

The Golden One stepped forward, shimmering under the spotlight. "Dr. Asalvo has been under a great deal of pressure. I'm sure once he's able to rest, he'll be fine. We'll win this court battle. We've won before, and with his vision we'll do it again. He believes in the potential you kids have, even if you don't. The Rotenberg harnesses will set you free, once you learn to work within them. You'll truly learn how to fly with the Thunderbird."

She was choking up on her own horseshit. The secondhand aversive equipment was an ABA "treatment technique" that had come out of the old Judge Rotenberg Center whose PTSD-twisted survivors wore their shock-burn scars as badges of honor. The old U.S. FDA had once banned the things, but there was still a market for them in the troubled teen industry. The trusties had been tormenting us for days about CABA having made the winning bid. Up on the stage, the intern closed by saying the treats we were supposed to get after we were fitted would still be given out. She seemed disappointed by all the leaden faces.

Trusties passed out individually labeled baggies of jelly-filled cookies. I pushed the one with my name away unopened. Angela wolfed hers and then grabbed mine. I started to say something and stopped myself. She stuffed her face, her eyes darting around.

She gave me a lurid grin. "Peeped in on them mixing up our batches. Barbital, baby—good times. Sleep easy tonight, maybe sleep through my own execution, pray-da-*Lawd*-mah-soul-ta-take." She fluttered her fingers like the feeble ghost of a holy roller. "Best a born-to-be-hanged injun-nigger can hope for. Too bad you didn't get yours."

The trusties collected the empty baggies. They checked under the tables and patted us down. A couple of kids who'd stashed their portions were detained after we were sent to bed.

...

Angela snored heavily. I stared at the ceiling, waiting for the lock to click.

...

I drove deep into myself, my heartbeat belonging to someone else, someone floating in the depths of the ocean, soundless and vast. My eyes were rolled back when Broken-nose pulled my eyelid up to check whether the barbital had done its work. I did pass out briefly as he hoisted me over his shoulder, my hands dangling as he reached around my thighs to tamp me in place. My display of the soup-stained sanitary pad seemed to keep his hands from straying too intimately as we crossed the security perimeter into the cold night air.

Broken-nose grabbed at one of my meager breasts. "Not worth the trouble except for the sport. She'll put up a decent fight. Nice of Matthews to give 'em over, but you got the better one. Pretty Doctor Ariel does hold a grudge—worth remembering." He reached up and patted my ass. "So do I. Mmm-mmm—so do I."

There was another voice, grunting under a weighty burden. "Shit, you got the easy job. That one's nothin.' You get to carry the big bitch when we get there." Then the sound of a heavy load being dropped, a vehicle door opening, and an engine starting.

...

The rusted steel of the pickup bed kept banging my cheek as it bounced up the rocky trail. The stars were clear overhead. I kept my body loose, letting it slide into Angela's against the tailgate. From under my eyelashes I caught a glimpse of the broken-nosed trusty checking on us through the back window of the cab. A shovel and pick slid around the bed, ringing against the corrugated metal.

...

Angela lay half-hidden in the winter weeds about a dozen yards from me; she barely moved when Broken-nose's friend kicked her.

He picked her head up by the hair and screamed into her face. "Get up and dig, cunt!"

She gave him the slobbery shadow of a Dark grin, and her eyes rolled back. I tried to mimic her overdose symptoms. The trusties cursed that someone had screwed up the doses—we were supposed to be able to stand by then. The Golden One had promised them their sport. In the cold glow from a small LED lantern, they probed between scrubby trees filling in an abandoned field. Broken-nose had left me mostly face down, but I could see through the dried grass that they were using the pick to break through the few inches of frozen ground to the deep-plowed loam underneath. No one was coming: no headlights, no sirens. It was time.

I was up, sprinting through the brush like my feet had wings, but Broken-nose was right behind. He'd been waiting for it. He kicked the back of my knee and twisted my arm behind me as I stumbled. Something extremely sharp pressed against the pulse in my neck, and a trickle of warmth cooled as it ran down my collarbone. A brief, high scream came from near where I'd seen Angela. I felt Broken-nose's face pressing against the back of my head, his tepid breath moist on my nape, and then he turned toward the scream, calling for his friend. I was staring into searing blue-white.

There was an urgent, familiar voice behind the light. "Drop and take the cut, Scope—Now!"

My legs did as I was told. I crumpled sideways, unwinding my arm enough to separate myself from Chill's target—the knife dug into my neck, but as a shallow slice that slid across my throat and quickly up behind my ear. A cracking flash deadened my hearing, and the body behind me drew itself by its grip on my arm to fall on top of me.

...

Gabriel was rubbing Angela's hands and gently slapping her cheeks. She blinked and flopped forward into her uncle's arms, sobbing softly. Gabriel had set his smeared knife carefully on the ground next to Broken-nose's friend. The friend lay on his back, motionless. A dark pool widened around his head, spreading from a broad, clean gash in his throat. A man with a kind face was dressing the cut across my neck; he wore a tan uniform.

Chill held my hand. "Scope, this is Deputy Tom Webster, the one from the sheriff's department I said you could trust. You need to go with him now. I gotta be scarce around here for a while."

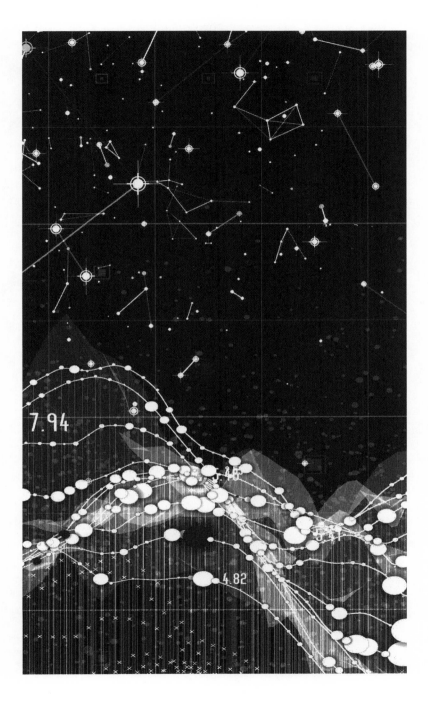

W E, WHO ARE GATHERED HERE on this day fraught with implications for the future of our people, must act with farsighted courage. It is our duty to protect our citizens' right to privacy, and further, the right of our law enforcement as they undergo their perilous charge must have even more of that precious freedom, commensurate with the burden they bear to protect this great Republic in its time of birth.

Therefore, we shall boldly go against the grain of popular appetites, of common dissolution and of yielding to the lowest and weakest of impulses of the lowest and weakest among us. We declare that this Republic will not allow any recording capabilities in any communication device in our territories: no camera, no video, no sound. There will be no more selfies for the selfish, no more traps laid by those who might tempt us to ill behavior, no more spread of vile misinformation against our bravest and most productive citizens.

Keynote speech, North Heartland Republic
Constitutional Convention of 2033
Senator Frank Lewiston of Wyandot

It was quite a scene, with the Nugent White Buffalo Partiers rubbing shoulders with Coon-skinners and Buckskins, coming together to decide which yoke they can let Laithbourn Cap put on the rest of us if they force a secession referendum through. They won't get it this year or next, but eventually they'll strangle the education system sufficiently to sell a hopelessly ignorant electorate on their Brave New Snake Oil.

The Conventioneers, in their day jobs in the Legislature, have already sold our water, our land, our timber and our health. The only threat to Laithbourn hegemony seems to be from Free Quebeckers flooding the market with unregulated pharmaceuticals in defiance of the corporate healthcare monopoly—taking vengeance for the outright swiping of their water by deluging our impoverished sick with cheap, effective, good-quality black market medications.

PoorJaredsAlmanac@TheUrbanHowl.press, blog post 8/12/33

TOM WEBSTER'S FAMILY took me in. They'd never had their own babies, but they'd permanently taken in a couple of "special needs" boys and were fostering another one, so it wasn't unusual for them to have an extra, slightly offbeat face showing up. Tom had worked for the Sheriff's Department since he graduated high school, and his wife had been in the military and taught in the public schools until her job was cut. They lived on a scrubby farm a few miles outside Deep Lake. The food they raised was cleaner and cheaper than what the store in town stocked, and farming kept the kids too tired to get into trouble.

The Websters expected me to start school come fall and to have an identity that I could stick to by then. I wasn't supposed to tell anyone my real name. I was to use the Webster name on anything official, as if I'd been legally adopted. Mostly they called me "girl" in a friendly-distant way. Tom and his wife didn't want their sons to know anything they'd have to lie about.

It wasn't much of a farm: a couple of dozen laying hens and a few breeding milk cows. Every few weeks somebody I knew outlived her usefulness and ended up in a stew pot. The males weren't around long enough to be useful. I hardened to it, but I never got over being brushed by inch-long eyelashes while nuzzling against a big, bony, coarse-haired face smelling of sweet hay, and then a week later seeing the same huge eye staring blankly at the sky with a clean, humane gunshot wound next to it. Tom had me pruning and raking in the apple orchard, keeping the woodpile stocked and the barn cleaned. It was easier to shovel cowshit than to look at their appreciative faces when they were being fed, knowing what I knew. Tom tried to teach me to drive the tractor, but I couldn't get my parts coordinated well enough to control the equipment.

There was a big void in what I knew about what had happened after Angela and I got carried out of that field, and I gut-knew it was supposed to stay that way. Uncle Gabriel still drove across Wyandot County to Deep Lake once a month to cut my hair in the Websters' kitchen, but he never talked much about Chill. and I felt I wasn't supposed to ask. He came on me one day when I was breaking up a stack of pallets with a sledgehammer to feed the wood stove. I was bashing out of my mind the terrified bellows of a smart, feisty bull calf hauled off to be a meat-slave. I could forget everything in the world when I swung a big hammer. My breath was a thick, hot fog in the cold March morning as the rage turned into shattered scrap lumber. Gabriel had been observing a while before I realized he was there.

He applauded and called to Tom to come out a moment. "I believe I have a given name for our girl, Thomas. Scope, if you'll accept it, I dub you Our Lady of the charnel grounds, Dakini Webster, Wielder of Hammers, Spinner of Illusion-nets."

Tom and I gave him a blank look.

He went to his truck for his phone, but it was hopeless to get a signal. I offered him mine, but he was reluctant to use it.

He told me to go onto a Buddhist information site. "Tibetan minor goddesses: very fierce, often rule in wastelands. Dakinis bring enlightenment by smacking you upside the head. Buddhist names were popular in the city a decade and a half ago among the hipster set."

Tom continued to look blank, but I scowled intently at an elegantly precise line drawing on my phone screen; it showed a petite, delicate-faced, dancing woman with a ferocious frown, staring eyes, an ornate band of skulls around her lithe hips, four arms, a weapon in each hand, and a savage grin with long curving fangs.

I said, "I like it."

...

I sat at the dinner table with Tom and his family. He and his wife called me Dakini instead of the usual "girl" or just "would you kindly..." The boy who seemed the oldest, a little younger than me, was hyperactive and whip-smart. He got it right off. I think he got that it wasn't my real name, too, but he kept that to himself. The middle kid, who was twelve, didn't have speech, so no one was likely to try to get information from him. The "baby" of the family, the little foster Liam, looked a couple of years younger. He carried himself like a benevolent emperor, despite being painfully small. He had Down syndrome and a speech impediment; he struggled to get his mouth around my new name. Anything much longer than a syllable wasn't likely to work for him, even though he could keep up with his sixth grade classwork. The closest he could consistently get was "Dakth." I said I could go with "Dax," as if that was what he'd meant to say, and he gave me a sweet, goofy smile that reminded me so much of Archer it hurt.

I'd be Dakini, but my nickname was Dax, as christened by Liam, and I needed to learn to answer to it like it was something I'd heard from before I could remember. Gabriel decided I needed a talisman to keep it in my heart, and he offered to take me to get one.

...

The twenty miles to Deep Lake were mostly fields of tacky pseudo-mansions, empty and falling apart. Whole streets of them, never completed, had weed-trees in the yards and faded bank sale signs roped onto the fake Euro-manor gates.

Gabriel shook his head. "Stupid. Stupid. Stupid. Fucking lemmings: no anchor, no roots. Who were they going to sell to?"

He told me about the dairy farms that used to be there. "The land's ruined now, all the topsoil scraped away—crap clay fill brought in."

We pulled into the stretch of buildings that had once catered to Deep Lake fishermen. Most were boarded up, but several sold retro-New Age handmade trinkets and homespun clothes by people like me who have a hard time holding a regular job. Some "spiritual center" types had set up there—crop circle tricksters and their co-dependents taking advantage of the cheap rent. Only the one next to the boat ramp still sold tackle. We bought a couple of bottles of water there. Gabriel said he used to drink from the lake as a kid, but he wouldn't do it now.

We walked along the gravel to a storefront that exhaled patchouli incense. The woman behind the counter had the same look in her eyes my mother did when she was in the rare mood to like me. When Gabriel asked to see a velvet display box of brownish cast bronze pendants, she asked if I was his daughter. He chuckled softly and said no, but we were related. The woman pointed out a pendant with an incised design very similar to the one I'd seen on my phone. The etched lines sharpened when she buffed the smooth metal to a somber golden sheen. Gabriel looked at my face and bought it without saying a word. I was stimming my fingers on the polished surface as we walked out.

When we were back at the truck, I remembered to thank him. I asked if we could take a walk around the lake. He said he'd drive to the place where he used to fish.

When we pulled off the dirt road, he sighed. He pushed aside the heavy undergrowth from the surge of humid late spring warmth as he walked ahead of me. The woods were full of trash from drinking, sex, and other dangerous habits. I knew enough to watch for needles before he warned me. Invasive vines draped and choked out the taller trees. After we plowed a few hundred yards through the condom-spangled neo-jungle, the shore opened out. The glacial gravel bay held the moldy corpse of an inflatable raft, a carpet of plastic bottles, and nests of six-pack rings half-floating in the shallow water. The sky was heavy overcast. Chirps of a few surviving peeper-frogs and rumbles of distant thunder felt close across the miles of leaden water.

I thought about what Gabriel had told me. When developers blasted the ledge out for a bigger ramp for the bloated white people who were going to buy all the bloated new houses, concussion shock had killed the fish, and the toxic muck it dislodged had left the lake poisoned for a generation. They'd skimmed the dead out and buried them with a backhoe in the topsoil they'd hauled off the farms. Beautiful lake trout under the loam, holding the heat with humid breath, their stench leaching into the world...

It felt like rain.

I murmured, "'Quand le ciel bas et lourd pèse comme un couvercle sur l'esprit...'"

Gabriel raised an eyebrow. "The low sky presses on the spirit like a pot lid? Baudelaire? Appropriate, somehow. Still full of surprises. Gabie—your 'Chill'—said I could count on that."

"Thank you. Tell Chill to send me a text sometime."

...

A couple of days later, Chill sent me a picture from some nasty club in a part of the city I'd never seen. I was glad to hear from him, but his photo was skanky. It appeared he'd landed a catch of Barracudas. On one side of him, flushed and awkward, was Bern Solomon—the tall, gentle guy who'd given me my phone, smiling vaguely into the camera flash. Bern looked like he was putting on weight, and he didn't appear comfortable with the situation. On Chill's other side was Jeff Arrington, the guy who'd made me feel weird after he caught me watching his ass while he was waiting to take a serve at the Sterling Island Athletic Association tennis courts. Chill looked older, and his clothes were a lot smoother than the club. The walls were plywood, with faceted clear LED Christmas lights strung around the top.

Jeff was still trim, but his not-quite handsome face was blotched and swollen, his lower lip purplish and lopsided as if he'd been in a fight recently. It didn't surprise me. Chill's grin was full-on Dark-wicked and he was holding Jeff hard by the wrist.

Jeff didn't appear to like it, but he wasn't doing much about it. That surprised me.

Chill's message was long. I wondered if he'd gotten a phone from Bern like mine, or if he was writing from a computer somewhere.

Hey smallstuff- glad ya still want me to stay in touch- me likes your barracuda boys. Bern misses you like breathing, ya know? We be celebrating his passage of the bar exam- you got yerself a genuine lawyer on the hook now. Ya could do worse than go back to him after yer next b-day when you won't land him in jail if you get caught doin yer stuffs. 17- age of consent in paradise soon as the law kicks in- if you need me to come get ya best tell me soon. Gonna be doing some contracting with yer boys long distance once we pull the gig together.

Jeffy came to terms with me on it over the weekend- this is the way we shook hands on the deal since we gonna have to work together closely and like you said, Jeffy thinks he's all that and anyone else's share of it too. I had to have an in-depth discussion with him about that. Anyway, Bern's gonna front the investment and not ask questions.

Hope Tom's treating ya right. Bern says he's good to put you up at the Island Hostel like he did before if it gets too wholesome for ya. Was almost wrecked enough last night to tell your "B"ern the whole story of that sweet piece of equip he gave ya- told him it saved yer ass- but didn't tell him where you were keeping it when it did #i_winks_atcha_from_afar. Anyway, check your paypal- Bern sent ya somethin nice to remember him by. Stay in touch yourself- G.

Chill was doing well with my old Sterling Island contacts. When he'd looked over my phone and then batted his eyelashes at me in the old scrub pine grove at Thunderbird, he'd probably been figuring the angle he was finally getting to play. I wished Bern would forget about me for his own sake, but I was glad he was helping Chill. Jeff was a piece of work, though. He'd made my skin crawl back when I was a runaway, and I hoped Chill knew what he was doing if he was gaming him.

...

I'd had a rough night, dreaming about Liam staring at the sky with a bullet hole next to his eye, magnified huge, blue and round in the lens of his strong glasses. I couldn't shake the image of that bottomless pupil with nothing behind it and the red-rimmed hole with more nothingness in it.

I was riding to the one good-sized town in the county with Tom for the monthly shopping. We pulled into the big box store parking lot to wait for his wife and the kids in the other vehicle.

He turned to face me. "Dax, you probably don't want to get too attached to Liam, for your own emotional health."

I gave him a sharp look.

He shuffled in his seat. "How old do you think Liam is? I know that's not your strong point, but guess."

I said ten, maybe twelve, since Down syndrome kids were usually shorter than average.

"He's older than you are, Dax. He's never had enough circulation to grow properly."

I started to object. I knew my own growth had been stunted by being spayed so young. I'd figured Liam had been neutered to "improve his quality of life."

Tom cut in. "He has a heart valve that will fail soon—no way I can pay for surgery and not have the family end up homeless. Barbara and I are trying to give him a few happy months and keep him out of CareWell until he hopefully passes in his sleep."

CareWell was Wyandot County's warehouse for indigents waiting to die. It was known as "Farewell" and was a taxpayer-funded enterprise owned by a for-profit corporation. The codeword was "cooperative venture," and the reality was hell for anyone not courteous enough to expire behind a dumpster as a well-behaved pauper should.

I felt tears starting.

Tom slapped the dashboard softly. "Damnit, I tried to adopt and get him on my County insurance. Youth Services had him in the system as a Social Liability. I already have two the county pays for—no more exceptions. I'm fifty-two. This isn't the world I grew up in, but it's the world I deal with. If the Heartlands secede, I—we—won't have that much protection—everything goes private and no way a low-grade public servant like me can pay for any of us."

He turned to me and rubbed my shoulder awkwardly. "Oh, hell Dax... please don't. Don't let him see you crying. You're the best thing that's happened to him in a long time. He has kind of an idea what it means, but I don't think he really understands it. For the best—I don't go out of my way to explain. Just let him enjoy his time, OK?"

CHAPTER EIGHT

Good afternoon and welcome to the show, Duke O'Brien here at Wyandot Broadcasting Foundation, the Rock of Your World. FreeWill Church-supported First Amendment Radio since before you were born.

And in the news On the Brink today:

Laithbourn Security has stepped in to assist what passes for Wyandot law enforcement in the crackdown on unauthorized pharmaceuticals entering from Frogland by way of Lord Douchebag's Privy. They do seem to forget they're just Canadians up there, reverting to their European inbreeding and getting along like perfumed Parisian and paint-faced London pansy-boys batting their eyelashes at each other now they've split up. I guess it makes it more exciting that way. Anyway, they're doing their best to poison us, and they're getting help from the inside, in this reasonable man's assessment. My Coonskinner sources tell me it ain't all rosy-pink-cheeked health pills these farogs and their indigenous whores are peddling. It seems our public servants know, or sure as hell should know, who's running this stuff.

O'Brien on the Brink, WWBF AM 58 and Webcast
brinksman58.press, 11/2/33

I HELD LIAM'S HAND as I took care of my part of the shopping list for the big box store. I hated the popu-lescent soundtrack punctuated with jolting announcements, garish smells and omnipresent greenish sixty-cycle fluorescent glare buzzing in my teeth, but Liam's smile made me hold all that in. He looked at the shelves like he was in a fairy kingdom. He never fussed about wanting things the Websters couldn't afford, but Tom asked me to keep an eye out for something small he'd enjoy.

I caught sight of Uncle Gabriel by the power tool section; he was talking to someone big whose body language took up even more room. I hadn't known Gabriel was back from Canada. He'd said he'd be gone another few weeks. I sidled close enough to hear they were speaking French. The big man had a corporate logo I didn't recognize on the back of his tan canvas jacket: a fleur-de-lis with crossed war-hammers over it. Gabriel caught my eye and gave me a look like it would be a good idea to make myself scarce.

As I slipped away, Liam gave me a slant-eyed look through his thick glasses and lisped juicily. "Your boyfriend's jea... lous of me. I can take him."

He thrust his round jaw out and puffed up his chest until I laughed in spite of myself. He grinned like he'd done his job well.

We were absorbed in discussing the conflicting merits of cling peaches in heavy syrup— the concern that they contained hormone disruptors in the can linings versus the fact that they tasted really good— when I found myself looking up at the man who'd been talking to Gabriel.

"Allo, dear. Sam Champetty sends 'is best." The man tipped an invisible hat.

There was a pistol holster strap crossing his chest under his jacket and a bulge below his left armpit.

I froze and tried not to visibly tremble.

"Not to worry, little lady. I'm family, your other family." The man nodded toward Gabriel. "I've 'eard much about you. Sam's gettin' married to the lovely Angie now he can wi' the law change. I'm thinking it might be that I could employ you to give them a personal wedding present, being as you are recommended as a whore of some rare qualities. Sammy says you 'ave quite a nice way about you with Angie."

I held the dakini pendant so tight I could feel it starting to bruise my fingers, but I wasn't going to loosen my grip enough to show the tremor.

Liam pushed in front of me to face the stranger and folded his arms. "Don't you talk that way to Dax."

The man gave a winking leer. "Dax, eh? That's quite the gallánt you have there, Dax. See you be worthy of the lionheart. I'll be 'round should you wish to talk terms."

He tipped the invisible hat again and walked away. When I looked, Gabriel was gone. I breathed deep a few times until I quit shaking and then put Liam's peaches in the cart.

...

I pushed the school counselor's office door closed, stared at the IEP papers and told Tom he'd better be joking. He'd said if I wanted to stay under his roof, I had to go to school and stay there. That meant an Individual Education Plan. I was autistic and therefore an Additional Burden on the System., and all such Burdens had to have IEPs.

The plan talked about me in the third person as though I wasn't old enough to read it, let alone be competent to agree to it. "Dakini will ask politely for permission to test out of subjects she feels she knows, rather than addressing the instructor in terms that disparage the instructor's intelligence, at least eighty percent of the time," and "Dakini will remain in her assigned seat for the duration of the class period at least eighty percent of the time. If she requires a lavatory visit, Dakini will request a monitor to accompany her, or the visit will be considered an unexcused absence. The frequency of these visits will be included in the calculation of her variance for successful plan fulfillment."

I turned to the putty-faced academic advisor. "I spent my fifteenth birthday learning how to do sick sex I got paid more in one night for than you see in a week. I could go back to the guy I did that for any time I want, but I like to think I'm worth more than that. I spent my last birthday negotiating for my life with a pedophile corrections officer. I'm not going to spend this one getting chewed off at the knees by sheep."

Tom hid his chuckle behind his hand. "I take your point, Dax. How do you think you'd feel about a vocational program? There's a building trades one at the community college if you can pass a high school equivalency test. I think you can still register for the fall term."

I said to give me the damned test, then.

...

I walked with Gabriel along the edge of Deep Lake. He said Chill was asking if I'd ever made that phone call to Bern. I'd used a haughty tone when I'd told the school official about what I could go back to, but in the light off the sickly water, Bern's kindness didn't seem so contemptible. He'd never been anything but good to me. He'd given me something valuable, and I'd never even bothered to use it to thank him for it. The words had sounded righteous as they'd come out of my mouth, but the aftertaste had an unpleasant tang.

There wasn't a lot holding me to Wyandot County anymore. I'd finally learned to drive an automatic transmission, but the rides I'd promised Liam were too exhausting for him. He was too tired to talk, got frustrated with pastime games, and wasn't interested in being read to. Gabriel said he was going to be gone a lot more for the foreseeable. He'd apologized for the way the Québécois man had talked to me in the store, but hadn't elaborated on it.

Two years of trade school loomed like something around a corner as I watched myself in a dream too unpleasant for a first-person viewpoint. I'd registered for classes and gone to the orientation, but I couldn't believe I was going through with it. I hated the way I resented Tom after all he'd done for me. Fall was coming on; yellow leaves floated in the gray water. The freshly exposed nape of my neck felt the nip of the wind. I rubbed the rough velvet of my new-cut hair as Gabriel looked across the lake.

He took a pill bottle from his jacket. "Picked these up for you in Montréal. Good-quality replacement hormones and strontium for your bones. You'll be thankful later. You don't want them getting brittle so young. Promise—I mean it—promise you'll take them according to the directions. They're genuine Canadian pharmaceutical. I'll get you a steady supply. This is six months' worth. You'll have to pick up from a connection... I know I can trust your discretion."

I nodded and put them in my pocket. Gabriel skipped a stone out into the shallows, its impacts making a sentence of interlacing rings until it ran out of energy and sank into the reflected sky. I pulled my phone out and turned it on for the first time in a few days.

I'd decided I was going to tell Chill to come get me because I couldn't face any more schooling when I saw he'd already messaged me the day before.

Smallstuff- this gonna be my last to you for a bit. Not sure why you haven't been texting much lately, but I get you're not too happy. Gabe's around more than he lets on- keep his # handy if ya need anything. Send a couple words back if you get this- just let me know it came through. Heading out and down w. Jeff tomorrow, this # wont be reachable anymore. Will send new one if I get back in one piece- wish me luck.

Gave Bern the pic you sent of you & Tom with yer brand new equivalency HS diploma so he'd know for sure I wasn't conning him abt being yer friend. Congrats abt that, btw- I never got that far. I told him you said to give it to him. Made his whole week. Bern's your sub- I get that thanking him might not exactly be the best thing, but try to think of something. Luvya and bye- Gabe.

Gabriel took the phone out of my hand as I was pulling my arm back to toss it in the lake. He turned it off and tucked it into my coat pocket. I took the hug when he offered it.

...

Tom wagered a pin-money check for every A I got in trade school, along with a small bonus if my average was over 3.9. I knew I could kill it. I felt almost bad about sealing the bet, but I wanted a little money of my own outside of what I had from Bern. The Heartlands Regional Coalition was getting nosier about people's accounts, so it could be risky to access it with my new name, but I liked knowing it was there. I did write a thank-you to Bern with a request to say hey to Chill if he heard from him, but deleted it without sending it.

Around Thanksgiving I brought home polymer clay from school. The assignment was to make a cast of a piece of architectural molding and then replicate the impression in the shop. Liam was interested enough to come down from his room and watch me get up on a stepladder and press the clay against the old egg-and-dart crown in the dining room. There'd been a piece missing out of it for the last sixty years. Liam thought it was magic when I brought back a resin composite section that dropped right into place. When I got my check at the end of classes, right before Christmas, I used it to buy him clay and a toy oven to bake it in.

...

The night Liam died, he'd reached for my hand when I went to say goodnight. He hadn't spoken much the last few days, but he'd wanted my company. As I adjusted his covers for the night, his pupils were wide—a shimmering deep blue I wasn't sure could find me. He was blind as a mole without his glasses anyway, but he'd found my arm and slid his icy fingers down to my hand as he stared into another horizon. I'd been entertaining him by making impressions of different objects in the clay I'd given him. He'd roll the hardened plastic negative around in his fingers like a stim, but it seemed more intelligent than the stimming I did. I'd made an impression of my pendant for him. He'd traced his finger over the fine raised lines of the dancing goddess spooned in the inverse of the convex pendant and smiled a little.

He held it loosely against his soft, hairless chest as I kissed him on the forehead, and then he said, very softly but quite clearly, "I'll see you soon…"

I'd lain awake in the room next to his with the door open, listening. The moonlight seemed particularly bright for a moment as I dozed off, and then I heard a huge sigh. The snow was falling thick outside, and it seemed strange that the moon should be shining. I couldn't find it as I glanced out the window, and then I pulled myself all the way awake. I fumbled to get up. When I had my slippers on the right way, Tom was already next to Liam's bed, feeling for his pulse. I watched as he patted Liam's limp hand and stroked his hair back.

He looked at me standing in the doorway. "All done. God bless us, every one."

CHAPTER NINE

*So, here we are, staring down the barrel of another year as one of the
Northern Heartland's few remaining, barely surviving cities. No surprise Frank Lewiston won reelection with, as they used to say in
Russia, 110% of the vote; they hardly need the gerrymandering anymore. As Senator Frank goes, so goes the Legislature—and with it
any hope for crawling back into this century, or even the last one.
Lewiston's platform always was "less public money for the public
benefit, the weak deserve the dregs, freedom for women to be slaves
to 'family values,' run the faggots out on rails, etc, etc." Those of us
with any sense have already left for brighter places.*

Editor's Page, TheUrbanHowl.press, 1/1/35

T HE WOMAN who taught field surveying was almost six
feet tall and in her mid-twenties. I didn't care; I was taking
a run at winning her. I'd learned not to leave my tongue
hanging out when I saw a beautiful woman, but Tom approved of
my few stammered sentences of respect when he'd asked how I
was doing in Petra Sexton's class. The only other class I'd connected with at Wyandot Tech was interior demolition practices;
I liked using a sledgehammer, and I was pretty good with it for
how small I was.

I didn't know what I was going to do at the end of it, but I'd
turned eighteen still in school. Looking forward to Petra Sexton's
Introduction to Practicum and Principles of Field Surveying for
Construction, Timber Management, and Geo-resource Extraction
was a large reason for that. When I saw her name show up on my
class schedule for the final regular semester as both my instructor
and my career counselor, my stomach did a pleasurable little
butterfly-quake.

Petra's arms, usually revealed by the rolled-up sleeves of her man's shirt, were hard, smooth, and well-crafted as a good piece of polished natural oak-branch furniture. I imagined the rest of her was too, except the parts that should be soft and fair. It was a pleasant speculation. Everything about her was in shades of warm woods and bronze. She wore her heavy chestnut-brown hair braided down her back, with a bandana tied around her forehead; when she pulled it off, her skin was clear ivory above her thick eyebrows. Her eyes were the color of my pendant when it had lain inside my shirt all day and the somber gold I buffed it to each morning had softened to a mellow tarnish. Her smile was bright against her weathered face, and its shine felt clear and real.

Most kids in the program were guys. That campus was generally known as the Wyandot Testicle Institute. Petra did what she needed to be respected. When the male instructors called her Pete, it acknowledged her right to be among them even though the culture in the skilled trades was tough on women. Petra's profession required more education than most, but that got her no deference. There'd been serious rollbacks to women's legal protections, and those for queers were gone. We were reminded so if we took public exception to being leered at or given an overly familiar "friendly pat." We were on our own to handle covert groping, and developed a female's quiet martial art of elbowing, toe-stomping and finger-twisting to maintain our body boundaries. No more appeals were being sent to the Federal Circuit Court until the secession referendum; still Petra made no effort to hide what she was. She held her head higher and pushed herself harder because of it.

I'd always been a clod about recognizing when someone was attracted to me, but she seemed to like it when I came in early and hitched a ride with her to the field site. We hadn't had a formal counseling session yet, but she'd suggested we could talk things over on the half-hour drive. On this particular spring morning, I hopped a couple of times and hoisted myself into her raised-suspension off-road pickup.

She offered a strong, callused hand to assist. "One day I should put a step bar on this thing so a proper-sized girl can get in without spraining something."

I chuckled and took the hand, finding myself hauled firmly into the seat a lot closer to its owner than I'd ever been before.

Petra grinned. "Sorry 'bout that. You don't weigh what I thought you might. Shit! That didn't come out right." She fussed with her seatbelt. "Been meaning to ask. Tom Webster ran across something, a piece of property out of Sam Champetty's bankruptcy."

I gave her a blank look.

She threw the truck in gear. "After he lost his job at Thunderbird, just about everything's for sheriff sale. Laithbourn scarfed up the good stuff near town, but no buyers for anything out in the sticks. Anyway, when I ran the titles for Tom, I saw a piece that came out of the Archer family—probate dockets going back a couple hundred years, out in Littlefield near the Darks' compound. Previous owner was Solon Archer—not a real common name. Sold it to Champetty about twenty-five years ago. Tom knew it was your dad's name. He let me borrow the department log-on and his password for the Regional Registry. Was the same Social Security number for the property transaction as the one we found for your dad."

I shot her a look that was probably pure panic.

She gave me a sly grin. "Don't imagine you have too many secrets from me. Tom loves to talk, and he doesn't have many he can talk to—just me and a couple of the Darks, god bless 'em. The school doesn't know, don't worry. Tom asked me to look out for you. He thinks you have cash stowed. We can help you get to it without getting Revenue Collections all interested if you need it. Didn't know if you might want to go look sometime."

I asked her if I was particularly interesting, or if she ran background checks on all her students. Her cheeks reddened underneath her deep tan.

...

Petra squeezed in behind her venerable metal desk. Her swivel chair was trapped so close to the wall that she had to perform a kind of acrobatic half-vault to get her long legs into it. The student chair was equally ancient, wedged in against the desk at right angles with just enough room for the door to swing in. I was getting better hardened to my queasiness from fluorescent light-ing, but the buzzing glare was strong in the windowless room. Petra had made me feel so at ease that it was only the lighting I struggled with. We traded jokes as I leaned on her desk, curled around on the chair to see the files she wanted to review with me.

Petra looked up. "Kick that door closed, would ya, Dax? Thanks. Don't want one of the Testicles barging in while we're talking."

She fiddled with a pair of school file folders; one had a couple of brochure packets in it, the other held my academic records. "Dax, I've never worked with an autistic student. I need help here. To be plain, I just don't see you as disabled, even though that tat of yours gets us a nice pack of greenbacks from the Feds for you every semester. That's changing, most likely, but you'll be graduated by then."

She tapped her pen on the desk as if I was supposed to say something.

She frowned. "You've been pretty closed-mouth about your past, but you should maybe start singing the tune Tom wrote for you. Some's suspicious in the front office even if they don't want to look too hard. Better hope they never catch onto the whole forged identity and med history Tom made up for you. The fake disability claim's paid off for him and the school, but I gotta ask: is the tat a fake too?"

I stared at her. "Ms. Sexton... I... yeah, I'm autistic. I don't— didn't know..."

It was Petra's turn to stare, but she did it kindly. "Shit. I'd have thought he'd tell you. He made a claim for a Fed scholarship for you like you were his real kid and some of the shit his wife was exposed to as a National Guard vet caused the autism. Damn... and call me Pete, please, or at least not 'Ms. Sexton.'"

I swallowed and stared at my feet. I felt a black fissure opening inside me.

My eyes teared in spite of myself. "There's a lot that people who know me don't tell me, Petra... I'm autistic as hell, actually, test out as more severe than a lot who don't talk. I saw a quote once: '"Mild" autism isn't how I experience being autistic, it's how you experience my being autistic.' It's the lies. I can't keep them straight, so the ones who need to sell them don't share them with me. Tom just told me to keep my mouth shut. It's one thing I do really well. He knows I can sell it for a few hours if I can go home and collapse for at least as long—as in don't try to make me talk, or I'll have an old-skool reetard spaz-attack.

"I make good grades, but I dread burning out before I graduate. It took a year to learn to drive an automatic. Can't keep my debit register straight to save my ass. Being on my own, filing my taxes under the right wrong name, keeping my med account paid up, making car payments on time—the whole mess makes me panic because I KNOW I CAN'T DO IT. Tom's wife wrote me instructions three times, each version more babified than the last one, but I still get lost in the variables."

I felt my words trying to slip away the way they used to when I was in the school where I first cut myself. Petra made the kind of mumbled objection I'd heard my whole life.

I wasn't having it. "DO NOT TELL ME everyone feels that way sometimes and I'm smart enough—I KNOW I'm smart. Smart doesn't help when you forget how to make words come out of your mouth. It doesn't help you keep sounds from glaring or touch from screeching. It doesn't help when stress reduces you to each breath you take, and if anyone gets near you, you don't know how not to kill them unless you tear your own skin off.

"In the textbook there's one right answer and the variables are defined. Humans aren't like that. I don't get half of what anyone's talking about. If I get stuck in a crowded room, I have to hurt myself to keep from curling up under a table... and on top of this I need to remember I'm not the person I was born as, and who knows it and who doesn't??"

I heard myself yelling, and I bent over in stifled sobs with my arms around my head.

Petra put the file folders back in the drawer. "These can wait. We do need to look at them soon, but let's not do it here, OK? No tears at the Testicle Institute. I'll stop by the farm over the holiday break and we can look at them with Tom."

...

Mrs. Webster was visiting her sister in the NorthEast Union for Easter with the two boys. It was the first time she'd gone in the year since Liam died. She'd spent the first weeks like she was sleepwalking and still spent a lot of time sitting silent. I found myself liking her more since she'd let herself get angry. There was a sour edge to her that was there before, but it had hardened and sharpened within her silence.

Tom, in uniform for work, put on a fresh pot of coffee and thawed store-bought pastries in the microwave. He hummed pleasantly. I watched Petra as she swung out of her truck, pulling a worn camo-patterned messenger bag after her. She trudged up the gravel walk to the house. Tom asked me twice to open the door before it registered. She waved when she looked up and saw me at the window, and it sank in that I was a long, long way into unknown emotions over her. I'd only thought I was in love with Angela. I was beginning to understand I hadn't had a clue what feelings could come from the sight of a person striding up a hill toward me.

She dropped the messenger bag on the kitchen table, and I took her jacket to the hall. As I raised it onto the coat-hook, I wrapped my arms around the cool outside of it and let my face rest in the scented warmth of the satin-quilted liner. When I came back, Petra and Tom were sitting on either side of an empty chair with my folders open in front of it. Petra smiled proudly. Tom's mouth was trying for a smile, but his eyebrows were saying something very different. I felt like I could faint.

The folder I'd seen in Petra's office that had the edges of a couple of slick info-packets visible now displayed them; one showed the plain sans-serif lettered logo of Laithbourn Capital, the other had the same fleur-de-lis and hammers insignia I'd seen on the jacket of the man who'd forwarded Sam Champetty's greeting to me in the store, above the words "Martel International Development, LLC/Martel Société d'exploitation internationale."

I cleared my throat. "Those are my internship offers?"

...

Tom had left for his regular shift of fifteen hours driving around the county. I stayed with Petra, a cup of cold coffee, a half-eaten pastry, and very few secrets remaining.

As I'd sat down, Tom had gently pulled the "high functioning" autistic-targeted Laithbourn packet with its gleaming heavy-stock paper, touting opportunities for the unique talents of "Special Citizens," and laid it on the floor next to his feet. "Pete, I think we need to set this one aside. It's a long story, and it has to be in hard confidence. Dax, do want to tell it or should I?"

I'd managed to make some kind of sound come out of my mouth, nodding in his direction. He'd sanitized the tale of my stay at the Laithbourn-owned establishment for wayward youth, leaving off the dead bodies that had accompanied my escape. My fingerprints and DNA would still register against Laithbourn's internal record of escapees in a background check. Tom briefly referenced the Darks having been of major and ongoing assistance to me. He seemed to expect the heavy frown that crossed Petra's face when he did.

She'd pushed the Martel International folder in my direction. "Well, I guess that leaves this. If you're in with the Darks, you should coast pretty well here. It's a barely second-tier outfit with a not even third-tier reputation, but at least you'll get healthcare and not have to register for Workfare. Helluva thing to have to settle for with your grades. Somebody had to know you were attending the Institute for you even to have gotten this. They hardly ever send us shit, particularly if they see Laithbourn Cap is offering. When Laithbourn stakes a claim, they don't expect competition. Usually when Laithbourn pisses on the corner of a kid's transcript, everyone else backs off."

Tom had rubbed his temples. "Easy, Pete. It's not like she has a choice."

Petra's face had softened into something beautiful and compassionate. "Hey, at least most of their work is up in the north end of the county, out where that property that came out of your dad's chain of title is. Good reason to go look at it, huh?"

Tom had excused himself to go to work, and she and I had spent the next two hours talking. By the time she'd left, I'd agreed to put a deposit on the house and land, sight unseen.

...

Mosquitoes hovered around the flashlight. The sky was deep orchid, and a clear half-moon broke the black treeline at the horizon. With the failing light, it was harder to follow the slumped sections of low fieldstone wall sunk into the soggy meadow criss-crossed with deer tracks. The remnants of the wall strayed by several feet from the fragmented red thread of laser light from the transit back near the trees.

Petra's breath showed as a faint cloud when she whooped triumphantly after I tripped on an unexpectedly post-like piece of granite jutting out of the ground. "Son-of-a-bitch! Ya fell over it! All this time we were looking and you fell over the damned thing!"

She ignored me nursing my twisted ankle and pulled a steel brush out of her jacket. I raised myself to watch as she swept lichens and grime from the squared-off stone.

She spoke as much to it as she did to me. "Damned near three centuries this thing's been here, since the early guys laid out this territory in rods and chains. Range lots—that's what you got, kiddo. This is the monument your deed description starts from. Hard to read the letters on it, but thar 'tis."

She was so intent on what was incised into the marker that she missed me drawing myself in to pounce on her. I had her spun around and on her back before she even let out a gasp. When I pinned her arms over her head, she grinned. I kissed her before I knew what I was doing, but I knew exactly what I was doing when I slid my hand into her jeans and down her hard belly, hunting the warm honey that called me in with its sweetly insane scent.

CHAPTER TEN

The LePen Heritage Party has formed a coalition within Parliament, based on shared goals of reduction in immigration and reparations against the fragmenting United States for vital resource theft. Other parties in the new coalition are advocating joining with the nascent NorthEast Union Region in a common action in the NATO international tribunal against the builders of the illegal pipeline, as well as seeking NATO recognition of how severely pressured Free Quebec is by the influx of refugees fleeing poverty, intolerance, and the toxic environment.

The LePen coalition released this statement: "Water pulled illegally from the lower Great Lakes has depleted the St. Lawrence watershed and damaged aquifers south of the Bouclier; this is undeniable. We shall seek just compensation for this damage, as well as for the drain on our resources caused by the inverse pipeline of unsustainable immigration that runs from the Northern Heartland through lower New Albion and into our homeland."

*La voix du Québec libre, édition en ligne anglaise
(for our international audience) 3rd March, 2035*

I N THE MORNING, I checked the fuel level in the new kerosene heater beside the wall with the water pipes behind it, filled the generator tank, went down to the dirt-floor basement to stoke the rusted wood-burning furnace, and then sat next to the yard-wide heat grate on the first floor of my ancient new house. It was an indulgence. The cold morning had frozen the few inches of murky water in the disconnected rain-barrel, but I couldn't even see my breath inside the house. The fire underneath me used an extravagant amount of wood, but I wanted it burning, so I burned it.

I'd felt a calm I'd never known when I'd lain on the frozen ground behind my own house and stared at the cold, clean night sky after Petra left in the wee hours. She made it clear she wasn't staying, despite the fire we'd lit between us. That had hurt, but it felt honest and right, too.

...

My house was empty except for a few pieces of decent flea market furniture the Websters had set me up with. Mrs. Webster had made a new check-off form that I could actually use, and I'd been able to follow through on my first set of billing cycles. I was so proud of myself for it that I'd called to tell her. She got choked up on the phone. I got confused and we had to hang up, but it was a triumph for both of us. I'd thanked her for putting up with me for the last three years, and she'd laughed aloud.

I'd gotten the house for almost nothing; the expenses would be in repairs and upkeep. Tom had got me started working out a budget for that. I'd begin my paid internship for Martel International once summer came. It was to be a probationary apprenticeship. If I did well for a year, I'd have a job.

The well water had passed a contaminants test by the one company Petra trusted. The stream on the property was clean enough to drink from in a pinch. The geology directly underneath was too unstable for drilling, and every wild thing in the county that couldn't stand the fracking noise seemed to have settled in around me. I sometimes shot and ate them, but I tried to be honorable about it. The coyotes accepted me as another predator in the territory we'd inherited from the long-gone wolves. Tom had taken me along when he went hunting whenever he could: turkey, deer, and partridge. It felt more honest than eating farm-raised animals that had never learned their proper fears.

Petra often seemed to find a reason to be in the area, even though she wasn't working in that part of the county. She said she'd promised Tom she'd look out for me and that we were "dating," whatever that meant. In my mind, dates were what I'd done with the Sterling Island boys deep in the park woods on the off-season. I told Gabriel that she and I were "seeing each other," although I wasn't much clearer on the meaning of that. What I liked best were the evenings that made Petra call me a cheap date. She'd drop by with a six-pack and a couple of pre-made sandwiches from the mid-county grocery, and I'd light a dinky fire in the huge, drafty fireplace in the kitchen and fight with the damper until it sputtered to life. Before we cracked the beers, she'd go over my list from Mrs. Webster, add a few things to it, and joke with me about what I'd forgotten; then she'd say she'd done her duty by Tom and we could relax.

After a bit she'd pull me upstairs to my crooked little bedroom, and I'd try to act like I knew what I was doing when she gently took my clothes off, almost worshipful like she was unwrapping some kind of rare artwork. I felt more confident after she visited a few times, and she got more assertive in what she wanted. I don't know what kind of radar she had, but she never pushed into places I was uncomfortable, and I had plenty of those. She liked that I was more at ease being the one in control. It made me sink even deeper into how I felt about her, and that was hard to live with when she wasn't there.

I didn't like it so much when we went on regular dates. She'd taken me to a couple of places where they seemed to know her well. All I could think about was trying not to embarrass her. I sometimes heard the name of Chill Dark taken in vain among her friends. I kept my mouth shut, even though it made me uneasy to let him down that way.

...

Gabriel sometimes stopped in, but he rarely wasted words with me. The Dark family compound shared an access road with my house; the track appeared to have been traveled for generations. I hoped for an invitation to visit, since I was only a couple of miles away, but I didn't get one. He seemed to know a fair amount about my property: where the well head was, and the location of the range marker I'd tripped on. He asked whether I was happy. I said that was hard to answer. He was a little more talkative about my upcoming employment situation and told me to let him know if I was having any problems. When I asked what the connection was between Martel International and the Darks, he said Chill's mother was part of the Martel family. I asked how

Chill was doing. He said as far as he knew, he was in Mexico. That was the end of that conversation.

As summer got closer, he warned me Sam Champetty was working for the Martels. He mentioned the marriage to Angela was rocky, but they'd had a son. Gabriel didn't seem happy about that. He was concerned that Angela had the baby so young. He'd murmured something about the child perhaps having some developmental issues, and then he'd gone quiet.

...

The office I reported to on my first day was a modular box that dated from before the millennium. It sat on cinderblocks in a graveled clearing with an unmarked access track. It was a quarter mile in from the un-maintained county road that intersected the Dark compound access road. I was going to have to save for a better vehicle; the teeth-rattling two-mile drive would break apart my ancient little city SUV come winter.

There was a sleek white helicopter in the lot surrounding the anonymous office. It was the only thing around other than my new chambray shirt and the sticker on my toolbox that had the fleur-de-lis and hammers logo on it. I dreaded running across the man who'd been with Gabriel in the store, but the two men in the office were quiet and well-spoken with slight Québécois accents. They welcomed me politely and offered a folding metal chair until the other new hires arrived. I stared at a county map with pushpins in it until a new crewcab pickup pulled in the lot. Three men in shirts like mine got out, speaking with local accents. I was introduced and my toolbox inspected and the contents approved. I was complimented on being well-prepared.

The bosses made it clear all on the crew were to be considered equals. No harassment would be tolerated. Crews would be assembled by the job; my next assignment would probably be with different coworkers. Company supervisors might drop in at the job site any time, and employees would be replaced if they gave cause. Our work-order was laid out: a quick, cheap renovation of an abandoned house nearby. I recognized it as one of Sam Champetty's properties that had been up for sheriff's sale at the same time I'd bought my place.

I'd ridden in the crewcab to the site in silence, put in a full day with only the usual worksite chatter, and gotten let out again back at the gravel clearing. The helicopter was gone, and the office was locked and empty.

The next day I reported to the still-empty office, and the crew-cab was waiting for me. The workers were mediocre framing carpenters. If they had anything to say about me or my trim carpentry, they did it out of earshot. There was no apprenticeship involved; there wasn't anyone on the job I would have asked for advice. I got the extra-hand help I needed when I asked. I went in after the framers and hid the shortcomings. A Martel supervisor spent half an hour looking around one day when he brought in a plumber and electrician. At the end of the week, the helicopter was back, and one of the polite men handed me a respectable old-fashioned paper check written for Federal dollars, not Regional scrip. I thought to myself, "I can live with this."

...

Petra was helping me eyeball a run of molding along the wall of my house. The low, crooked ceiling made her look even taller. There was no point using a level; there wasn't a straight, plumb, or level line in the place. Most of it was old enough to have been put together with hand tools. Petra stood across the room and gestured higher or lower, finally giving a thumbs-up. I set a finish nail to hold it in place with a crisp puff from the pneumatic gun.

I cleared my throat. "So... do you think you might ever want to stay here?"

Petra leaned down and switched the intermittently deafening air compressor off. "Pipsqueak, Tom seems to think we were made for each other, but if they hadn't just changed the vice laws, you wouldn't be old enough to drink. He's maybe giving you a little too much encouragement. I'm not the committing type, and I keep learning ways you're, well, a lot younger than you seem at first. I'll look out for you—you can count on that—and enjoy our time together, and I hope you do too, but I need my own space." She shuffled and got a wry look. "But hey, you got a view of the compound access road. Maybe we can catch a peep of Angie Dark sneaking around."

I tried to smooth the seize out of my voice when I said I didn't
know she was around anymore.

Petra looked down at her huge, dusty work boots. "Saw her at
the club in town last week... thought you knew. She had a full-
scale cage fight with Champetty over her letting the baby wander
off. Left her a mess. Kid's gonna make it, but he's in rough shape.
Got himself caught in a leg-hold trap out by the old family strip-
mine, and how he got that far off is an interesting question.
Angie's working herself into her old ways, even if she ain't quite
jailbait anymore. Moved into a trailer on her uncle's back land,
signed her rights to her son away. Having a kid at eighteen probably not the best thing for anyone. I know you're close to the
Darks, and they're behind your paycheck, but it's a good clan to
keep some distance from. Just my opinion..."

The "club" Petra went to was a low-profile, members-only
queer bar. Since the Northern Heartland had re-criminalized
"homosexual acts" over the summer and removed privacy
protections for Regional Network communications in defiance of
a U.S. Supreme Court order, clubs were one of the safer places to
make connections. The Dog and Pony was a popular spot.

I mumbled a question about Angela being at a queer club.

Petra snorted. "Jeez—and you two were in the kiddie pen together? I know you don't get into other people's business much,
but I'd have thought you'd get that. Angie's kind of hard to miss.
She's at least as much of a freak as her brother. Just because they
roll around with whoever pays the bills doesn't mean they don't
get seriously mutant when they're shopping for their own fun.

"Angie's got the flesh to die for, but I keep telling myself..."
She paused and took a long look at my face. "I keep telling myself
I got a good thing started here. I know you've been through hell,
and it says a lot for you that it hasn't taken away all your innocence. I won't go to the club anymore without you, OK?"

She walked over and held me. I hugged her hard enough to
feel her ribs moving as she breathed, and tried to keep my heartbeat steady, my eyes dry, and my mouth shut.

...

If I had a deer I needed help with, Gabriel would come by and we'd get it hauled out and hung in the shed attached to my house, the hooks and floor darkened from generations of Archers using it for the same things I was learning to do. He seemed reasonably impressed with how I was managing but reluctant to help me with my list. With the failing communications systems in Wyandot, it was harder to reach the Websters, but I didn't feel I should rely on Petra so much after our last conversation.

Gabriel did invite me to the compound for a clan dinner, finally. He told me to keep what I might learn to myself, that there were things that Tom didn't know and didn't want to, and that it could be dangerous to mention them to anyone else. He said I should meet Chill's parents since I was working for his mother's family and Chill's dad was a "longtime employee."

..

The compound was a neat group of single-story white houses that the autumn dusk had painted a soft amber. When I drove up, Gabriel came out and apologized, saying Chill's mother Luce was a tad "under the weather." I gathered she was drunk, from what Chill had told me. I breathed more smoothly once I was fairly sure Angela was nowhere around. Gabriel introduced me to Chill's father Michel, shuffling with his jacket pulled close against the bite of the evening air. He'd seemed disinclined to unwind himself enough to shake hands, which was fine with me. I nodded to him and wrapped my own hands snugly into my pockets even though I wasn't that cold.

I learned that Chill's father, Gabriel's older brother, had known my dad. The Archers had abandoned Littlefield when my dad was in his early teens, but Chill's "Pappy Mike" remembered the family clearly, for better or worse.

Once upon a time, Mike must have been handsome as a celebrity, but age sat hard on him. His long hair had wide streaks of sleek black remaining in the gray and his eyes were clear blue, but his brittle-looking shoulders had a weighed-down hunch. Gabriel told me he ran contraband for his in-laws and had been using the merchandise a long time. Luce's family tolerated minor sloppiness in the inventory accounting out of consideration for her.

Mike and Luce's marriage was held together mostly by that structure. It looked like the grim horizon of it burdened him, as if the years ahead were heavier than the years he'd passed.

The Martel operations were primarily pharmaceutical. The "development corporation" allowed them to cross the border with commercial credentials and keep their accounts unscrutinized under the protections of Regional business regulations. The demand for genuine Canadian pharma products was huge, whether for therapeutic or recreational purposes. Runners like Gabriel carried medicines prescribed by practitioners for those who couldn't afford or didn't trust officially-sanctioned corporate healthcare. Runners like Mike handled the other stuff. I was part of the camouflage behind which they operated. There was a small wildcat oil and gas unit, but it wasn't nearly as big as they tried to present. The news wasn't a surprise, but it was a disappointment. Gabriel warned me to keep my eyes on what I'd been told to see and leave questions unasked, even of the Darks—especially of the Darks, if I wanted to continue being invited to dinner.

There was a bonfire in the graveled space that served as a square for the compound. Rotisserie supports made from exhaust pipes were set up; the young fire between them still smelled of accelerant. I sat next to Mike as he tended it. He looked at me with the light-eyed, seductive grin he'd passed on to his kids.

His soft voice was full of shaded laughter like Chill's, but even higher pitched, like he was choking something back that wanted to climb out his throat. "Y'know we're related?"

I gave him a blank look. He chuckled and poked the fire.

His sleeves were rolled up and the needle tracks on his pale, spindly arms showed clearly in the orange glow. "Archers, Darks—same name. Your side translated it, mine got transliterated. We're both D'Arcs. Long separation of branches—same tree. Your side assimilated, mine kept the frog-talk mongrel heritage. My ma was out of one of the last good Catholic residential schools outside Montréal, but she always kept connections here. Us, we come by the shadows naturally. Your side had the crackpot hermits, mine had psychos."

A grungy female voice yelled something complicated; it could have been in French, but I wasn't sure. It came from the house furthest up the small hill that nestled the compound.

Mike muttered, clearly enough for me to hear, "Va te faire foutre, sale conasse."

I was reasonably sure he'd just told his wife do something rude to herself and that he didn't have a good opinion of her hygiene. Gabriel came out of his house, knocked on the door of another one, and then he and the sturdy-looking man who'd answered headed up toward the voice.

Mike said "Soup's on.... not. Hope you're not too hungry. She didn' get to the part that goes inna oven."

He reached for his wallet and dug out a laminated photograph of a jaw-droppingly beautiful Métis woman in elegant clothes from perhaps a half-century before. Up the hill, I could see the two men coming back out of the house, carrying something on a pole between them.

Mike put on the cigar-store injun pidgin Chill used when he was pissed about something racist. "This my mother. Me tell-um sacred story of our people, since you no hear-um before.

"Schizo mother got cast out of Kingdom of Frogs, come here to cuckoo part of family like her. Her bring-um blessings of whoring and magic snow: teach-um broke crazy clods real make-money medicine dance. Your side of family get all too good for it, leave for land of rotting crystal towers, sell-um D'Arc homestead to human pig. Me marry Frog Princess of Underworld. Her not crazy, just mean like only pitbull crawl-um out of ring alive."

He gave the fire a vicious stab, and the crown of it tumbled into the fierce red coals; their deep color signaled they were ready to roast the side of venison that Luce had dressed and run through with a spit rod before she'd gotten too drunk to walk outside.

CHAPTER ELEVEN

The New Confederate Region has joined in a mutual-benefits pact with the North and Central Heartland, SouthWest and LoneStar Regions to further commercial development and resource-sharing. Representatives of the RedVote Pact Regions have agreed to stand firm against any rulings of the NATO court on water rights and to mutually defend against, by force if necessary, any outside interference with sovereign pipeline systems.

Voice of the New Confederacy, 11/15/35

I GOT A QUEASY FEELING when I saw that Petra had already staked out a bar table at the Dog and Pony. The jukebox boys didn't like her claiming one inside the invisible boundaries of their territory. I was supposed to meet her at nine, and it was still a couple of minutes to, but it appeared she'd been there a while. I was learning Petra was a heavy drinker. She didn't drink hard every day, but when she did, she meant business.

There were two empty high-backed stools at the table, one with a large-ish jacket hanging on it that was too femmy for anything of Petra's. She waved me over to sit down. As I crawled onto the unclaimed stool, another pair of hands slid along my shoulders.

A puff of alcohol-breath came up behind me and slid along my cheek. "Hey there, Stranger. We just been bitching about Runt. Uncle Gabe won't tell me where he is, but I bet you know. Last I heard he was moving in with his new boyfriend in Mexico—but who gives a fuck? Don't tell Uncle Not-Daddy I'm drinking, OK? He might get all parental and make me cry. He don't like it when injuns drink, particularly injuns who need to be careful not to run their mouths."

The stinking feather-touch of Angela's breath set off a twinge of neuralgia in my face, and I shuddered involuntarily. Petra stared and muttered something about the county being a pleasanter place without Chill-fucking-Dark. I took it she was trying to start a fight. The last thing I wanted was to be the neurocrippled bait-dog for a couple of drunk dykes to rip apart. I tried to slide off the stool, but Angela held my shoulders from behind. My back prickled. I told her to let go.

Her strong hands clamped hard on either side of my neck. "Stay a bit, Runt-ette. Like I was telling your friend here, you've been a lot friendlier to me in the past. You seemed to like it at the time. Truth or dare, Runt-girl, fess up. I told the T and the whole T—nothing but the T might be a stretch. I said you wouldn't do it as a wedding present. I was looking forward to that. I missed you, and I wanted to think you missed me. Poor Sammy saw Paradise, and then it was gone. I'm so sentimental, I kept the toys you left behind. You can play in any hole of mine you want since Sammy's not calling the game. Huh, Pete?"

Petra's face was clenched hard as she leaned around the tiny table and slid her big palm into the back pocket of Angela's tight pants. Angela cocked her hip to receive it.

There was a lot of liquor in Petra, but her voice was tight and cutting. "Sure, Angie. I thought my girl was something clean and untamed. Seems there were aspects I hadn't seen in her. Maybe I shortchanged her. My heart's kinda chewed up right now, but I have to admit my groin is interested—really, really interested."

I yanked Angela's hands away and pushed her at Petra. "Chill was right about you, Angela. You can't stand anyone having anything good. You have to destroy it. What I did with you wasn't my choice—that was your game, you and your... whatever that disgusting thing is to you. You sold him that you were doing it as a sweet little present to his dick. I still have nightmares, if it's any satisfaction, so just get the fuck out of my way."

The whole bar leaned in to catch the boiling T getting poured.

I turned on Petra. "You could've asked me if you wanted to know what happened. It was something I did to save myself from something a lot worse. Isn't a subject I like to dwell on—doesn't mean I wouldn't give you a clean answer if you asked."

...

I was unlocking my pathetic beater car when Petra caught up with me. She tried to take my keys. I wrapped my fist around them and plowed it into her solar plexus.

She caught herself, bracing in a deep bow over the car hood. "Guess I had that coming to me, Pipsqueak—respectable—gut-shot—kid..."

Deep laughter came from the darkness a half-block away, followed by a straight-guy chorus of whistles and leering calls. There were other private drinking clubs nearby, and relations between their patrons could get risky. I popped the doors and told Petra to get the fuck inside. She braced herself to keep from smacking her head on the dash, still doubled over as I dropped the gas pedal and the ancient vehicle lurched toward a better-lit neighborhood.

I drove to her apartment, a walkup over an empty storefront. She'd turned crossways in a fetal position with her arms over her middle and her back against the door. She tried to uncurl and asked for a couple of minutes. I turned the car off and stared at the jagged shadows on the street as the windshield fogged up. She was making my car reek; bar-stale secondhand cigarette smoke saturated her clothes, and her skin exhaled her heavy drunk. I wanted her out, and she knew it. She pushed her face into the worn upholstery and started to cry. I wasn't prepared to deal with that. I opened my door.

She reached toward me, her head still turned away. "Fucking Darks... poison... poison the whole godforsaken world... Please, Dax... Don't... let it..."

I told her I was going to help her up to her room, make her a pot of coffee, and then I was gone, for good. She made a soft, sobbing wail, bit her lip, and nodded.

...

It wasn't a good winter after I broke up with Petra. Some windows at my house were bashed in by three guys I'd pissed off when I'd thrown them off my property for hunting without permission. I had it posted. They'd ignored the signs; I got nasty. They took it personally and came back to make a point. I'd fired my rifle at the vandals' truck as it blocked my driveway. I guess they thought they were going to trap me in and I'd just let them do it. They sped out with a shattered windshield. I was scared enough to be hot-crazy, but I didn't know how long I could keep it up.

I called Gabriel after they took off. He was in the city but drove the six hours in as soon as I told him what happened. He made me stay a few nights at the compound until I could get my house closed up. None of the other Darks interacted with me, but Gabriel was a gracious host. He put me up on his comfortable couch, and fed me cooking like I hadn't eaten since I was a kid. There wasn't much to learn about him from his small, immaculate house. I felt if he left so slight a mark on his own life, I needed to be out of there before I left a messier one.

I didn't have enough in my regular account to cover the repairs and security reinforcements. I'd dipped into Bern's money, and that drew the attention of Revenue Collections even though I'd followed the usual precautions. The account was under my old name; it was seized. I was told I could avoid prosecution for tax fraud by forfeiting it. The Feds had frozen all revenue sharing, and the Heartlands weren't taking in enough for basic government operations. They were grabbing whatever they could under any pretext from the ones who couldn't fight them. I'd taken the offer and counted myself fortunate for not having my house held as collateral while I worked off a Sisyphean indenture for using a false identity. They didn't care who I was, which name had come first, or how I came by it, as long as they could confiscate my Federal cash.

In the panic from that, I'd missed a couple of items from my list since I didn't have anyone to go over it with me anymore. My regular web-cellular service was cut off, and I missed some important messages. Gabriel had muttered several times about people encouraging me to bite off more than I could chew in trying to run my own house by myself.

...

On one blizzard-warning day when it wasn't safe to drive my disintegrating vehicle, Gabriel had given me a ride to the Martel office. I'd called him with Bern's phone because my regular one was still cut off; he was one of the few people I felt safe calling from it. I'd thought about walking since it wasn't that far, but I didn't think it would be smart, as cold as it was. I made damned sure to thank him properly. I was starting to feel like the kind of autistic burden the blue puzzle-piece, freak-awareness, find-a-cure fundraising campaigns depicted.

Gabriel made it clear he'd be out of the lot before I opened the office door if the helicopter was there. That morning, the helicopter was there but the office was locked. Gabriel was gone before I could catch his eye. Someone had been there to meet the chopper passengers; the lot was full of fresh tire tracks. There was a new crew guy there, sitting in the cab of a Martel-marked truck. When he saw me shuffling outside the locked door in the frigid weather, he waved me over.

I look at the memory of myself and scream at that person shivering in the pre-dawn light to set off walking when the bosses didn't show, whatever the risks—to never get in that truck, no matter how hard the wind-driven snow hit against her skin going white from the cold, no matter how afraid she might be of losing her job if she left that miserable place.

Instead, I stepped into the warm cab of the plumber's idling truck and accepted a cup of coffee from his thermos. I've marked the years following that decision in a timeline of breakages— breakages in the places and things around me, and breakages within myself.

I've only role-named a few people in my personal cast of characters. It's an autistic habit I try to avoid. I've been told it sounds like the self-centered, mechanical-minded sociopath stereotype of autism. My friends, or even adversaries, usually have their own names if they loom large enough to warrant the effort of remembering them, which isn't trivial. Role-naming is a tactic for autistics to effectively map their worlds, and I'd be less emotionally exhausted if I did it, but I understand I owe humanity more than that. It reduces them to things in my mind, like the way I look at people's eyes that unnerves them.

In some cases I'm OK with that. It lets me grapple with the ones who've done me damage in places I have a hard time getting to in my head. I role-named the Thunderbird psych doctors, and I role-named The Big Mistake. That's all I'm ever going to call him.

...

I'd waited nearly an hour, drinking my cooling coffee, trying not to talk too much. The Mistake was surprised I hadn't gotten the text that there wouldn't be a regular crew going out because of the bad weather. He said he had to wait, because he'd been called in to inspect a new property. I said I'd been having trouble with my phone. I didn't say why. He looked edgy after a while and checked his tablet; he said the message to stay in the office lot was from a Montréal exchange, but not the one he generally got instructions from. He asked if I'd mind if we went into town and waited at the diner.

Before I could answer, a huge-tired Martel SUV came skidding into the lot, spraying snow and gravel down the side of the truck. The Mistake whirled around to open the door as four men spilled out of the SUV. One of them waved him back in, screaming, "Sortir ce foutu camion d'ici—s'ils voient que le logo vous est mort!" as he dragged one of the soft-spoken bosses between him and another big thug. The boss was bleeding heavily from a darkened hole in his fawn-colored cashmere coat, and he struggled to get his footing as he was hauled along. The third thug followed close, tripping on the boss' trailing cordovan shoes when he couldn't keep his feet under himself. The Mistake looked at me the way I find myself looking at people.

I said, "Roughly I think it means we should get the hell out of here, and probably ditch the truck once we do."

The Mistake spun the truck around, nearly hitting the trailing thug as he pushed the well-dressed wounded man into the chopper. We crossed a ragged red line melting into the churned-up snow leading from the SUV toward the helicopter, and then we hit the county road flying.

...

I told the Mistake to take my access road. I'd seen the running lights of another vehicle pulling into the lot in the rearview mirror as the chopper lifted over the trees, lurching in the gusts; any pilot with a choice would have stayed grounded. The wind was full of bursts of gunfire, but I couldn't tell whether the chopper was still airborne. I prayed no one had seen us. The blizzard was driving crystal-dry drifts that would cover our tracks in minutes.

I'd said to park behind the ruins of my barn. As we'd looked out my new front windows, we'd seen a black SUV drive slowly along the county road in the distance. Every few seconds another squall would blast it out of sight. It stopped at the entrance to the access road, and the Mistake reached for his waistband. He was better armed than most plumbers I'd known. The SUV moved on, and he'd sat down at my kitchen table without being asked.

There was sweat on his lip. "Dunno if you were praying, but if you were, tell me who it was to and I'll convert."

He noted the new security windows and said it seemed like I'd been prepared for something. I said it wasn't what had just happened that I'd been preparing for.

He laid a formidable automatic pistol on the table and extended his hand. "Maybe we can look out for each other then, young lady. It looks as though you could use some help around here, and most likely neither one of us has a job anymore."

I reached out and shook hands, sealing the deal with The Big Mistake.

CHAPTER TWELVE

In a skirmish that may become drawn out, New Albion border police confronted a small squadron of Laithbourn Special Operatives inside sovereign NA territory. The Laithbourn troops were captured after an exchange of small-arms fire; when questioned, they claimed to be in hot pursuit of Franco-Canadian drug traffickers.
<u>*New Albion Courier, Online Edition January 18, 2036*</u>

I T WAS SILENT until the blizzard stopped in the small hours, then some kind of fury came down on the Dark compound. The Mistake and I went up into my attic and watched out the tiny dormer window at the smoke rising to the east. There were booms and crashes and paramilitary-type sirens, but no gunfire. The Mistake asked how heavy equipment could come in without passing the house. I said the access road was a loop, and the far end wasn't as steep as the one I used. I could smell the tension-sweat off him, but I was glad he was there.

...

As soon as the sky began to pale, I left the Mistake to watch the house and started walking to the compound. I avoided the track, slogging through the woods to the crest of the hill above the settlement. As I looked down, my breath caught. Only the house near the top of the slope remained; all the others, including Gabriel's tidy home, were destroyed. Tracks of heavy equipment zigzagged across the lot where I'd shared in the roasted venison.

Something touched my arm. I spun around, dropped my shoulder and tried for a linebacker's run into the solar plexus of whatever had startled me, only to stumble into emptiness.

There was a fast, harshly-whispered joual curse, followed by a soft, alcohol-scented chuckle. "So you're the one I was too skunked to meet. Not as bad as it looks for a Laithbourn hit. Some of the boys got beat up pretty bad. Had to stay smart and let 'em do what they came to do and stay alive in the process. Done a medical convoy to the Motherland. Probably most of the clan will stay up there 'til there's some kinda armistice."

I was looking at a small black-haired woman in a camo coat. There was blood on her hand. It was Luce Dark, Chill's mother. I asked if she was OK.

She licked the blood off the fresh cut. "Well enough, all things considered—this injun-juice cocktail in my veins is good for something. Takes more than a bunch of bellowing cornfed white boys to catch a half-breed Martel. Watched them try to get that 'dozer up this hill for a half hour before they gave up. Good thing they didn't get the propane tank set off—they almost took themselves out when Gabe's blew."

She licked the cut again. "You got halfway decent reflexes for a city-bred—made me nick myself getting outta your way. I'll tell ya us savages usually check to see who we're trying to nail before we do it. Saves the apology you didn't make."

I mumbled something.

She laughed quietly and waved it off. "T-bird must've taught you something. You're the only twat I ever heard my faggot son talk about with any real fang in his grin. He seems to think your breed of neuro-fucked is interesting enough to ignore the alien-lifeform drainage fixtures."

She offered me a mostly-emptied bottle of Canadian whiskey, and I accepted. The deep burn in my throat was welcome. I nodded my thanks and passed it back. She lit a cigarette, saying she could finally enjoy one without the smell calling attention to where she'd been hiding all night.

She held the bottle in both hands and dropped onto her thin haunches, looking out over the wreckage. "The Abrahamists say the Archangels begin and end us. Gabriel lights our lamp and Azrael the Chill snuffs it out."

She made a face like an Aztec skull mask and her voice came out in a low hiss. "'They take the noose and go out at night to strangle others. They break into well-protected places. But they shall come to regret their actions... Azrael, the Angel of Death, shall crush them like sesame seeds in the oil-press.'"

She pulled a deep drag off her smoke. "Ah, who the fuck am I kidding, railing and shaking my bony fist at the sky like some poor old Palestinian biddy cursing in a flattened olive grove? Scriptures are for the ones trying to save themselves when the noose is already around their necks. My kid's a hardass and smart as vinegar in a cut, but he's no avenging Angel, and if he's all that smart, he'll stay in Mexico. He doesn't need Martel shit."

I asked her if she'd heard anything from Chill recently.

She shook her head. "We don't talk much. If he had his umbilical cord he'd burn it, and I wouldn't blame him. He seems to think well of that friend of yours he's working for, says he's kept their mercenary butts from getting shot off more than once. I have a hard time forming the picture, but that's all I know.

"Anyway, it's been a pleasant chat, girl. I hope we get to do it again, but this ain't quite the place. Think I've waited about long enough for Mike to get his ass home and find it thusly. He'll have to deal with it on his own—I need to get out of here. Listen, if Gabe or my Gabie comes back and wants to take you somewhere, go. Don't go with anyone else. Look at me and register that, OK?"

She snapped her fingers; I caught her fierce black eyes.

When she was sure I was focused on her, she repeated herself. "Do not go with *anyone* else. I know Tom's decent, but he's a mouse in uniform caught in a dogfight. Don't count on him being able to do much. You need to lay low—don't stand out. DON'T talk to anyone about any damn thing. If they think you're a retard, go with it—get as stupid as you need to."

She snuffed her cigarette carefully in the snow, buried the butt under frozen leaves, and disappeared into the woods.

...

When I got back to my house, the Mistake had made himself a sandwich and left the fixings out with an extra plate. His work tablet was on what looked like an internal corporate Martel International web page.

He gave me a look when I came in that I wish I'd understood better then. "Was getting worried there, young lady. You do a lot of dangerous things on your own for such a small package. You didn't even take a gun, for fuck's sake."

I muttered something about the Dark compound having been leveled and there wasn't anyone around to shoot.

He pushed the plate at me. "Eat something. If I'd have known how you like it, I'd have fixed it for you. We got a long road ahead here, gotta keep our strength up."

He tried to rub my shoulder and I pulled away reflexively. He apologized and said he'd noticed my tattoo and that he knew it meant someone who had touch issues.

I shrugged.

He made an effort at a pleasant smile. "I know it might've been nosy, but I didn't have much to do with myself. I can get my tools up here—I found a few things I could fix... and... um... I saw that list you have posted up on the fridge. Looks like you missed a car payment?"

I mumbled that I hadn't had anyone checking my list with me recently. I tried to put together in my disintegrating brain how late my payment was. I felt my face falling apart. Tom had set the loan up for me. The regular payments instead of an automatic withdrawal were supposed to teach me responsibility. Tom had cosigned, and they'd come back on him if I defaulted. I tried to explain and to keep from crying; neither effort was working.

The Mistake pulled his chair next to me and cautiously rested his hand on mine. "Shit, I'm sorry. Can I help you with that? I'm pretty good with talking to folks. I can call and say I'm your guardian or something. I saw you're on the payroll as a Special Needs—I can make it sound like it's not your fault. Would that help?"

Some stupid, grateful words came out of my mouth.

...

I drove the Mistake to his house to pick up his guns, a jacket without a fleur-de-lis, and paint supplies to make his Martel International truck into a camo-style, local-looking thing that wouldn't catch the eye of Laithbourn's mop-up crews. No one was issuing or checking registrations anymore, so he burned the papers from the glove box.

The Mistake's house was small but tidy. The dishes were washed and the floor wasn't sticky. I wish I could've said the same about my place. It wasn't that I didn't care; I never had enough left in the tank when I'd get home from work. I'd start and then phase out and find myself sitting in the middle of the floor with my eyes watering from trying to keep them open when I just really needed to go sit in the dark and recover my ability to think.

I was never good at assessing people the usual way, but the Mistake looked to me like he'd been single a while. His clothes were mended by someone who'd never learned how to sew correctly, but they were clean. His pants had folding creases along the side seams, not front and back, so mommy probably never taught him. He was a strong, good-sized man with the start of a paunch. His thinning, buzz-cut hair said he was at least a decade older than I was.

He made a pot of coffee and disappeared into the sole bedroom of the ranch-style house; it was off a cramped central room with a half-century-old kitchenette at one end, a small round table and a couple of chairs in the middle, and a couch and huge Pyongyang Sensimmersion multainment unit at the other end. He came out tucking in a fresh shirt, carrying a respectably large docking tablet and keyboard.

He put the dock setup on the table, saying he wanted to show me something. "Somebody should've set you up with something like this I found. I can copy you the program—it's freeware. See, the calendar pops up and important things flash red. You can set when you want to be alerted, when you want the yellow warning, how much lead time you need. For something like First Wyandot where they're not gonna give you any more grace after this, you can get it to give you an urgent flag earlier. If it looks like you're gonna make an overdraft, it'll give you the flag. It links to your account balance sheet."

He looked at my face. "Or I can do it for you."

...

The Mistake and I loaded his electronics into the back of the camo-painted truck, cushioned with a couple of bags of clothes. His guns and tools were already at my house. He'd gotten an email from Laithbourn Special Operations acting under the authority of the Provisional Government of the Northern Heartland Autonomous Region warning him they were "aware of his activities" as a paid operative for Martel International's contraband smuggling and distribution network. There would be an officer and support personnel at his home within twenty-four hours, and the property would be seized as forfeiture for having participated in those activities.

We'd had sex. I did what I did when I'd done it for money—not the type of sex, but the attitude. I'd found something positive to focus on, in this case gratitude, and gone through the very vanilla motions. My payments calendar was set up; the missed installment on my loan was forgiven; my faucets didn't leak anymore; after a couple of well-timed bursts of "target practice" automatic rifle fire coming from the back of my house, the jerks who'd broken my windows had left me alone.

I was very grateful. When I could offer the man a refuge when his life was ripped out from under him, I was glad to do it.

2.34

1.89   1.84
2.86   2.57
2.02 2.10.   1.87   9.65
2.90   4.27
2.93   1.57   5.19   2.42
2.33   92
.93   2
5.58 3.02 2.4
0.92   1.93   2.26
1.77
1.07
0.92
0.00
2.74   2.63 4.02   1.22
2.75
4.67
7.94 1.84
.08   3.84
5.22   5.46 2.55
1.92
1.90   5.41
1.57 2.04   7.06   2.01 2.79
.08 25 2.07
3.86
1.10   1.4

WHEREAS *there has been an unrelenting flood of reports of violence perpetrated by persons with a diagnosis of autism, and*

Whereas *persons with that diagnosis constitute a significant and disturbingly large minority of our population, and*

Whereas *persons with that diagnosis are rarely fully employed, productive members of society, and*

Whereas *the Act under the United States body of laws formerly named The Combating Autism Act, while having suffered from dilution owing to misguided sentiment in previous years, contains new and valuable provisions in need of further strengthening,*

Therefore, *the Legislature of the Northern Heartland Autonomous Region finds it provident to enact the provisions of the existing United States Autism CARES Act under its own authority, subject to the following alterations and together with the following additional provisions to further mitigate the danger to the public and the increasing drain on Regional resources incurred through the burden of unsupervised and unproductive persons afflicted with autism...*

Preamble to the Northern Heartland Regional Combating Autism Act of 2036

CHAPTER THIRTEEN

Well, they've done it.
Editor's Page, TheUrbanHowl.press 3/21/36
(on the joint secession of the RedVote Pact Regions, splintering
the former United States)

I WAS WALKING around the house in the small hours. The Mistake was snoring and taking up most of my bed. I looked out my new steel-barred, wire-reinforced shatterproof glass windows, wondering if I needed to tend the furnace. The road we'd watched the black SUV inching along on the day Martel International fell to Laithbourn Special Ops was inundated with runoff from torrents of early spring rain. The cloud-veiled moon glinted off the pond in the dip where the county drainage system had failed, and gleamed in the quarter inch ice slick covering the steep driveway. The floodwater pool was freezing over, the serrated fretwork closing in from the edges as I watched.

The Mistake had been with me a couple of months, but it was beginning to feel like he'd been occupying my world since the Stone Age. I was grateful, but other emotions were creeping in. When I looked at things straight on, I was in control, but if I caught sight of my life from another angle, it appeared for a shadowed instant like something was coming down on my neck. I wasn't adept at turning the picture around in my mind; the flicker of instinct would vanish as soon as I focused on it.

The temperature outside was in freefall; the lingering drizzle had turned to crystalline fog drifting in dry wisps across the glazed ground. I put my hand against the big heating grate in the middle of the first floor hall; it was barely warm. I went to the basement to feed the wood fire before the embers died and I'd have to relight from a cold start. Even though I'd faithfully kept the pile stocked, the Mistake had put more cordwood on it in a day than I could in three. He was nearly double my weight, and despite his bit of belly, he wasn't soft. The muscle he brought to the chores made me feel it was worth putting up with the way he was crowding in on me.

As I climbed the precipitous stairs back to the kitchen I thought I saw a dim bluish flash, and the ground shuddered with an enormous booming crack.

That was quickly followed by a thud from upstairs. "What the dickin' fuck was that?!"

I waited for aftershocks; there weren't any. The Mistake bellowed again like I hadn't heard him.

I checked the kitchen fireplace masonry for fractures.

The single sharp, isolated bang had made the answer plain. "Cryoseism."

The Mistake lumbered downstairs and glared at me. "Huh?"

I didn't like the way he was looking at me like it was my fault.

I returned the look with some "back off" in it. "Cry-o-sei-sm— ice quake. From the cold, saturated ground and the rapid temperature change—like the cracks you hear when you pour your drink into a glass with ice in it. It can make a weak lighting flash from the electrical discharge. Happens around here sometimes—it's more exposed to weather shifts than where your house was."

The Mistake muttered something about speaking of drinks, and pulled a beer from the fridge. "Wish to hell you could talk like a normal person—not a fucking digi-pedia with an attitude problem. I thought they were supposed to teach you that in your special classes. Yeah, I miss my place. I miss a lot of things, so just don't bring it up—ever."

He used opening the beer bottle as an excuse to avoid my eyes. "Christ, I hate this dilapidated piece of shit out here in Woodsnigger Heaven. Should've been this house Laithbourn leveled— not mine. Wonder how many fleas they set loose bulldozing your buddies' rat-colony over the hill—makes me wanna shake out the sheets just thinking about it. They could've sold my place, instead of knocked it down—they didn't have to destroy it. Just do not bring it up."

He took a deep swig that drained half the bottle and gave me a strange, jagged smile. "If you want my help keeping your sorry mess of a life from caving in on you, you better give me some respect there, little cripple-brained attitude-girl."

...

Once the sun rose, I went to get a look at the outside of the house. There were few new fine cracks in the horsehair plaster inside, but nothing that looked serious. The security windows had held, but the flashing around one had separated. I made a note in my pocket-list to caulk it when I got back from checking to see if my contraband pills were in at the veterinarian's office. The cryoseism had had the positive effect of jarring loose the blocked road drainage; the pond had emptied out, leaving a saw-toothed edge of ice that had begun to drip from the hint of warmth in the morning light.

I hadn't heard from Gabriel. I'd tried to reach Tom to find out if he knew how any of the Darks were doing since the compound had been demolished, but he hadn't answered my texts if he'd gotten them. He and Gabriel had both told me they might have to keep their distance if things were to get messy over Martel, Inc. I planned to wait until I was on the road before I pulled Bern's phone from its hiding place behind my broken dashboard to check if anything had come in since the day before. The Mistake might have said he loved me a couple of times, but something told me I should keep my last-ditch safety line to myself. Given the way he was inclined to poke around when I wasn't there, I thought the vehicle was the better choice for stashing it.

The Mistake seemed to put aside whatever had eaten its way under his skin in the middle of the night. When I'd said I was headed out, and to please throw some salt on the worst spots in driveway once the sun hit it, he'd given me a stiff smile and said "Sure, girlfriend." It wasn't much of a smile, but it was something. I joked that I could get down the hill fine; it was getting back up that would be the problem. He smiled again, and it looked more genuine. He went back to watching his morning news on the big tablet. They mentioned the ice quake "in a remote part of rural

Wyandot County," but it was mostly about the upcoming secession referendum. The Mistake raised the volume when one of the
blowhards he liked started venting about the Feds.

The tablet lost the signal, and the Mistake snarled something
about the f-ing middle of nowhere. I slipped outside. A couple of
heavy duty cam-drones marked with media outlet logos zoomed
around like bicycle-sized bumble bees. One of them dropped in
close and a screen flipped down to show a reporter's face. He
asked if I wanted to tell his audience anything about the ice quake.
I said there wasn't a lot to tell, that everything was OK, and waved
him off.

Every cold front was offered by the telegenic puppets in front
of the cameras as a refutation of overall environmental heating,
despite the "tipping point" United Nations report being more
than a couple of decades old. No one with just a curriculum-
approved Heartland public school education had the science
background to challenge that mindset. Trying to explain would
only get me digitally erased by one of the many people who didn't
want to broadcast what a digi-pedia with an attitude problem
might have to say.

...

I pulled into the old Martel office lot for a private place to
check my phone. The pre-millennial modular was a burned-out
shell. Some animal had left nesting materials drooping out the
doorway. The door had been ripped off the building by heavy
equipment. It lay bent up on the ground with shreds of sheet
metal from the siding still attached to it.

Gabriel had texted late the night before.

*Darling- your medication is waiting for you at the usual place.
Afraid I must ask you not to contact again- for your own safety. Am
removing your number from accepted calls in case my phone is
seized- please use our law enforcement friend for emergencies. Something else there for you as well- calming techniques. Gabie thinks you
have the mind for it, asked me to send them along with his best- Love
G. (elder) with love from G. (Chill)*

...

The Mistake was out when I got home; that was probably the
only reason he'd salted the driveway. My stomach twisted when

I saw the big truck gone—no note, no message on my regular phone. As a solitary autistic, I needed him and he knew it. I had a bleak sense the power games would escalate, but I was too tired and stressed to think things through. I checked to make sure his toolbox, guns and electronics were there. He'd be back.

I used the chance to slip Gabriel's chip drive into my phone to play his meditation coaching. I thought it would be something Chill had found, but it was Gabriel's voice explaining the seated posture, gently guiding me to be aware of my breathing, mindful in my body. He'd added a simple slideshow of images—lotus blossoms opening out, water, and quiet flames.

By the time the Mistake stomped in, I was smiling calmly. It pissed him off so much he took a half-hearted swing at me, but we both knew he was too drunk for it to mean anything.

...

When I saw the Sheriff's Department SUV sliding and churning up the driveway, I ran to meet it. I'd tried calling from a public landline to reach Tom, but all I'd gotten was a recording saying that physical wire and cable connections would no longer be maintained and to use my mobile device. That was a joke; the tower coverage for Heartland-legal phones was spotty even at the southern end of the county. The service provider had been at war with the utility commission over not repairing the signal relays for years, and then the utility commission was dissolved because it was interfering with free enterprise and hurting the economy. Somehow the net bill never went down even as the services bundled into it got thinner and less reliable. I figured Tom had had the same problems at his end and was solving them with a personal visit.

As I watched the uniformed driver get out, the joy drained from me.

His unfamiliar face met my fallen one as he extended a legal envelope toward me. "Dakini Webster? I have papers for you."

...

The document was a notice from Social Services saying that since my employer was no longer licensed to operate outside the Independent Territories of Canada, I would be considered an unemployed autistic under the carryover provisions of the

Combating Autism Act of the United States and the Disabled Citizens Responsibilities Act of the Heartland Regional Authority. I
would be required to register for Workfare and must report to
the county office within ten days.

...

The freezing rain made slushy ponds in the road again; my
balding tires wallowed and fishtailed through them. If I'd had a
choice, I wouldn't have been driving in that weather. I'd waited
until the last day to register because my face needed to heal.

The Mistake had taken another drunken swing at me, but this
one had connected. He was on his knees as soon as he'd seen the
blood, wailing his apologies with his arms wrapped around my
legs, but he'd still managed to tangle into his sorry words that I'd
somehow made him do it. The split, discolored swelling in my lip
had finally gone down enough for me to show my face, and I
needed to be up for serious eye contact.

The woman at the workfare office had dug up my file on her
ancient computer, complaining it was missing half my information. I didn't help her, but she wasn't expecting it. She
practically called me a "ree-tard," but I took Luce Dark's advice
and went with it. She grabbed my arm to verify the tat on my
wrist, flipping my hand over like a hoof filed for a horseshoe. If I
hadn't had years of being handled that way behind me, I would've
given her something to remember me by before I'd known I'd
done it.

She handed me a printout of two available positions. I had to
choose one or be declared an unmarried non-compliant indigent,
whereupon I could lose anything of value I owned and be sent to
an institution/warehouse paid for with the proceeds. The Mistake
had mentioned that if I were to marry him, I could declare myself
a "housewife" and never have to worry about Workfare again. I
wasn't sure whether he was joking, but I decided it was a good
idea to act like he was. Once I saw my placement options, I wasn't
so sure of myself. The jobs were, of course, at sub-minimum
wage, while there still was a minimum wage. I was a Burden on
Society, and they were doing me a big favor paying me at all.

One job was for general help at a meat processing plant. When I recoiled, the woman said it was in there because the office director had read "that Temple Grandom's book" and so he knew autistics would like the job. She apparently thought because autistics were psychopaths that shot up schools they'd enjoy working in a slaughterhouse; she looked relieved when I wanted no part of it.

The other available job was for unskilled labor at the county nursing facility CareWell, mostly janitorial and "basic client care," which essentially meant changing incontinence pads. I'd clenched my teeth and said I'd take it.

The loop of that decision replayed itself in my head on the drive back until my boulder-filled driveway loomed in front of me. What gravel hadn't washed away was furrowed and slicked by the freezing rain. I tried to stay mindful in the moment the way Gabriel's meditation instructions said. I took a run on the slope and managed to get nearly to the top before my tires started to spin. The brakes did nothing. The SUV slid backwards a few feet and then swerved violently. There was an impact, and then I felt like I was in a washing machine. When my head cleared. I was lying on my side looking through a fretwork of cracks in the windshield at the scuffed bark on the trunk of a pine tree.

I heard the Mistake bellowing from somewhere. I used my last functional brain cells to fish my phone from behind the dash and hide it where I'd always kept it safest.

...

The Mistake's truck radio blared the secession referendum results. The Northern Heartland was now free of the constrictions of the United States Constitution. The new legislature would have the voter-approved draft of the Regional Constitution ratified in an all-night session.

The Mistake was driving me home from work, as he would drive me anywhere I had to be for the next half-dozen years. He'd declared I was too inept to have ever been allowed behind the wheel, and "blamed himself" for not taking control sooner. I couldn't have bought another vehicle on my own even if I could have afforded it. There'd been a small loan fund and some trained assistance at County Services to help people with social disabilities handle things like that, but the program had been cut the year before.

I was feeling less and less competent, and the mandatory girly-pink scrubs with the blue puzzle-piece pattern I was issued at work didn't help. They identified me as female sub-par labor, not to be entrusted with important or strenuous tasks, and they were very effective at keeping the wearer from feeling dignified enough to stand up for herself. I pulled my coat around me and vowed to remember to bring a change of clothes for the ride home tomorrow.

I tried to shut out the noise from the radio and the images in my head from what I'd had to do at CareWell. It seemed like each day of the couple of weeks I'd worked there had left me with something I needed to forget. I attended to my breathing and tried to meditate, but I couldn't get it to take. I rested my face against the truck door and watched the low clouds hanging heavy above the overgrown fields, my eyes blurring with tears.

I felt myself starting to rain.

A lotus opened slowly in my heart; its center was as black as deep space, and as empty.

CHAPTER FOURTEEN

Well, dear listeners, I must say this reasonable man is On the Brink of busting out in a little jig—we can finally clear away the disease that's rotted our society from the inside. We've won this round, but now there's work to do. Secession is the first step of a long march back to productivity and decency. Yes, dear listeners, It Is Time to Get to Work around here—let's Clean House, Ladies and Gentlemen...

O'Brien on the Brink, WWBF AM 58 and Webcast
brinksman58.press, 3/21/36

I WAS ON what was supposed to be my lunch break, but I could never eat anything during working hours at CareWell. I dutifully stopped in at my supervisor's desk and told her I was going to get some fresh air.

Her Mrs. Santa chubby cheeks raised up, but her eyes stayed vigilant.

She fixed me with her "understanding" smile. "Don't wander too far, sweetie angel. If you're not back in fifteen minutes you know we're going to have to put a little tracker bracelet on. I still think it's a good idea, just to be safe. Your fiancé thinks so too—you're lucky to have a man like that to watch out for you. A lot of regular girls would be happy to have him—Lord we are grateful. I tell you what, why don't you sit out front where I can keep an eye on you."

I clenched my teeth; the grammatical structure of her last utterance was a question, but it wasn't optional. "Lord we are grateful" was her favorite phrase; it meant one would be wise to act as if whatever followed had been divinely inspired. I was wandering again, but they'd have to shoot me with a tranquilizer dart if they wanted to clamp a tracker on my autistic body. I'd always been sidetracked by beautiful, miraculous, elegant things like plants with floating seeds and moths with powdered wings caught by the wind and moving down some deep channel of space, away from the human world. Stress made it more magnetic to follow that compass bearing of quiet wonder.

Time was getting away from me at levels large and small; my work breaks vanished into the fog, and so did the seasons I'd once tracked so intimately. I wasn't allowed to hunt anymore, since I'd become "valuable" at work, and "vacations" for those of us who came to be employed under Workfare were an abstract concept designed for a different class of people than we'd ever reach.

Back when I was free, Bern had once trekked after me for miles along the shore of Sterling Island as I tried to read the parting words of the dying lake written in vast stretches of sand punctuated with artifacts of decay. I hadn't realized he was there until I'd turned toward the keening of a gull and seen him sitting on a chunk of cement, watching me as the sun went down. He'd smiled and put out his hand.

The more I tried to do the right thing, the more I'd come to appreciate Bern, even though in society's eyes, with his masks stripped off, he'd have been a pedophile pimp aroused by the idea that friends who shared his kinks would pay a lot to play with his precious pearl. He never pushed me to do anything. I came into his life determined to live from my sexuality. I'd had a fairly clear idea of what I was headed into, and it was preferable to what I was running from. Autistics as a relentlessly honest group have fewer social illusions, and I grew up in an environment that allowed even fewer. My so-called childhood would probably have killed me if I hadn't gotten away. At almost twenty-one I found myself wishing I had the strength and confidence I'd had at fourteen. I wasn't likely to land on my feet twice the way I'd done on Sterling Island.

I'd been damned lucky to have found someone like Bern to look out for me. He was a decent human being, kind, compassionate, and deferential—and I sorely missed him. I thought about how I'd been annoyed when he'd tried to leverage his friendship with Chill into just getting me to send him a few words. I'd been ungrateful enough to think about throwing his phone away, when I should have been using it to talk to him. He hadn't tried to make any contact since Chill had asked me those few times to call him. Now the phone was dead, and the chance was gone.

I tried to air out the smell of adult diapers and disinfectant from my pores in the heavy, humid heat of midday, and played with the wisps of hair coming out of my regulation ponytail. It'd been a long time since I'd had a decent haircut. I struggled to construct a way to get out of my life alive, but I couldn't make it work. When I'd run away as a kid, I'd had a little money and I was in the city. I tried to see what might be open to me in post-secession Wyandot, but I couldn't come up with much. The Mistake had almost caught me with Bern's FedWeb phone a few weeks prior. I'd dropped it out my bedroom window when he'd shoved the door in, popping the wobbly old lock to see what I was doing. Fortunately, I'd been cutting myself as I'd searched the bandwidths for information from the outside world. The blood got him to back off without trying to search me, but the battery pack didn't survive the drop. The Mistake had bellowed that I was one sick piece of shit as I'd grinned with my teeth and drilled him with my eyes. His pupils were wide and his voice quavered as he'd backed out of the room.

I'd laid the phone parts to rest under the floorboards of the butcher shed, leaving a smear of my own juices on them like a talisman, beneath the row of ancient blacksmith-hammered iron hooks. The tiny structure had doubled as a smokehouse before the age of refrigeration; no matter how many times I might sweep it out with bleach solution, it would remain black as its plain purpose. The Mistake, for all his guns and manliness, couldn't handle hunting and its aftermath. He couldn't even take his kill to have it dressed by someone else. He'd eat a factory-farmed hamburger that held more hidden horrors than any honest field-kill, but he'd never look the thing he did in the face. He never set foot in my shed, surrounded as it was this time of year by a buzzing requiem of flies. My dead phone would lie undisturbed until the resurrection.

I was so deep in my own ruminations, I didn't notice a tall figure walking stiffly toward me until it was close enough to touch. I avoided eye contact and made a move to head back to work. I didn't want to interact with anyone. Even knowing someone outside CareWell had seen me in my humiliating pink scrubs was painful.

A voice that was familiar, but more subdued than I remembered, called softly. "Hey, Pipsqueak, hold up. I've been looking for you. They won't tell me anything here, and I don't dare go to your house anymore."

I rushed to Petra's arms, my tears caught in the dry trap of my throat. She winced, and I pulled back to see her face like the bruised ghost of my own, but she was missing a tooth and another was broken near the gum. After that first time, the Mistake was always careful not to visibly mess me up too much.

I murmured an aching question about her injuries.

"It's open season, honey-girl, and your Neanderthal has buddies who're happy to have an excuse to beat up a dyke. Listen, Tom's taken his family to the NorthEast Union—he tried to reach you before he left. Told me to tell you when I could. I'm headed there. Got to get my mouth fixed or I'll never work a decent job again. Come with me—now! Just run—"

I took her hand and nodded, but the whoosh of a swinging glass door made me look toward the CareWell entrance. A pair of large orderlies were trotting toward us as my supervisor watched with folded arms.

I whispered as I pushed Petra away. "Do not turn around. There are a couple of guys coming for you who know how to take people down. I'm gonna sound mean right now, but don't remember me by it..."

I snarled loudly for her to have a good life in the Union as I shoved her toward the street.

The supervisor gestured for her human attack dogs to hold up at the gateway that marked the edge of the CareWell grounds. She watched Petra hobble quickly to her truck.

The supervisor gave me a smirking sneer. "Best all them types are leaving. The air's cleaner around here already."

I was damned if I was going to let her see tears in my eyes.

...

I put the Mistake's food in front of him. I'd learned to fix what he wanted, even if I wouldn't eat it myself. It was a small price to pay for peace.

He had one of those illegible expressions that meant there was a storm brewing. "Your boss says you sent that bulldyke away that kept asking about you. Glad to hear it."

I noted the faint twitch of an autistic reflex to argue about the definition of a bulldyke, and how far beautiful, bruised, broken-toothed Petra was from that. It was pointless.

The Mistake had steady work recently; he muttered that some of the farog supervisors he'd worked for before were crawling out into daylight again, and they'd done him a favor or two. I perked up to hear the Martels might be back in business. I asked if I could join one of his odd-job crews as a trim carpenter so I could get out of CareWell and maybe draw an actual paycheck instead of lunch money.

He pushed his food away and yowled. "For god's sake, you lit-tle freak—whoever the fuck you really are. I knew about the dyke thing. Pretty hard to miss, kinda funny, and the guys helped me deal with the competition. This is different. This Champetty pulls me aside today... I just thought I was putting in a bathroom for him. Thought him and the guys were friends of mine—go out, have a little fun sometimes. Turns out it's a whole other thing. Now I'm the entertainment. He likes to play all kinds of games, him and his farog friends."

I started to say something, but he slapped his hand on the table to shut me up.

"Don't open your mouth. So, Champetty says he's been want-ing to fill me in on a few facts. He tells me what you were, from back when you were in detention. So I guess I didn't even know what your real name is. You think you're going to go in and watch me look him in the face after that? I got no choice but to go face him—but your slutty ass ain't gonna be there. Yeah, I bet they'd love to see you again. I can't turn the work down, it's all there is to keep this goddamn rotting hulk of yours from caving in over my head. You're killing me..."

At one time, my stomach might have twisted itself into a bloody knot to hear that. By then the shock was so muffled by the depth of the hole I was in I barely felt it.

I sighed. "Thunderbird was five long, long years ago—and you know my real name. I left all that behind. Sam Champetty belongs to a piece of my life I want no more part of. Didn't think it was the kind of thing you wanted to hear about."

The Mistake pulled his head out of his hands.

There were tears on his face. "This is a nightmare. I swear I'm gonna pull the trigger just so I can wake up."

Something in me was sorry enough for him that I went over and rubbed his shoulder. He wrapped his arms around my waist and wailed into my belly.

...

My supervisor and the Mistake had some mutual admiration thing. He'd stop at her desk when he picked me up in the afternoons even though I was aching to get away. They'd do that cutesy thing that normals do where they're talking to each other about you with quiet voices, but they make sure you hear certain parts. I heard the Mistake moaning how he didn't understand how to deal with me.

My supervisor said "think like a donkey" with an icky wink. When he looked blank, she explained coyly that all he had to do was pretend he was a "stubborn little [mumble mumble] ... jenny-ass... tee hee hee" and he could figure me out.

I heard her ask when I was going to marry him, and he'd murmured something that gave her warm chuckles. He was a Good Man who'd reached out to lift a mentally deformed sinner into the blessed light of day for no reason but the kindness of his heart.

I became a Redemption Project. I was pulled off food delivery, cleanup, and diaper and linen changing to work in the main office a few days a week. My supervisor reminded me to repeat "Lord we are grateful" to myself often. Her name was Miss Ellway; she became "the LWAG" in my mind. I was kicked up to non-disabled wages with provisional permission to wear regular slate-gray CareWell scrubs, but with a nametag that had the puzzle piece prominently on it. It still meant as much as the raise to get that pink off my body.

During the days I worked in the wards, I was indeed grateful for the stupefying drugs the "clients" were steeped in, even though I hated myself for feeling that way. I didn't have to interact with them much, other than to wash their flaccid bodies of the incontinent mess of the side effects of their chemical straitjackets.

I thought of them more as individual patterns of sagging skin and blotched, swollen ankles than as humans. I reminded myself it could have been any of plenty of people I'd cared deeply for who inhabited the discolored flesh-sacks in numbered beds, threadbare chairs and strap-crossed wheelchairs designed to be pushed, not maneuvered by their occupants. I'd been bludgeoned by the smells and textures so much they barely registered anymore. My senses were going dead, and I was grateful for that.

The nameless beings in their stained, ragged gowns still shuffled through my dreams, sometimes with Liam's sweetly pudgy face, sometimes with Petra's bruised one. I was always trying to talk to them in my sleep, whether or not I recognized their faces. When I was actually there washing stuff off the corners of their mouths, I never tried to interact.

There were a couple of wards I wasn't permitted in without a senior orderly; those felt more like Thunderbird. When the LWAG pulled me off that duty, I was conflicted. At least those patients seemed to be still fighting for something.

...

It took me a while to do the data entry because I was always a clumsy typist, but I was careful. The LWAG had left me alone in the office with a virtual pile of long overdue intake information and backlogged reports, together with an inch-and-a-half physical stack of papers that might or might not contain the same information. As I followed patient IDs through the system, I kept ending up at an admin-access-only password-protected folder. The LWAG had told me my job stopped when properly categorized client transcripts entered the cache for that folder. She would handle them from there.

That was interesting. Usually transcripts landed there when a client died, but not always. Sometimes the client left the facility,

but that was rare. Sometimes it appeared the client was trans-
ferred to another ward that was off the books, because certain
information still came in about them.

The record-keeping was fatally shoddy in the transparent
parts of the system, and I had no expectation anything would be
different within its hidden lairs. What could be or wasn't in that
folder wormed through my mind as I tried to follow my instructions. The system could be stupid, malevolent, or both. It was a
puzzle that woke up my brain for the first time in far too long.

I couldn't take the temptation anymore. I checked the camera
monitors up and down the hallway. The day shift secretary had
been let go in the last round of budgeting, so I was pretty much it
for office staff. The LWAG did her own typing and answered the
phone, and she'd left for her church-and-government cooperative social services seminar. The head orderly had no interest in
anything that would disturb the poker game that had started immediately after her departure.

To avoid unnecessary login attempts, I initiated a dummy
user identity for myself in the hopes that the process would give
me password parameters. The minimum requirement for the
creaky, outdated municipal software was nine characters with at
least one letter and one number. I pulled up the LWAG's
username, scratched my head for all of thirty seconds, thought
like a donkey and tried "WeRGr8ful." I was in.

CHAPTER FIFTEEN

A mysterious hacking group continues defacing various Laithbourn sites, and has managed to freeze up a number of RedVote Pact governmental servers for extended periods. The individual Treasuries have come up with workarounds to continue meeting their obligations...

Voice of the New Confederacy, 5/5/37

I WAS DOING my client updates while trying to cover for having been in my LordWeAreGrateful boss's private files. After my initial triumph at getting in, there wasn't much to get excited about—just more shabby bookkeeping, incomplete client records, and links to swoony Christian romance blogs. The folder I'd been so intrigued by led to one on the network main drive that required a more formidable access key. It wasn't worth getting caught for, and I wished I'd let it go as a waste of time before the LWAG and the Mistake had walked into her open office and started talking about me in front of my face. She was calling me CareWell's little Aspergeek Angel.

I was no geek. However, I could apply common sense and usually get the machines to do what they had to if I was left in peace to do it. To deflect attention from the open file tabs, I said just that, in the flatly mechanical, nerdy voice they expected of me. The religious country music station the LWAG kept on was bad enough; I mentioned once again that I couldn't keep the lyrics from showing up in what I typed, and I could get my work done in half the time if I could get away from the "blessed" radio. She and the Mistake were nodding along to some piece of incessantly-repeated treacle as they yammered. They weren't even hearing it, but they were still moving to its marionette-strings.

The Mistake leaned over on my desk. "Wish you were this well behaved at home when things aren't to your majesty's liking, little princess. Your language is more, umm, 'colorful' when Miss Ellway isn't around. I should invite her up to supervise you in the kitchen so I can have an evening without that foul stuff that comes out of your mouth when I'm trying to eat my dinner."

The LWAG simpered and cooed. She was flushing and her perfume reeked from the warmth of her dumpy body. "Well, we hope that she doesn't make herself sick with those naughty words. We can't get by without her..." She leaned against the other side of my desk, up close with the Mistake. "It's a good thing the ones with autism are honest, otherwise I'd be really worried how much she could get into." She craned around to get a look at my screen. "Fortunately, you aren't interested in us boring ordinary people and our silly lives, are you, Angel?"

I'd managed to get her file closed, and I was tired of the bullshit. "I'm interested in getting my job done. You asked me to do something. I'm trying to do it. You're the one with the Master's in psychology—you tell me how I'm supposed to work in the middle of everything with people leaning on my desk and talking. Just dealing with the smells from the hall takes half my brain capacity."

As if on cue, an orderly came up to the window counter and bellowed at me that he needed another pallet of Laithbourn's proprietary disinfectant that the Regional Authority was contract-bound to use in its joint healthcare venture facilities.

I slammed my hand on the desk.

It seemed like a strategic moment for a tantrum. "I will not swear, since that's Frowned Upon, Mister, but if you actually cleaned anything with that caustic fluid instead of slopping messes into corners to ripen to a full eye-wateringly glorious stench I'd be more inclined to do it for you—you just pour it down the drain by the hundred Federal Dollar bucket-full so it looks like you're doing something when you run out of it." I turned my bulging eyes toward my supervisor. "If. You. Want. Me. To. Do. My. Job. Give. Me. The. Blessed. Space. And. Silence. To. Do. It. —Please."

The LWAG looked at me round-eyed, and turned to the Mistake. "I do see the potential for a potty mouth, but we mustn't get our Angel all in a fret about cleanliness. The delicate autistic olfactory mustn't be subjected to offenses—we've certainly had a textbook illustration of the result."

The three of them started joking about the vomiting spell I'd had the week before. The same orderly had left a bundle of fouled laundry in the hall in front of the office. The bag had torn and left a smear from the elevator to the laundry chute, and he pointedly hadn't cleaned it up when I complained. I'd gotten up to get it myself, but I hadn't worked in the wards for weeks and wasn't as hardened as I'd thought. I'd started throwing up and couldn't stop. I'd dragged myself to the restroom and curled on the floor, raising myself every few minutes to force out a little more into the puddle at the bottom of the stained porcelain. It was like I was trying to puke up my entire life.

...

The LWAG had waited a few weeks to move me into the network server room in the basement to make it clear my tantrum hadn't been the reason she did it. I didn't have a window anymore, but the trade-off was worth it. I hardly noticed the weather anyway. The old pipes clanged around me, and the HVAC system roared. It still felt like blessed silence. The room was off a mezzanine balcony surrounding the furnace platform, so any flooding wouldn't reach the equipment. There was only one surveillance camera down there, pointed at the furnace to watch for malfunctions. I rarely even had footsteps by my door. The room had fluorescent overheads, but I'd taken the nice LED lamp I'd used when I worked overtime at night down with me.

There was a decent single-stall unisex bathroom on the mezzanine; since smoking was re-legalized in public institutions after RedVote industry lobbying, nobody bothered to go out of their way to use it. I only saw the sun when I came up to get paper records. I usually got wireless network downloads from the staff tablets. I worked a ten hour "daylight" shift starting before dawn, plus another half-shift after all but the skeleton staff had left.

I tried accessing the main server drive, but it simply hummed and blinked its green and amber lights, disdainful of me, locked out of its ruminations. It was a warm black box with a mass of spaghetti emanating from it; the computers feeding it were hard-wired. Whoever designed the system, probably before I was born, felt wireless connections were too vulnerable to hacking. My attempts were like throwing pebbles at a cement wall. I tried to convince the LWAG to let me take care of entering the completed weekly reports onto the main drive for her, but she wanted to be the one signing them in. She said the CareWell server was connected directly to the parent company network and they were very particular about security "upstairs."

I made sure my productivity improved and stayed up. I didn't want anyone second-guessing my new work assignment. It kept me away from the Mistake; he'd drop me off in the morning, and in the evening I'd get a ride with the second shift secretary back to a fracking commissary a couple of miles from my house. I'd call the Mistake as ordered before we left, and he'd pick me up from the commissary lot when he was damned well ready if deep snow or sodden summer rains were too heavy for me to walk.

I thought I might be anorexic. Even that far from the wards above me, I smelled the sickness of the place. I could only choke down a few crackers through the day. The Mistake was letting up on me; I was fading into the shadows so far he hardly needed to bother. I hadn't had one of his easy-to-hide but heartstop-scary punches to the breastbone in more months than I could remember. I just stared at my bony hands on the keyboard day after day. The money went into the account the Mistake had supervised ever since he moved in, and he drank it away.

...

The Mistake had come in to demonstrate the pro version of his favorite malware-ridden bookkeeping program that he'd showed me back when I first met him. He earned a cashback credit from the company for every paid account he referred. The LWAG gleefully greeted him over the Turkey Day fast food advertising on the radio. Thanksgiving wasn't an official religious holiday in the Heartlands; it was now a 'secular celebration' that didn't merit paid leave, but the Black Friday hawking was inescapable. The LWAG had barely signed back onto her desktop workstation after lunch when she'd called me up to repair her latest mess. I was trying to concentrate over the ads while I got her intakes straightened out when he'd sauntered in.

The two of them were bending over me while they leaned on the swivel chair I was sitting in, spinning me a few inches from side to side every time one of them gesticulated while they gave me contradicting instructions about downloading and installing the program. The pro version needed to go on the shared network server drive, and the system kept telling me I wasn't an administrator. I started to get up as the LWAG reached for the mouse, but I changed my mind. She went to a folder on her personal drive I'd thought was full of old crap she couldn't bear to delete. She opened an official CareWell administrative document that looked like all the others, except it had a long ID number of some kind in the upper right of the page. She cut/pasted it into the admin password, hit "enter" and the system bent over and accepted whatever piece of digital toxicity she had jammed into it.

She gave the Mistake a coy smile. "I never can remember that key number so I put in on the first document I ever generated here, the first intake I ever put into the system after I was promoted by Laithbourn Healthcare. It's my proudest thing."

She gazed in rapt admiration as the Mistake showed her the marvels of the program. He muttered something about me not being smart enough to use it and not to ask me. Every computer he'd ever put the thing on had slowed to a lockup-prone crawl, but he insisted the pro version wouldn't be like that. I bowed my head and followed Luce Dark's advice about letting people think I was as dumb as they wanted to.

The LWAG reached over to sign herself out of the corporate network and shut her workstation down.

She patted my hand while looking at the Mistake. "It's a good thing our Aspie Angel doesn't know my login. She could get into all sorts of mischief now."

...

I waited a couple of weeks before accessing the server to look around without opening anything. It was an on-ramp to some kind of Laithbourn superhighway. The complexity was daunting enough to keep me out until my head was clearer. I'd started using my time after I was done with my morning tasks for a session of Gabriel's mindfulness meditation. It was beginning to work, but there was a big part of me that didn't want that comforting dissociative fog to lift.

One slow afternoon, I decided to see if I could practice on the Mistake's financial program. I thought I might get into Care-Well/Laithbourn files that way, and I needed to learn how to appear unobtrusively professional to headquarters. I indicated on my timesheet that I was going on break, and disabled the LWAG's keystroke tracker for my machine. I tried creating a dummy account from random digits; the program rejected several as invalid. I didn't want to touch my personal account because the Mistake kept a view log on it.

The number from my old seized account was seared in my memory. I thought it might work since it had been valid at one time. The program appeared to accept it; a new screen asked for an identity. I didn't want my CareWell username setting off anything, so I entered "scope archer" without thinking, and then hit a high panic as the screen flashed. I tried to pull back as window after window flipped. I pressed "backspace" and "delete" and tried for a shutdown. I was reaching down to pull the power cord when a new screen with a familiar image on it popped up.

The Guy Fawkes mask with its crown of lightning bolts that had been on my old phone showed, with a pane asking for my password. I gave the one from my phone, and watched as the seized account came up, with thumbnails of court documents streaming down the side of the window. There was a hokey effect as the mask's eyes and crown of lightning bolts lit up, and then each bolt flashed in turn around and around, as a "please wait" indicator. Finally, the screen stopped playing with itself and a page of instructions appeared.

I didn't know whether what I'd stirred up was going to save me or destroy me, but at least I felt fully alive. I watched as my

Sterling Island remuneration flowed back into the voided account and the court documents appeared in order and then flicked away, stamped "deleted from Northern Heartland Docket Archives Registry, no evidence of hardcopy found." The instructions warned me the account was now under my new name, with a fictitious record of its creation. The new pedigree would be sent to the email I provided.

I thought I was done for the day, but the program had other ideas. I didn't know what it might do if I antagonized it. It was too creative and too fanboy to feel like a Laithbourn trap, but I couldn't be sure. I decided if I was going down, it would be in a blaze of glory. It asked about my contact device. I presumed that meant the phone, and I entered that it needed a new power pack when asked for the reason I wasn't using it.

The Guy Fawkes mask flashed its eyes again. "Do you wish to make a report?"

I pressed the "yes" button, and entered everything I knew about CareWell's files onto the screen that followed.

...

I was walking home in the December darkness. The deep ruts in the road looked bottomless in the strafing moonlight. I was enjoying the way my breath rose up toward the clear, starry sky. I didn't want to turn the curve that would show my poor old house at the top of the hill, kitchen lights glowing as the Mistake worked on his fifth beer and his foul mood as he waited for me to fix the dinner he was bound to find unsatisfactory.

I was jerked from thought by the sound of crunching gravel. It came from a sinister, huge-tired, night-vision equipped vehicle like Laithbourn agents used. I took off for the woods. A slight figure jumped from the back, holding up a phone like an ID badge. It was a young kid. He didn't speak, but the screen he used to identify himself was the lightning-crowned mask. He pressed a battery pack into my hand, along with a chip drive in a tiny sleek case. He slid back into the vehicle and disappeared—the black SUV running without headlights, rumbling quietly into the night.

...

The screen on my revived phone showed my full biography—Thunderbird Mountain, my University Hospital autism diagnosis, when I started using my new name—it didn't appear as though I had many secrets from this entity, whatever it was.

The mask with the same cheesy eye-blink effect came up on the phone. "Is this you?"

"Yes."

"Please insert the chip the courier provided."

This time instead of the cheesy-looking mask, the image that appeared was the Little Dipper. The North Star brightened and blinked to indicate activity. The phone illumination flickered and it made a slight whirring sound I'd never heard from it before.

The backlighting on the LCD panel went dark and it turned slightly iridescent, with a word-crawl underneath it. "Please press your right palm firmly to the screen for fifteen seconds."

I did, and the palm print remained in the panel for a moment. "Verifying."

The normal appearance of the screen returned. "Identity confirmed. You will be corresponding directly with Polaris Constellation momentarily. Please extend your keypad."

A texting format appeared, with a standard message pane. "What level of risk are you prepared to take to further this investigation?"

I typed, "Deadly. Kill or be killed."

"Are you prepared to become a Constellation operative?"

"I am."

"Welcome to the Polaris Network, Scope. We are honored to have you among us."

CHAPTER SIXTEEN

*I still haven't found anyone to confirm what happened at the Dog &
Pony queer bar out in godforsaken Wyandot County. It appears from
the relatively safe distance of this great metropolis like a good old-
fashioned lynching. At least three unfortunately appropriately-appel-
lated faggots were hung, and more, including several females, died a
worse death when the place was set afire and the barred windows
intended to keep the pitchfork-and-torch crowd out served instead to
trap the patrons in, lit up like xmas rum-raisins by the quantity of
alcohol on the premises.*

*Whatever joy the poor sots strung up and flambeed by the cross-
wielding mob may have found from their attempts to love one another, I hope to hell it was worth it.*

PoorJaredsAlmanac@TheUrbanHowl.press, blog post 6/18/39

I COULDN'T SLEEP. The air was hot and dead still. The power
was out again, and the secondary generator needed gas I
didn't want to waste running one ceiling fan. The primary
backup that ran the refrigerator growled from a safe distance under the open window. The Mistake moaned from his room across
the hall; he was prone to nightmares when he added pharmaceuticals to his drinking regimen. I considered one more time
whether to offer someone behind the Polaris mask everything in
the account they'd gotten back for me to dispose of him. I didn't
have allies left in or out of law enforcement to help me get him
out of my house, but at least I'd gotten him out of my bedroom.
I'd met him at the doorway a couple of weeks before with my
demolition hammer when he'd followed me up the stairs bellowing that he was going to have to start beating the crap out of me
again because my attitude had regressed. I told him it was time
for him to sleep somewhere else, and to bear in mind that he was

facing a woman with a sledgehammer and a clear conscience. He went to the other bedroom and locked the door behind him. I never had to sleep next to him again.

Getting him out of the house was another problem. Realistically, whoever was behind Polaris wasn't the solution. If they could get my money away from the government that easily they could get whatever they wanted, and I probably couldn't go through with it anyway. I rolled over. The Mistake's snoring came through the thick plaster walls. The peeper frogs sang so shrilly in the trees along the creek that I cursed being lucky enough to have them; drilling runoff had poisoned most of them in Wyandot.

I stepped carefully across the creaky boards of my crooked little bedroom, slid back the hardened steel slide bolts I'd mounted to the lopsided oak door, opened it so slowly it barely groaned, and gently turned the key in the rattle-prone passage lock behind me. I slipped into the low-ceilinged hallway, down the narrow stairs, through the kitchen and out the back. Even though the tiny citrine-colored frogs were making the inside of my skull ring, I wanted to go cool my feet in the water. I trod cautiously through the firefly-spangled grass at the edge of the clearing, trying to make enough ruckus to get any snakes to move on without making so much they'd take offense.

I let out a sigh as my feet hit the cool muck under the dark trickle. The weather had been humid, but the rain wasn't coming. The creek was low enough that the wide, flat boulders in it poked up from the water, their usual coating of wickedly slick algae flaking away in a gray, musty-smelling powder. I sat on one before I thought of what kind of mess it'd leave on my underpants and the ragged man's shirt I slept in, or tried to. I figured I was up until dawn anyway.

I hadn't heard anything significant from Polaris since the winter, back when I'd watched the faceless hackers use my information to get into the infuriatingly blinking server box. I was discouraged from poking around in the server on my own. I occasionally got an alert to watch out for some person or another who might be coming through the CareWell system, but I'd never been able to help. I'd pointed out the file folder into which a number of "clients" had vanished from the official records. If Polaris had found anything useful in it, it wasn't telling me.

I sat on the filthy rock that was gradually warming from my body heat and tried to forget how much I wanted to hear from someone; at that point I didn't care who. The air was finally cooling enough that the frogs had softened their frantic song, and clear moonlight touched the movement on the water surface. I folded my legs into a lotus position, my feet leaving dirty smears on the inside of my thighs. My autistic hyper-flexible joints allowed me to sit easily, but there were other ways the practice was less comfortable. I was finding meditation brought out muttering mirages in my head that were unpleasantly like what my mother described when she was too far out there to worry that people would call her crazy.

I wasn't sure if I was in the best headspace to be so intimate with my own workings, but I needed to get control of my despair. Dancing with the gibbering foxfires between my ears was preferable to getting pulled into that. As I'd dropped deeper into relaxed concentration, I began to hear soft, distant hooting. Owls had once hunted in the woods around me, but they'd long fled the drilling rigs and chainsaws of the modern forest, or so I thought. I wondered if it was coming from inside my head. I'd only heard recordings of owls, and I couldn't have said what kind it might be, but it sounded like it might be my idea of what an owl's call should sound like. It was time to pull up and blow the fairy dust out of my skull.

I stood and brushed the dried algae off myself. The owl still hooted faintly, barely audible but from a distinct direction. I felt better about my sanity. I followed it, stumbling and skinning my knees up the ravine forming the far boundary of my land, and found myself on the overgrown track to the ruined Dark compound. I trudged contentedly along the ruts edged with brittle weeds. My feet were callused from all the barefoot wandering I did; a few months back I'd found myself shoeless in the snow, a quarter mile from the house.

The owl's voice got clearer as I approached. There was a playful flourish to it unlike any wildlife recording I'd heard. I knew I was being drawn to the compound. I picked up my pace and stopped trying to locate the source of the intermittent sounds. The powdery dirt whispered against my soles, and my ragged shirt flapped in my own soft wind. I hadn't run in years. I opened my arms and let my feet fly until a sharp, clear, marijuana-like smell hit my nostrils. My heart stopped at the sound of a baroque owl-hoot that ended with a cutting chuckle.

A familiar, sardonic grin caught the glow of a small fire in the middle of the compound lot. "Achh! You make the calling—no guarantee what answers it. Now nothin' better's gonna come. Va te faire foutre, moult-dirty little white-chick spirit-bird." Chill's father Michel put his cupped hands to his mouth again and made a flute-like hoot, modulated with the flutter of a long, skinny palm.

I said "'Go fuck yourself' yourself. Sounds like you say that to all the girls, anyway. Don't call me a skank or I'll take it personally."

Mike Dark grinned and told me to pull up some gravel and sit. He wafted the smoldering sage smudge stick at me and then doused the bundle in a small dish of water. I nodded my thanks at the gesture and asked if it was something I should learn about.

Mike raised an eyebrow. "Don't kid yourself, Archer-girl; you don't got enough indigenous in you to qualify for the back of the bus. Best be careful drifting around in these woods—my Maman used to have tea with the windigo that owns this place, and it will—" he made a snatching gesture that made me jump— "snap your head off and suck your soul out if you don't respect the rules of our shadows. If you came when I called in my blood-spirits, was because you're a nutcase, not because you belong here."

I told him maybe he was honing in on my call, not the other way around, and that he was the one with the blue eyes and probably the paler skin if he wanted to compare.

He gave me a hard smile. "Brown ain't in the flesh, or the eye of the beholden. Your family did all the right things to wash the savage out of yourselves—you're no skin-sister of mine."

I let him feel my autistic stare. "So what am I then? My dad never talked about where he came from, or much else for that matter. What are you that you can kick shit in my face? For my-self, I've spent a lot of years in hell paying for it but nobody's really told me what it is."

His aquamarine eyes caught the light before he lowered them, deferring but not apologizing. "DNA test's a rich man's indul-gence. Who knows? Our line had the Indian killed out of us to save the Man in us, to paraphrase the residential school motto. We dunno. Gabe and I have different dads due to the occupa-tional hazards of Maman's profession—from the look of him, his papa was a purebred Red Injun, but even if Maman knew which client he was, he'd be the King of France if you asked, and she'd believe it when she said it."

Mike pulled a tiny pipe from his pocket, loaded and lit it with-out offering to share. "Your side had a taste for lily-white crazies—diluted the muddy all out of you. Beautiful pale ghosts full of the light that shines through the cracks in the world, ones with mathematics music in their brains like tuning crystals to the universe but couldn't leave the house with their clothes on straight. Maman thought you Archers were the nobility of the family. Broke her poor crackpot woods-nigger heart when you sold her great-granddaddy's house to that swine that fucks my daughter."

I glared hard enough to make him drop his gaze again when he raised it.

My words came out like trying to swallow stones. "—Well—I bought it back again, for the price of a used truck—it's got no gas under it, it's too steep to farm with anything but hand tools and the house is falling down—any of you Darks could've had it if you wanted it, but I actually did, because it belonged to my father. Now, if you want to help me get the asshole out of there that I made the mistake of turning to for help when the Darks left me high and dry, I'll be happy to discuss it. If you can make him gone, as in all gone, I'll listen politely."

Mike's eyes sparkled in the firelight. "OK, Archer-girl, I know you been through some shit and Chill likes you. So does my brother Gabe, and those aren't easy likes to get, but best not to count on too much from this side for a while yet. I stay up there in the old place sometimes when I'm running stuff for the wife's people." He nodded toward the house at the top of the hill that the bulldozers couldn't reach. "But you ain't seen me. Big Brother-in-Law Martel might be watching over us more than you know, and that might or might not be comfort. Ain't none of us really here—I'm just something you dreamed. I'll put a word in and you might hear something one day."

He looked hard at my face. "Patience, Archer-girl—the mill-stone of the world turns slow, but it grinds down all things." He looked toward the pinkish, paling spot on the horizon. "Rosy-fin-gered dawn is reaching for us. Better get home and out of your dancing clothes before your man wakes up, sees you been con-sorting with spirits again, and beats your snarky little ass."

...

It wasn't long after Michel Dark and I disappointingly an-swered each other's summonings that I began trespassing in the CareWell internal network. I'd found security camera feeds from the wards that weren't officially on the books, and I needed a wit-ness, even if it got me killed. I patched the camera feeds into a Polaris-encrypted fake-but-authentically-revolting cis porn site. Most office computers had sign-ons to porn; "upstairs" didn't bother with tracking them so long as things didn't get too obvi-ous. It was my best shot that Polaris would see what happened in those wards where the clients' files had all been "mislaid."

I had no place else to report the rooms full of people who had no legal existence, kept in a chronic stupor, often in "medically appropriate" four-point restraints if they were aware enough to moan their objections. I told the LWAG I needed to get out of the basement sometimes, and started working in the wards a few hours a day. CareWell was so shorthanded they'd take whatever help I gave so long as they didn't have to pay me for it.

I traipsed after the senior orderly on the off-the-record rounds. On my first visit I counted thirty-seven diapers to be changed in the three non-existent wards. Those thirty-seven flaccid bodies all seemed in what should have been their physical prime, and all had a blue puzzle-piece tattoo on the wrist. I washed each face in its deep, drugged slumber, rolling each hip up to check for bedsores, discreetly pressing each limp right hand against my phone screen as urgently instructed by my Polaris handler as soon as the camera feeds had found their way to human eyes.

CHAPTER SEVENTEEN

Senator Frank Lewiston reminded the Northern Heartland Regional Assembly Thursday that rural areas gave the Secession Movement the most support. He indicated that the Urban Core has pulled back from infrastructure maintenance agreements but they're "perfectly ready to consume whatever remaining resources they can gouge out of Wyandot even if its lifeblood has to be hauled out in all-terrain crawlers." He explained that extensive areas in his district don't have any communications service except citizens' band radios anymore, which are to be used only for emergencies and have frequent outages.

The pullout of Laithbourn Capital's unprofitable development and resource extraction subsidiaries from Wyandot due to recent earthquakes and resulting damage to Laithbourn-owned facilities has left the senator's sparsely populated district without much leverage in the assembly.

Garth Carpetlayer, Senior Correspondent,
Heartland Freedom Herald, 12/19/42

I'D TOLD THE SECOND-SHIFT SECRETARY to leave without me after the emergency broadcast said the roads would close at sundown. I tried the citizens' band radio in the office to let the Mistake know I was staying over, but he wasn't answering. The blizzard had dumped two feet of snow through the afternoon. It was obvious I wasn't coming home that night and why, but the LWAG insisted he'd worry. The secretary said she'd try to raise him when she got in. The LWAG thanked her.

I had a cot in my basement office, my own coffee maker, and a locker with a change of clothes. I'd learned I should give myself sponge baths in the mezzanine bathroom after one of the nicer orderlies mentioned that it was sometimes hard to tell whether it was a patient or me who needed cleaning up after I'd spent a couple of nights at work.

I got down to my task of getting the year-end drug inventories to balance. I'd gotten a blank check from the LWAG to do what I needed to make them fit. The pilferage was jaw-dropping, and most of it seemed to end in disappearances from places only she would have had access to. She must have known I'd be hacking to cover for her.

Before she'd left into the snowstorm, she'd given me a stiff peck on the cheek as I'd sat at her desk with the inventory files open. "You don't get paid near enough for your loyalty, sweetie. I know it's your way of showing it... to do this... slaving away when everyone else has gone and left you alone with the lights on standby. I suppose you like it dark like when you work. Anyway, I'm going to see what I can do about getting you a performance bonus even though you're Special Needs. There should be a way to at least get you a Christmas check from Charitable Discretionary."

I saw the sentimentality pooling in the corners of her eyes. I told her to get out and drive carefully while the roads were still passable. She'd reminded me to put the panic button pendant on and then wakened the dozing guard to walk her out. I listened for the beeping of the keypad arming the security system. I heard her engine start, and then the guard's. I pulled the corrugated metal safety curtain down over the reception window the way I was supposed to when there was no night watchman on duty.

The skeleton crew orderlies and I had the building to ourselves. I checked the hall camera and saw the doctor who was supposed to be on duty trying to slip out. He told me to put my autistic rules-obsession where the sun didn't shine when I told him he wasn't allowed to leave us there without a physician. He said he was getting home before he was snowed in, and if anything happened, to go put on my tinfoil hat and channel an MD in from the Mothership.

I called him a chickenshit for not having the balls to leave when Miss Ellway was still there; I almost called her the LWAG out loud. The doctor snorted and told me to go back to my hole.

He'd come to CareWell after he'd lost his medical license in the NorthEast Union, and Laithbourn Healthcare had made him an offer because they couldn't get anything better. I noticed when he buzzed himself out, he didn't use his own passcode. The sequence wasn't assigned to anyone I knew of. I went back into the office and clicked the lock behind me.

I couldn't afford to have Laithbourn looking for discrepancies in the CareWell system. I was channeling so much information to Polaris through my machine in the basement that if "upstairs" inspected it, they would know they had a mole in the tunnels. As I got back to work on my year-end reports, I re-drew the picture of the inventory accounts to keep the pilferage from attracting the higher-up's attention. I left in a few controlled-substance swipes that were probably by former employees so we wouldn't look too perfect and the guilty parties wouldn't be readily available for questioning. I did cover for a small, regular, biweekly vending-machine food theft of a box of bagged nuts that had to have been by the secretary I rode with, but otherwise I left non-drug reports alone.

The risks I was taking made my pulse flutter when I looked at them square on. I was taking Laithbourn delivery reports and altering them at the source, wherever that was located in the real world. I was altering Laithbourn folders of CareWell requisitions on the blind assumption that no hard copies had been made in some office on the Gulf Coast. CareWell, a few small urgent care facilities, and Thunderbird Mountain were Laithbourn's last foothold in the Northern Heartland, and there were rumors that Thunderbird was emptying out. I had no idea whether that would make Laithbourn hang on to CareWell harder or just let everything go.

Laithbourn's energy operations had recently pulled out of northern Wyandot, leaving whoever depended on them spinning in the backdraft. A new round of seismic events had blown several wells out, killing a still-unknown number of workers. Some wells continued leaking, blasting like gigantic blowtorches into the sky, and the pitiful remnants of the municipal emergency response structure didn't have the equipment or training to handle them. Our Senator had called in a firefighting crew with the familiar fleur-de-lis and hammers logo to handle the blowout conflagration at the largest wellhead.

A big Québécois who looked familiar had grinned at the media cameras from under his thick mustache and quoted an old wildcat well-firefighter saying. "If you think it's expensive to hire a professional to do the job, wait until you hire an amateur."

I was jolted out of my ruminations by the sound of the perimeter gate opening, and some kind of heavy vehicle driving around the building. I switched the computer monitor to the exterior cameras. Whatever it was drove without headlights and had just pulled up next to the service dock. It was illegal to drive using only a night-vision screen in the settled areas of the county, but that never seemed to affect anyone rich enough to own one. Its doors now open, the big vehicle's interior lights flared in the swirling snow.

Six paramilitaries got out of the unmarked transport, moving crisply, their wind-shredded breath rising into the blaring security spotlights in the wide-angle view of the rear lot. An orderly was gesturing while he struggled to pull his jacket on against the blasting storm. The lead paramilitary pushed him aside and the group of them lifted a gurney with something blanket-covered on it onto the dock, careful as pallbearers. I switched to the close-focused dock camera. A small, obese woman with terrified eyes stared into the open door behind the orderly, her hands and feet strapped with professional tidiness to the gurney rails.

...

Polaris had been silent after I'd notified them about the woman delivered to the service dock entrance in the middle of the night. Before I'd returned home when the blizzard had broken, I'd located her in the anonymous wards, in a tiny room by herself. I'd noted the puzzle piece on her wrist and sent her palm print without being asked. I'd found what information there was on her in the files and forwarded that to my handler. I received nothing in response.

When I tried reaching my handler through the old financial software portal I'd first made contact through, I got back a terse admonition to learn fast to recognize when I needed to lie low.

Two days later I was told by a phone text to remove every trace of Polaris connections from the CareWell computer system. When I'd completed that, I'd tried to send a text to tell them it was done. The phone was dead as a brick.

...

The head orderly administered shots, discarding the vials in a plastic bin in the cart he pushed. He got farther ahead, out of sight and earshot. Once a week he'd make the round of injections, and I'd follow with another orderly on regular rounds. Recently I'd been working with the orderly who'd let me know I'd needed to pay more attention to my hygiene. He gently lifted the groggy bodies while I removed the soiled diapers and ragged gowns, sponged off pale, soft bellies and addressed the beginnings of bed-sores before putting clean rags back around them. From the way the orderly talked, he was the one who'd been on the service dock in the middle of that night blizzard when Laithbourn delivered the tiny woman with the terrified eyes.

We entered her broom closet of a room; when she saw us she attempted to flap her hands, but they were still in restraints. We weren't allowed to undo those without the head orderly present. The nice orderly leaned over and whispered something to her; she made a happy-sounding little wail.

He picked up a vial the head orderly had dropped and held it up so I could see it was some kind of hormone. I nodded, muttering that it was the same thing they all got. They got their individual meds and their horse tranqs to keep them quiet, and they all got those shots. I slid a gel cushion under the tiny fat woman's hip where she was getting a pressure sore from not being able to roll over. The orderly quietly asked her if she'd like to be sponged off; she made another happy wail and flapped her hands as expressively as she could.

As he supported her back, I slipped her gown up and undid the snaps over her shoulders. She gave me a softly relieved coo as I washed her; the orderly whispered something to her about trying to get her better diapers. She made an "ah-ah" sound and seemed to try to gesture at me. He leaned in even closer to her, whispered so I couldn't hear, and then winked at her. She looked at him with a sweet face just touched by a smile. From what I knew about growing up with my deep-into-the-indigo autistic cousin and his schoolmates, and some of the patients I'd helped care for, she was beaming.

He nodded toward her mounded belly. "Notice anything?"

Actually her color was better than most in that ward. Her soft, youngish body had no blotches or marks. I shook my head.

The orderly nodded in a gesture that took in all the patients in the ward around the private room. "OK, for the two hundred fed-bucks question: what's the same for everyone here, beyond the placement, anyway?"

I thought a moment, remembering all the bodies I'd washed. I couldn't think of anything on their stomachs that was common to all of them. There were thin, fat, male, female—some bellies even had tone to them when they'd arrived.

The orderly gave me a look like he expected me to be smarter.

His whisper was barely audible. "Hint: What do you have on your wrist that's like what all of them have?"

I reflexively looked at the blue puzzle piece tattoo I shared with every patient in the secret wards.

The orderly was forming the words when it came together for me. "No scars. The boys have all their equipment. That's why hormone shots, to keep them from getting frisky... they haven't been spayed or neutered."

The orderly gave me a sardonic smile. "No shit, Sherlock."

CHAPTER EIGHTEEN

Our tin-shack neighbors to the south have again gotten themselves in hot water over their excessive reliance on a single commercial enterprise. Mega-conglomerate Laithbourn Capital has run from its Northern Heartland base with its tail between its legs after being unable to cope with problems of its own making. Even its so-called "healthcare" leeches-and-exorcism cash cows appear to be in danger of tipping on the unstable terrain. The collapse of the monopoly puts to rest the risible notion that a fragmented United States might constitute any threat to a solid, robust union of Anglo- and Franco-Canadian power.

"Ringing in the New Year" The Anglo-Canadian Observer writing for The New Albion Courier Online Edition January 3rd, 2043

I'D JUST RETURNED from the errand the LWAG's temporary replacement had sent me on. She'd asked me to ride with the polite orderly to get sanitary supplies since we hadn't received a shipment in nearly a month. The LWAG was on a Laithbourn-approved church-group missionary sabbatical for six weeks, and her understudy didn't have the same wheedling skills with the home office. As the orderly and I passed the receptionist's window, I noticed there were uniformed men looking at the office computers. I heard someone tell the temp to stay off the intercom and phone because no one else needed to know the parent company was there. The orderly muttered to keep walking. I did as he suggested, slinging the plastic trash bag of supplies over my shoulder so it hid my face.

When we got to the elevator, he hit the button for the basement mezzanine. The car coasted down half a floor. The lift motor stalled, and the overhead light dimmed for a couple of seconds until the backup generators roared on. When the orderly steadied himself, his left hand was near my face; as the light flared and the motor surged to life I saw faint scarring on his wrist. He jerked his undershirt sleeve back down over it and shooed me out when the doors opened. He didn't make eye contact when he hit the button and waited for the doors to close again.

...

I tracked what the Laithbourn auditing team was looking at from my basement computer. They were scrolling through files I hadn't seen, staff files with clearance settings and patient files with more detail that I'd found. I copied/pasted file addresses and tracked password keystrokes into an open document. I managed to keep up for a couple of hours, tracking everything happening on the five office computers upstairs. I was fried when the lull finally came. I shut everything down and copied my Polaris-encrypted document onto a cheap little jewel drive, and then I wiped the encryption app from the computer. Even if someone got hold of the drive, my now-unreachable handler had promised the encryption would hold up. I'd never be able to decipher it again. I pulled up the CareWell inventory accounting page and started entering the supplies I'd just helped buy.

I heard soft, quick footsteps on the metal stairs. I checked the outside security cameras. A couple of Laithbourn vehicles were pulling out of the lot; one unmarked limo remained. The basement camera showed it was the usually-nice orderly whom I'd heard on the steps. I unlocked my door, rested my hand on the kitchen knife I kept in my drawer and waited. The orderly knocked. When I said, "it's open," he stood leaning in the door frame. His face looked like it had been slapped around.

I looked up at him. "It has to be exhausting, passing as well as you do. I'd be willing to bet that's not your real name on the tag you wear."

He sighed. "Correct on both counts."

I stared at him a while. "Who's behind the mask?"

He folded his arms. "Ursa Minor."

I pulled my hand out of my desk drawer. "Have I been reporting to you all along? Fuck... just fuck you."

He reached in his pocket and chuckled when I flinched. "I was warned you'd be a handful. You almost blew us out of the water enough times to warrant putting a nanny on you. Plus, if Laithbourn pulls out fast, they may shoot the livestock before they go. We don't want you rotting in the sun for the Indians to find."

He leaned over and handed me a microdrive. "Here, plug this into your phone in about a week. Can't say exactly when we'll be ready with new secure channels, just keep trying. Radio silence for now.

"Fortunately we Thunderbird graduates know how to take a punch. I was in the class right after yours. Anyway, you missed Mrs. Put-That-Back-Where-You-Found-It from housekeeping's stash of pills she was dealing out of here. She made the requisitions herself and then canceled them out. She didn't hide them as well as you hid the Boss-Lady's shit, but all of us got the thumbscrew treatment. I wouldn't bank on Ellway not cracking when they talk to her. Lucky for you nobody suspects the free-range ree-tard in the basement—"

Loud voices echoed above us. I hoped he was right about the not-suspecting thing.

The orderly looked up. "Got anything for your last report? I gotta run."

I tossed him the jewel drive. "Just nearly every keystroke from upstairs for the last two and a half hours."

He kissed the tiny piece of electric blue junk jewelry. "Sweet. I hope we can do this again sometime, but Laithbourn's too close now. That woman they brought in—her name's Amelia Price— she's been trying to tell anyone who'll listen about what goes on in the Laithbourn 'sheltered workshops.' She blogs at..." He grabbed a piece of paper from my desk and spoke as he wrote "...fattyinthefire.difability.freemednet. You can't find her by searching—she's been wiped out of all the engines. You have to enter the address. Try not to get her in any more trouble than she's already in, but if they move her out of here, use the phone. A Polaris proxy contact will be in it."

An alarm siren announced the elevators were going out of service. He hissed "learn that and flush it" and nodded toward the paper. I tore a corner off it and scribbled the late-shift doctor's sneak-out passcode on it. He studied it, passed it back and gave me a quick salute before slipping into the innards of the basement.

...

I couldn't find Amelia's blog at the address I'd memorized. When I checked for mirrored sites that might be storing some of her posts, I got a message from my malware-tracking program that my movements were being followed by newly-activated root-level spyware. An alert flashed that my program was blocking an attempt by my computer to access an unknown network port. I pulled out, erased my browser history and rebooted. When the screen reappeared, there was a Laithbourn Healthcare window over it that said unauthorized software had been removed from my terminal. I had to click "accept" that I understood that employees were not allowed to install personal software or applications of any kind on Laithbourn-owned workstations.

...

Over the next few weeks Amelia faded into the same pasty cocoon that eventually wound around every CareWell subject. Her skin turned yellowish and blotchy, and her sweet-faced almost-grin vanished, even though she was out of the restraints. There had been a red flag in her intake file that she was a biter, but the softly whimpering creature I saw couldn't have managed that level of fight. Her ID wristband had a different patient number from the one she'd arrived with; patients never had last names, just given names and Laithbourn codes, like farm animals. Her bedsores and the chafing on her wrists and ankles weren't healing. Her diapers had a slightly industrial smell. Her mouth looked unhealthy even though her breath was sweet. There had been a warning in her original file that she was diabetic. That didn't stop her from getting pancakes with thick, sugar-based syrup, donuts, candy, and soda. When I raised the issue with the temporary supervisor she just said that was all Amelia would eat. She was losing weight in spite of it.

The temporary supervisor told me I wasn't allowed extra time with Amelia. When I ignored her, she said she was going to put a note in my file for when Miss Ellway got back. I said, "Fine." I figured Amelia used a communication tablet to write her blog. I found an ancient one in the office confiscations box; it was still set up for the person who'd brought it with him years ago. The depleted battery took a charge but didn't hold it long. I turned the volume on the synthesized male voice way down and closed the door to Amelia's room before showing it to her. I sat on the bed, holding the tablet for her like a book-rest, and asked permission to set her elbow on the crook of my knee to support her hand. She rolled her head affirmatively and scrolled through the tablet like a pro. The pages flashed past, too fast for me to read. She brightened once, her quiet laughter gurgling when she came to a page headed "commonly used" and pressed a few of the big on-screen buttons; the tablet had sworn in decidedly florid language, forcefully instructing someone to back off, stop touching, shut up, move over and/or go fuck him/herself. It was clear why the open-ward orderlies had confiscated it.

She played with the outdated writing program but lost interest. She was gently evasive when I tried to converse. She used the synthesized voice to ask if she could access the internet. When I told her the tablet connectivity had been inactivated when it was confiscated, she turned her face away. I set the tablet next to her on the bed and asked her if she wanted anything before I left. She flailed her hand weakly for me to just go away.

...

When I came in early the next morning, Amelia's tablet lay broken on top of the wad of trash in the wastebasket outside her room.

As the night orderly passed on his way out he snickered. "Too bad. She dropped it... shame about that."

She barely moved when I called her name. She'd vomited into her pillow, and her breath came in fast little gasps. Her flushed body glistened with fever-sweat. What appeared to be large hand-prints darkened her skin in discolored blotches inside her thighs and around her neck and forearms. Her sheets were soaked with urine, and her diaper lay torn and bunched near her feet. The abrasions on her ankles were festering, and her lower legs were bruise-colored with red streaks. The bedsore on her hip was pressing into the mess, and wept an ugly fluid in response. I went downstairs and dragged the night-shift doctor up with me as he was getting ready to leave, screaming at him that Amelia had probably been raped and was so obviously in diabetic shock that even he should have seen it when he made his rounds.

He checked my nametag and stared at me, his expression like cement. "Miss Webster, I have never been in these wards. These wards are not a part of this facility."

I felt myself starting to lose it. Someone from the orderlies' desk called down; the LWAG appeared and tried to calm me. She'd just returned from her sabbatical and was nursing a peeling sunburn with some kind of strong-smelling ointment. She took a stethoscope and pressure cuff from behind the desk. She inflated the cuff around Amelia's arm, and watched the numbers spike into the stratosphere. She pressed the scope against Amelia's wrist, muttering something about a rapid heartbeat.

I yowled, "No shit! Really?!"

The doctor snapped at a couple of orderlies who'd come to watch the show. One of them left and came back with a blood test kit. The doctor tied off Amelia's arm and stabbed the needle in. Nothing was coming. Amelia moaned faintly. He yanked the needle out again and squeezed; a few drops of blood slowly appeared, thick as warm honey.

He turned to me. "Probably an accurate diagnosis, Doctor Webster. She's not likely to survive without amputations. We don't do that here. She'd also need other extreme measures— probably a kidney transplant." He snickered. "I doubt she'd get a very high placement on *that* list. Well, we'll address the issue humanely."

He turned to the orderly who'd brought him the kit and asked for a drug I'd seen in veterinarian's offices. I felt my fist crash against the stubble on his jaw, then strong, practiced hands pinned my arms behind me.

The LWAG was trying to get me to look into her face. "Angel, it was sweet of you to stay with her, but we have to do the right thing. It's not kind to let her suffer."

...

The LWAG had talked the doctor out of calling the private county law enforcement on me. He'd had a high-powered taser held a couple of inches from my heart and was clearly aching to use it. I'd screamed myself out as one orderly showed him the euthanasia drug vial like it was a bottle of good wine while the other held me. The LWAG had had enough. She had reasons for not wanting me in official custody where I might get questioned about awkward subjects, but I was grateful for the way she stood her ground. There was a part of me that held out a fairy-tale hope she wouldn't let the doctor go through with putting Amelia down like a dog. She had another orderly take me to her office. I sat in her chair and swiveled and hummed and rocked myself until the Mistake came to pick me up. The two of them talked a long time in the hall and then they bundled me into the truck.

The Mistake was expressive as a tree stump for the drive home.

When he finally pulled the handbrake and killed the ignition, he turned to me and his face was on fire. "You. Have. Humiliated. Me. for the Last. Fucking. Time—*Freak!*"

He grabbed my shoulder and spun me around so his fist could impact me square on the sternum. It felt like a freight train. I moved my mouth, but there was no air in me. I gaped like a hooked fish, tried to get out of the truck, and collapsed onto the gravel. The Mistake dragged me into the house by the back of my shirt and my waistband.

...

The Mistake was passed out on the couch. The meds-and-alcohol cocktail he'd taken was likely to keep him there a while. He'd worn himself out hitting, yelling, weeping, and threatening to kill himself and me for three days without sleep. My ribs were so bruised, I hadn't taken a full breath for two sunrises. I'd finally told him if he was going to kill me to just fucking do it already. Instead, he got down to some serious self-medication. He dropped fast, the silence of the house broken only by his gurgled breathing.

I stuffed an old towel between the front of his pants and the cushions so the inevitable accident wouldn't ruin them. When the rhythm of his breath didn't change, I carefully pulled back his eyelid to see if his eyes were rolled back. He was out cold.

I pulled the keys to the truck from his pocket.

...

Even though the night air was early-Spring chilly, I had the windows down. The rifle sang its steel song on the rack behind my skull. This time I knew the owl-call in my head was in my head, but the owl rushed with me, its silent, speckled wings spreading on each side as I swept down the road. Fairy tales, dark fairy tales full of vengeful owls with claws like arrows might yet become real...

...

The CareWell building was darkened; the standby lights seemed dimmer than usual. One critical-systems backup generator was running; the other had gone dead. I'd let myself in on the doctor's code, using a tissue between my fingertip and the keypad. The console warned the alarm system had one hour and 38 minutes of functionality remaining. The electric eye watching the entry was dead; the red power indicator light had gone out. The lifeless security cameras watched over a sanatorium of ghosts. I rushed past the shuttered office and up the fire stairs to the secret wards. I had to use the code again to get the door for that floor to open. It was devoid of life.

Every floor was the same. I didn't go down to my office. Being trapped underground with the lights gone and the doors in auto-lockdown didn't appeal to me. Something urged me to the front office. I touched the steel curtain across the reception window and felt the call louder. I slung the rifle around, put my finger gently on the trigger, and let myself in.

The LWAG appeared to nap, her head resting on her arm laid across her bare desk. I came near enough to smell the sunburn salve arguing with her synthetic perfume. A palm-sized patch of her auburn-dyed hair had been torn out. Her face was bruised, and there were what looked like handcuff marks on her wrists. I checked her neck; her pulse fluttered, dim and fading. I put my ear near her chest and heard a faint, dry, sucking gurgle with her impossibly gentle breath. The arm stretched out under her face had been tied off and then released, the rubber strap lying loose and the crook of her elbow still holding the needle, the syringe empty. A neatly written note lay near her hand. I pulled it away carefully, without touching any other surfaces.

The note stated it would only be a matter of time before investigations revealed the facts of her crimes, and there was no point to dragging things out. She detailed her drug pilferage, including what she saw as my part in it, and the resale end, which I knew nothing about. She asked whoever found her to treat me mercifully because I'd acted out of loyalty to her and was incapable of understanding what I'd done. She said she'd let down not only her employer, but also the University Hospital which educated her and had put such faith in her. As I read the last sentence, she sighed deeply, and the sound in her chest went silent.

I folded the paper into my pocket, re-armed the security system behind me, put the rifle back in the rack, and drove home in the paling twilight. I parked the truck precisely in the spot it had been in when I was dragged from it. I checked that the Mistake was still in the same position on the couch, and slipped the keys back in his pocket. I replaced the sodden towel pressed against him with a clean one. He still didn't move, but his snores were loosening; he'd come awake with the hard morning sun in another couple of hours. I lit a burner on the propane stove, started the corner of the LWAG's folded suicide note on fire and rested the little burning tent carefully in the cast iron skillet. When the flame was done, I washed the ashes down the sink and started a pot of strong coffee to cover the scent of charred paper.

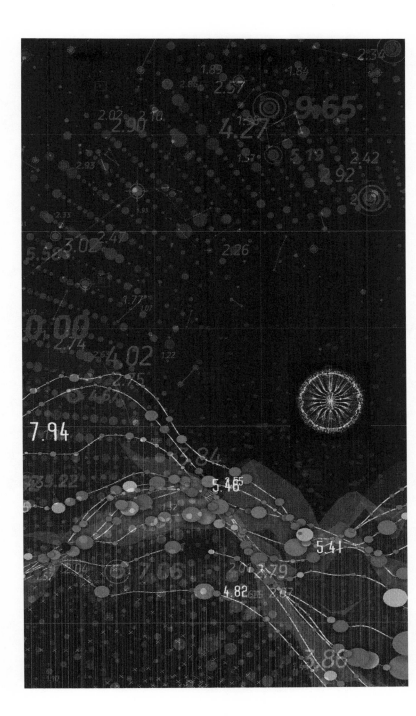

Ruling, Northern Heartland Regional High Court

*T*HIS COURT finds that the plaintiff has unilaterally abrogated its contractual obligations to provide those services specified under the terms of <u>The Northern Heartland Regional Development Pact of 2031</u>. This court further finds that the aforementioned Northern Heartland Independent Region, defendant, the contractual successor to the Northern Heartland Autonomous Region of the United States of America, is no longer bound by the terms of said Development Pact and is therefore under no legal or contractual obligation to make those payments demanded by said Laithbourn Capital under this pleading. Said pleading is therefore **denied.**

<u>Laithbourn Capital, LLC v. Northern Heartland</u>
<u>Successor Governmental Entity,</u>
<u>NHRHC 5, 203, (2043)</u>

CHAPTER NINETEEN

For the first time in many, many moons there is cause to rejoice here in the last bastion of civilized urban life in the old N.H.R. The Regional High Court has freed us of the yoke of Laithbourn Capital via an emergency ruling that cuts off public payments to them once and for all. Here in the city, we'll be getting to know the Martial Administration and Reconstruction Service as one of our private-contract emergency municipal services providers.

Laithbourn's pullout from Wyandot has been a messy business, with many highly disturbing questions left unanswered. The Care-Well skilled nursing facility that cared for indigent Wyandot citizens has been left utterly empty. The old Free Quebec-based Martel International outfit was summoned to break the locked-down CareWell building open. Their terse press release states that once they gained access, only the body of a single, badly beaten female administrator was found inside, under circumstances that suggest a clumsily staged suicide covering for outright murder. None of the between fifty and ninety clients variously reported to have been on the premises prior to Laithbourn's retreat have been located and all records on location have been removed or destroyed, according to the Martel security forces, who provided only a single photograph of the administrator's office crime scene.

Former Deputy Sheriff Tom Webster, long rumored to be behind whatever honest information occasionally managed to make it out of the Wyandot Sheriff's Department, has emerged from a safe retirement in New England to take over his old boss's job. We understand he's in negotiations with Martel operatives to gain access to the sites they now control. We wish him the best of luck, and whatever blessings this Vernal Equinox may bring.

Editor's Page, The Urban Howl Spring Preview Edition,
March 20th, 2043

I WAS ON A TRAIN headed west. It felt like an old train, swaying slightly, with clackety wheels. The lights were warm, but they flickered as if they were run by a generator off the engine. I couldn't see anything but black out the window. Michel Dark was sitting across from me, wearing all black, and he gave me that family grin, all fangs and seduction, and moved next to me. He leered and said, "Basilisk." I went to push him away but saw I'd been mistaken—it was Chill, and then I didn't mind so much. Chill said, "From a cockerel's egg," kissed me on the cheek, threw the window open, and the gush of wind sucked me out with the owl wings I'd felt when I was driving to CareWell with a loaded rifle in the rack behind my head. The wings kept spreading as if they had a dozen joints, unfolding from an invisible cocoon like webs of capillaries filling with newborn blood, and I was the wings and I spread from horizon to horizon, taking in wind more real than any breath I'd ever taken awake. My feathers, thundercloud gray, except the second one from the farthest left tip, black, infinite and conscious in every mile of me, aware. Lightning flared from the eyes I didn't have anymore because I was all sky, deep as midnight interminable, bottomless blue...

When I woke up, I listened for the Mistake snoring across the hall and snuck outside. I slid along the mooncast shadows to the ice-cold butcher shed. I lifted the blackened floorboard, slipped the microdrive the Polaris orderly had given me into my phone, and it came alive.

...

The life in the phone wasn't what I'd hoped, but it seemed to be working as a phone, anyway. There was no proxy contact in it the way the orderly had promised. Every bit of Polaris information had been scrubbed out of it. It was like a time warp. Even my old contacts list reappeared as it had been back when there was only Bern's number in it. The single-entry list was updated to the extent that Bern's number showed he was an attorney, with JD, P.C. after his name.

I told the phone to search for an active FedWeb band. It flickered to tell me it was working on it, and then locked in and gave a tiny chime to tell me I had something coming in. I silenced that sound I hadn't heard in years. My warm exhale caught the faint glow from the screen. I realized I'd been holding my breath and my pulse was running fast.

There was a text from Tom Webster, sent a few days back.

Dax- Please send something if you get this. I'm around. I never should have left- ashamed of myself and time to do the right thing. Know it may be hard for you to make contact. Try to let me know you're ok.- Tom

I hit "Reply" as if it had been just a few weeks ago I'd graduated tech school, telling him I couldn't risk him coming around, but I'd stay in touch.

...

I slipped back into the house. The Mistake was standing in the kitchen with that hollow look in his eyes that meant he was toeing his way along a thin, high edge. He hadn't been eating much lately, and he'd been drinking alone in his room.

The Mistake's face scrolled through a half dozen expressions before settling into one I couldn't read. "Where were you... out there, half-dressed in the cold and no light?"

I muttered that I'd had a dream that shook me up and I couldn't get back to sleep.

He said I hadn't answered his question.

I bristled. "Where the fuck do you think I was? Where could I go? You don't let me drive and there's a lot of nothing in walking distance."

His eyes started to glisten and his breathing came soft and ragged. I didn't want to deal with him crying, but it looked like that's where things were headed. I told him to quit worrying about me and go back to bed.

He swallowed and stared at his feet. "I was just about to go search for you. It's freezing out there, little special-girl... and the coyotes..."

I snickered in spite of myself.

"Don't laugh at me, Dax. You know they've picked off a couple of kids around here in the last few years."

I said I wasn't a two-year-old even though he might treat me like one. I wished I hadn't snarked as soon as I said it. There would be either fists or tears.

The fists balled up and I danced toward the door fast.

He wailed and the waterworks blew open. "No, no, no, no... I'm not... I won't... ahh!"

He sank to his knees, his sides heaving as he bent over with his hands resting on his thighs, giving me a view of his growing bald spot. That generally meant I was safe if I didn't provoke him.

I walked up to him.

He rested his head against my leg and grabbed my hand. "Baby girl, I gotta come clean..." He stared up red-eyed, pressing my hand to his wet, scratchy face.

I said OK.

He pulled in a soggy breath. "CareWell... it didn't just close up like I told you... Miss Ellway's dead—murdered... I didn't tell you my last Martel jobsite was the CareWell building. You remember the furnace there?

I said uh-huh. The furnace was a constructed-in-place megalith that sat on a massive platform in the center of the basement, ringed by the mezzanine balcony where my office and some storage rooms sat up out of flood danger. It ran on just about any fuel that was thrown into it, so long as the natural gas igniter got it started. The Mistake had worked on it a few times when the nozzles clogged.

The Mistake let the words out. "It was a—it was... there in the basement. Bodies... in the furnace—half-burned but it didn't stay lit..." He swallowed. "Not supposed to tell. They had me reconnect the gas. Stoked the thing up again, got the coal and wood burning, and finished the job. Bill Martel's overseeing the site—his brother's in from headquarters to supervise. Records from the vault... computers from your office down there, everything into the furnace. Make sure it doesn't clog up, shovel out the ashes... just keep it burning..."

I realized I'd dropped to the floor next to him. He buried his head against my stomach. I curled over him, careful of the tender spot in the middle of my chest. I regretted letting him get close enough to my body to have other thoughts come into his mind.

His breath came soft but harsh when he felt me stiffen. "Could you ever love me, Dax? After all this time, could I ever give you enough of me... that you'd ever...? I swear, if you leave me alone with this in my brain I'll put a bullet through it to finally have some peace."

I raised his head up to rest on my shoulder, put my arms around him and rocked him, making little shushing sounds until he cried himself out.

...

The Mistake got a nice bonus for his work at CareWell, anyway. He decided he was going to get a new rifle. A few years before it might have been a new SensuWorld multainment unit to invite Sam Champetty and the boys over to admire, but we didn't have the programming anymore, just an AM radio that could receive four stations on a good day. There was more cash in the strongbox than the Mistake could drink away in a week, so he had to spend it on something. He'd come up with the idea he was going to be a tough guy and start hunting. He wanted a rifle better than mine, and he had a nice fat pack of Martel Federal Dollars in his pocket to make sure of it.

The United States might have dissolved, but Corporate America was very much alive, and the Federal Reserve and its banks kept on like nothing had happened. The Martels were based in the Aligned Federation of Independent Canadian Territories, but they paid their hires in what continued to be the world's premier currency. AFICT money was good on the world market, but illegal to accept within any of the RedVote Regional Divisions. Most working saps in the Regional Divisions got paid in their Region's scrip, but their corporate masters dealt with one another in the greenback, same as always.

The Mistake had his packet of dollars ready to impress the guy behind the counter of Wyandot Premier Firearms, but someone had beaten him to it, and with a bigger wad of cash.

Chill's hair was long and tied back, with a few threads of silver in the black. I was surprised he wasn't covering the gray, but looking at him closer, it seemed in keeping. He was dressed well, but not styled up the way he'd been when I'd known him. I pushed the jolt down and tried to look at the merchandise. I knew I'd get clobbered if I said anything, so I pretended I didn't know him. He looked blankly at me with those pale eyes underneath heavy, un-plucked eyebrows and went back to examining a rifle, looking along the barrel with his snake-tattooed finger resting loosely on the trigger. There was sales-talk about skilled marksmen appreciating this or that feature. Chill laid down the cash for it.

The Mistake stared at the pile of Federal bills, dragged me out, and muttered something about where a woods nigger got that kind of money. That seemed to take care of the hunting idea. I didn't need to worry about finding a new place to hide my phone. The butcher shed would remain my domain.

The Mistake was in the liquor store and I was waiting in the truck when Chill came out with his purchase, safely latched into a new hard leather case with brass corners. I started to make a half-hearted wave, but Chill looked right through me.

...

There was equipment working at the far end of the drive. Construction materials were being delivered to the Dark compound. I thought I saw Uncle Gabriel by the creek, but whatever it was disappeared when I waved.

...

I told the Mistake I wanted to go to the new Martel office and put in an application. He sneered, and I left it alone. Not long after, while I was waiting in the truck while he picked up his pay, my old supervisor noticed and came over to the window. As the Mistake was coming out, the guy was telling me how he'd gotten patched up back in Québec after taking a Laithbourn bullet. He'd always been decent to me, and I was wishing him the best. He asked if I wanted my old job back, and I said, "Hell, yeah!" The Mistake shot me a look as I was shaking the guy's hand. I knew I was going to have to fight over it, but I didn't care.

I texted Tom to ask what it would take to get the Mistake out of my house. He said the new domestic violence laws didn't favor me. He had to maintain a working relationship with the Martels; they handled most security in the north end of the county while the re-formed Sheriff's Department handled the more populous south. Since the Mistake and Champetty were working together and sometimes drinking together, that made things even more complicated. I asked Tom if he'd seen any of the Darks, and he said he tried not to, but they were rebuilding with a vengeance.

...

Champetty and Chill ran afoul of each other at the gun shop at the start of hunting season. Champetty had offered the opinion that Chill might be a sharpshooter but he wasn't any hunter. Chill proposed they take their cleaned season total and match it up by weight, with each man having an observer from the other camp to confirm the kill.

Chill named Uncle Gabriel to follow Champetty, and Champetty decided the Mistake would shadow Chill. The Mistake never admitted publicly that he couldn't handle deer guts, and he had no idea how much of them he was likely to see. I wondered if Sam knew about the Mistake's queasiness; it would have been his kind of game.

After the first day of it, the Mistake poured himself a beer. "Creepy halfbreed. Slides up a stand like a monkey. Knows where the deer want to move before they do. Changed his shirt after he dragged a carcass out—faggot has black wings tattooed on his back. Sam says he was a friend of yours. Has the same kind of scars you do. Perverted little freak like that would be a friend of yours... I don't suppose you're going to tell me why you acted like you didn't know him. I'd like to think it's because you've finally learned something, but I'm not gonna bank on that."

I shrugged and kept my mouth shut. I enjoyed the Mistake getting rattled, but the wings sounded tacky.

Champetty made a good showing. He lost weight, and didn't drink while he was hunting. He bought more rifle than he could afford and wore his thin cotton gloves like some high-level assassin. Gabriel said it was a new pair every few hours because they'd get damp and useless. No hunter I'd ever known used gloves like that; most would use fingerless types if they weren't comfortable with the clumsy feel of full-hand gloves, but Sam claimed they kept his fingers warm without losing trigger-feel. He hung and cleaned his own take, even though that wasn't part of the bargain. He acted like the wager was already won.

When the season was done, Sam and his crew loaded the frozen carcasses into a couple of pickups and headed for the field between Littlefield and the Dark settlement, where a Martel arbitrator had brought in a truck scale. The Mistake wasn't full of team spirit; he had a better idea than the rest of the mob of what was coming.

The Darks had lit a bonfire. In front of it was a stack of frozen-stiff carcasses about four deer high and seven or eight long. Chill climbed on the pile, half-naked and waving his shirt around, immune to the bitter cold. He was skinny as ever. His arms were sleeve-tattooed with Japanese flowers. I saw the wings, and they were gorgeous ink—restrained and elegant, fresh enough to still be peeling. It was clear there didn't need to be any weigh-in. Chill started doing fake Indian war-whoops, slapping his hand over his steaming mouth, bending deep, picking his knees up high, stamping his feet fast and light. The Mistake bellowed at him to shut the fuck up.

Chill sashayed over and pointed his snake-wrapped trigger finger up close at the Mistake like he was daring him to bite.

I said, "That's not necessary," and he pointed at me.

I grabbed his hand and drove my autistic stare back into those colorless eyes. "Pretend you don't know me, Chill—that's fine—but don't work at making it worse for me than it already is."

He blinked and grinned. His scrawny chest was flecked with fine white scars and a few fresh pink ones. His face had aged hard and smart, like a seasoned predator.

He pulled his hand free. "You know, you do remind me of someone I used to know, now that you mention. Fascinating..." He cocked his head. "Name's Gabe Dark, look me up sometime."

He walked away, displaying his new wings, switching his skinny ass like an aggravated cat.

CHAPTER TWENTY

Last month our neighbors in the Northern and Central Heartlands took the final step toward reviving "science-based" eugenics under the euphemism: "Domestic Homefront Genetic Heritage Health Planning," as if their usurious "healthcare system" had ever been more than profiteering. They now seek openly to destroy any Heartland subject who cannot be made a sufficiently productive cog in their greenback-mills—the witch-hunt backed up by relentlessly efficient thought-control machinery that has turned parents against their own children found unsatisfactory by corporate standards.

We in the AFICT owe refuge to those trapped in a governmental system that plagiarizes its propaganda from pre-WWII American eugenics broadsides while ensuring that no person within its jurisdiction is sufficiently well-educated or has adequate access to uncensored information to make the connection to the roots of Nazi genocide. When we brand our fellow human beings, whatever their disability, as "nothing more than burdens on productive society," we are no better than the repressive troglodytes we look down on.

I am aware that this makes my position an unpopular one, but if I am to be relieved of my standing by the voters who once entrusted me to represent them, I shall at least have been brought down with a clean conscience. I will say this until my last breath: We cannot call ourselves a just, civilized society while we turn away those seeking to escape the grip of this lethal madness.

Speech before the 2044 Joint Session of Governments,
Aligned Federation of Independent Canadian Territories.
Rt. Hon. Dame Boadicea Sinclair, (Former) Speaker of
Parliament, Free Territory of New Albion

SAM CHAMPETTY sat at the kitchen table Tom Webster and his wife had given me as a housewarming gift and bellowed for the Mistake to get him another beer. The Mistake bellowed at me to bring them both more beers.

I said, "Va te faire foutre."

The Martel brothers, Merlin and Guillaume, looked at each other and smirked.

Guillaume, or Bill as he was called around the job, leaned back in his chair, stroked his beard and looked at the Mistake. "Where did your girl pick up that language? I wonder—you must not like her back on a crew of big, hairy farogs. You do realize she just told you to go fuck yourself?"

Bill was the large, unpleasant man who'd tried to hire me to whore for Sam and Angela as a wedding present. The intervening years hadn't made him pleasanter. Merlin, the chuckling, heavily mustached older brother, was the one who generally spoke to the news media. Merlin could always come up with something to say. He was a couple of inches shorter than Bill, but solid as a RhinePact tank. I was being triangulated for bullying by the others; he was the only one there who seemed to like me.

Bill nudged Sam with his foot. "Hey, Sammy, I hear this girl— she's a card-carrying professional, right? Now what kind of professional girl won't give her man a proper blow job?"

Sam offered that there were enough of them there to make sure the Mistake got his blow without getting his dick bitten off. I needed to derail the idea fast. There was enough alcohol, testosterone and power play in the room that it felt like it could get real.

I tried to hook Merlin with a gaming smile; "So... how many bodies in the furnace? The big man who's too lazy to get his own drink can't get himself to think about it. I changed a lot of adult diapers just to have those clients end up as an alternative fuel source."

Merlin twinkled at me from under thick gray eyebrows.

His tone was measured, but stayed light. "Fierce little Pixie... Sometime I'll show you the video we found when we cracked the CareWell building open." He patted his phone in his pocket, gave Bill a cryptic look, went to the refrigerator, pulled out a couple of beers and set them in front of Sam and the Mistake. "Don't be talking to the Pixie that way. I have plans for the Pixie—someday she may be giving you orders."

Sam popped his beer open without saying anything. He seemed to take Merlin's admonition as social jousting more than a real warning, but he wasn't in the mood to get into another high-stakes pissing contest while recovering from being outhunted by Chill. He took a swig from the bottle and gestured a thanks toward Merlin, who stayed standing at the kitchen counter.

Merlin nodded back and then turned to look down at the Mistake. "Good boy to keep your mouth shut about exactly what you saw. Not such a good boy to have brought it up in the first place, even to Pixie. Pixie has a dual identity, so I understand. I'm unclear on the story, but I'm finding I trust the Pixie. I appreciate the fact that her condition makes it excruciating for her to lie... But if someone were to ask her an inconvenient question about CareWell while we are still probationary in our Regional contract, her inability to prevaricate could make things awkward."

The Mistake was several beers ahead of the others. He'd started as soon as we'd come home from the deer-kill debacle after Chill wagged his finger in his face, a good half hour before Champetty and the Martel brothers had shown up after returning the unused truck scale to the company lot. The evening social was supposed to have been just for him, Sam and Bill. He didn't seem happy that Merlin had invited himself along.

The Mistake glared and muttered something about me making some kind of disgusting sick retard pass at that perverted half-Martel runt. "Little bitch-freak sure as hell lied about not knowing him. Autistics can't lie, huh? Bullshit."

Merlin's expression was perfectly illegible, his mouth concealed except for a thin line of lower lip visible under his mustache. "Careful... The company employing you is run—very efficiently—by my cousin Severin, who is at least as autistic as our Pixie. Severin has no need to lie. When lying needs to be done, he has one of us take care of it. I'd accept that the Pixie might not have shared the entire truth with you, but I'd wager she didn't lie. Think on it."

The boiling rage on the Mistake's face was plain enough.

I edged closer to Merlin as he stood next to the stove and said, "Thank you. No, I didn't lie."

The Mistake whirled at me, but I'd picked up the cast iron skillet I'd burned the LWAG's suicide note in and shielded my face with it. The sound of his fist hitting the metal had a meaty crack. He snarled and lunged past Merlin to the sink to run cold water on his shaking hand, retching as it puffed and blackened.

Merlin said, "You're both fired."

He said something to Bill in French to the effect that the last thing they needed was pathetic domestic crap on the job site with Regional inspectors around.

Bill stood by the door and said he expected no one needed to be told to keep their mouths shut, because it should be obvious that silence was the price of continuing to breathe.

He raised Sam's arm like the victor in a prize fight. "Our Sammy may not have bagged the most venison, but trust me, you do not want him putting on his white gloves for you."

None of them looked at me as they left. The Mistake blubbered at his hand with the faucet streaming over it full blast.

I watched the Martel truck pull away, taking my attention off the Mistake for the instant it took him to slam my temple with his good fist. My teeth snapped together, scissoring into my tongue. My mouth filled with blood. I fought to stay conscious. I gripped the skillet hard and swung it edge-on like a cleaver at his bad hand as he leaned on the table, but he was too quick. He charged, trapping me in the corner. I swore in a swollen, mangled voice for him to get the fuck out of my house or else just commit suicide like he'd been promising he would for so, so very fucking long. He stared at me while that sank in, and then he tried to kill me.

He pinned me with both wet hands around my throat. They were slippery, and it saved my life, but there was enough strength in the hurt one that something in my neck crunched as he tried to crush my larynx. I struggled to pull in a breath; black disks swam in my vision. There was a look in his eyes I hadn't seen before. I stabbed my fingers, pinched together like a bird beak, at those staring eyes. He pulled his face back, and I had the space to knee him in the groin. His grip loosened for a second as he bent over. I got my other arm free enough to swing, bringing the edge of the skillet against the back of his skull with a clear ringing sound. He dropped to his knees and then collapsed partway onto his side, flailing and pushing himself up on his elbow. I cudgeled him behind the ear with a full two-handed swing, and the sound was ugly. He slumped and stayed down.

I made sure he was still breathing, turned off the sink faucet, grabbed my hunting rifle, stopped at the butcher shed for my phone, and started walking.

...

The sun had set. The ground was covered in wet, heavy snow, and the air was bitter with the fading light. I started the long trudge to the Darks' settlement, sliding in the thawing mud at the edge of the track, wondering if I'd have a voice when my throat healed. I had to will my rubbery legs forward. I jolted as a big engine came at me from around a curve. If I hadn't resisted the temptation to walk in the more passable middle, Chill, driving fast and without lights in the last shreds of twilight, might have run me over instead of stopping.

He rolled down his window and leaned across the seat. "Heya. Didn't think you'd take me up that quick... or are ya just out night-poaching?"

Then he saw my mess of a face, got out, and helped me up into his truck. He slipped the rifle off my shoulder and set it carefully under his on the rack behind the seat.

He pulled out a pint flask from the warmth of his jacket, unscrewed the top, and offered it. "Firewater? O small one with a long story?"

I took a couple of sips. It was hellfire on the hamburger that was the inside of my mouth, but it filled me with life. He turned the truck around, flicked on the headlights, and we churned and slid toward the warm bath he promised me. He drove the way I'd seen him shoot, a long time ago: calm, intent, and relaxed. I didn't want to talk, and he didn't want me to. When we got there, he had me lean on his shoulders to get down from the running-board. He maneuvered himself to carry me inside, but I pulled away. I stumbled down hard, stood on wobbly legs, and stared up the hill to the soft lights in his window. He offered me his arm like a gent, and we marched sloppily to his house.

I don't know what I expected, but Chill's newly-rebuilt house looked like a good motel room. The wood paneling was waxed, there was a big easy chair, the dinette was clean, and his marksmanship trophies on the mantel above a built-in firebox had no dust on them. Coals glowed a deep, comforting ruby through the stove glass, and a neat bundle of split birchwood nestled in a black ironwork cradle. He had a full bookcase. A beautifully mounted buck head with a majestic rack of antlers hung on the wall; it was the only thing that carried an obvious sign of his personality—he'd put a crown of dark red silk roses on it and tied an old-style long silver-gray jacquard man's tie around its neck. It was a real, wild buck—not an overbred trophy freak from a hunt-farm.

The living room smelled of warmed cedar shavings in a bowl by the sleek woodstove, along with lemon furniture polish, dish soap, and some nice cooking smell lingering.

I looked at the door handle I'd just held; there was a bloody smear on the polished brass knob. My knuckles were raw, so I guessed I'd connected with the Mistake's face at some point, but that didn't account for the blood I was putting on anything I touched.

I realized I'd probably wiped my mouth with my hand.

My voice came out in a bruised croak. "Shit! Sorry, it's... I'm a mess."

Chill looked down at the boot-prints on his probably-ruined rug. "Don't worry about it—this is the most exciting thing that's happened to me in a long time, Smallstuff."

I wasn't sure if he was tweaking me.

He gave me a sly look. "Well, OK, let's get you cleaned up then."

He helped me to his bathroom, which was as spotless as everything else, and set out towels and soap. I flinched when I saw myself in his mirror.

His voice turned kind. "I won't intrude, but I'm here."

He backed out and closed the door. I started filling the tub, but I couldn't get out of my thermal undershirt. My shoulder didn't want to bend the way I needed it to. Chill must have heard me yipe; he was there before I called. He took a pair of scissors from the vanity drawer and neatly snipped the problem away over my mumbled protest. He shut the water off and sized me up. He was a small man, but still bigger than me by a couple of inches and fifteen or twenty stringy pounds that had turned more to steel over the years. We sparred with our eyes, and he took me under the arms and lifted me into the tub. The hot soapy water burned in my scrapes.

I flinched as he lowered me into the suds. "You better fucking not drop me."

He laughed softly. The warm water gradually eased my stiff places, and I slid down to soak my bad shoulder under the foam. He handed me a washcloth with a Greek leaf pattern cut into it, but I balked at using it.

He mock-scowled. "I don't keep burlap sacks for when I have guests over."

I managed to crack a smile, and then he asked if I wanted him to leave. I shook my head.

He started washing the blood off my knuckles. "Bet whoever you were fighting with is in worse shape than you right now."

"Hope so."

I sat up a little and he went to wash my back. I pushed his hand away. I never liked anyone touching me there, and he knew it. I muttered that he must have forgotten a lot about me since he'd seen me last. He said to remind him and went to do it again. I grabbed his thin, soapy wrist—tight. My grip was full of all the adrenaline in my system; I felt it close like a piano wire snare. He gasped, then a barely audible purr came from his throat. He kept his eyes on me while he arched his neck, assessing me with his head back and tilted, a slight grin flickering. There was some of the old Chill I knew, but someone new was in there too, and not someone I necessarily felt safe with.

I dropped my other hand under the water out of sight.

I set my grip again, clenched my aching teeth, and pulled him forward. "I am never going to be touched against my will—ever, by anyone—again."

He rested the long tattooed trigger finger of his free hand against mine clamped on him and began stroking it along my tensed forearm. "So what is your will, all-grown-up ferocious warrior-lady?"

I snatched his free wrist, my hand flicking out of the water fast as a snake. If I'd been trying to do it, I couldn't. It just happened. I held his wrists imprisoned together between us.

My voice came out hoarse and about half an octave lower than I expected. "This—like this."

We stared at each other; his eyes were sleepy-looking, but they danced.

He cocked his head to one side like a playful dog. "Well, don't stop there."

I didn't.

...

Chill got up off the bathroom floor, clearing his throat. I'd held him down by his neck, straddled him, and told him to unzip. For a few minutes, I'd listened to something inside me so crazy I'd forgotten how battered I was. Then it was over and I was left back in myself, feeling sore and awkward.

He looked at me sideways and grinned. "Haven't been fishing in a good long time. Not quite the way I remembered."

"You asked for it."

"Yep, I sure did." He kissed the top of my head, "Not complaining... maybe you should've been? Wasn't the most gracious thing of me to do right now, provoking you. Bad habit of mine, even if you are irresistible when you're fired up."

My adrenaline was wearing off fast, and my hurt body had stiffened. He offered me a Black Watch tartan flannel robe that smelled faintly of sandalwood, some ibuprofen and a glass of water, and guided me back to his bedroom. It was cozier than any bedroom I'd slept in since I'd lived with my parents. I said his house must be really well insulated.

He made a wooden Indian face with his arms crossed out in front of him and nodded stiffly. "Yup, heap good built teepee... Us tribe buildum so we no getum frozen backsides." He grinned at the smile he'd pulled from me. "C'mon, let me help get you under the covers. I'll be in on the couch if you need anything."

I told him I didn't want him being the one sleeping on the couch. He said his bed was too small for both of us, particularly since one of us was one large bruise.

He leaned in the doorway and folded his arms. "You cause me trouble, Smallstuff. You got me all turned around."

He went into the next room. I heard him open some kind of cabinet. He closed the door to the room and locked it. He set something by the front door and then something outside the bedroom door.

He came in holding a rifle and a box of ammunition.

He sat on the bed, loaded the rifle and set it against the headboard. "Don't know what's following after you, kid. Do know the probabilities. My fault for setting it off... Sorry about that, babe. You warned me. I fucked up—I fucked up a lot over you, and I keep doing it. I'm a douchebag. It sank in finally why you were pushing me away. I was out on the road headed to sneak up to your house to make sure you were OK."

I sat up as best I could and told him I was leaving. I hadn't thought about what I'd be bringing with me. I'd hit the Mistake hard, but not hard enough to kill him. When he came to, he could be anything from a whiny six-year-old to a cold assassin.

Chill shook his head. "Don't think about it."

He changed into pajama bottoms that matched the robe, turned out the light, and slid himself carefully under the covers next to me.

I said, "Thank you."

I dropped into a pit of exhausted sleep, broken by my body howling whenever I tried to roll over. Chill gave me as much of the bed as he could without falling out. Every time I woke up, he was looking at me.

In the morning I shuffled out and stared at the buck trophy as Chill made coffee. The gorgeous rack of antlers had been polished recently; a faint chemical smell said the taxidermy had been done that season.

Chill came over and rested his hand carefully along my shoulder. "Yep, I poached him a week early—he didn't even count against my total. Seemed like a good omen to come home to."

CHAPTER TWENTY-ONE

Well, dear listeners, I have some genuine gonzo journalism to report—news in which the reasonable man himself took part, if only as the sole outside observer. No one knows what this reasonable man might look like. All the better to see you with, my Darling, when you try to pull something off. I could be anyone...

So, I was told by my sources to watch the back entrance to the main building of the mighty University Hospital. As I waited in my anonymity, several empty buses with New Albion plates passed, and the security gates rolled open. As the drivers debarked, whom should I see as the leader of the fleet but Sir Lady Saint Bodacious herself. Now as you know, my feelings about this particular female are complicated. However I may view her politics—and the ridiculous picture of a skirt-wearing Canadian now-ex-parliamentarian with a dregs-of-the-British-Empire knighthood—I would not mind at all dubbing her a bit with my own knighthood if given the opportunity.

Be that as it may, what should I see pouring from the building but the sorriest parade of subhuman residue I have ever observed collected in one place: toe-walkers and hand-flappers, blinking idiots in the bright afternoon, moaning and gargling as they shuffled to the buses. Then the second wave—the floats—powered wheelchairs, paid for by whose hard-earned money I do not know, in incompetent formation, cretinous head-lollers drooling and steering around with their spastic hands taped to their little joysticks. Finally, the queen of imbeciles—and only a female would have the stomach for it—Saint Boadicea herself, pushing... pushing... a thing... a female thing, with folds of flesh as if it once were obese, but now a pile of flaccid, deflated flab... legless. Yes, listeners, at least there was the decency of a lap-blanket to hide the worst of that, but the outline of stumps was clear... but even that was not the very worst of the whole disgusting tableau. That Thing, that Thing... was... holding... propped by pillows because its arms were too full of congenital disease to even form a proper motherly cradle... an infant, puling and twisting away from the goodly light of the Lord's own sun. That most obviously un-sterilized Thing carried in its vile arms its own foul offspring to pollute our clean and decent world...

O'Brien on the Brink, WWBF AM 58, 1/9/44

THERE WAS A KNOCK at Chill's door. He shut the laptop and tucked it into a lower drawer of the kitchen silverware cabinet. I'd been watching live feed from a New Albion news station on it for hours. The Dark compound paid for access to an AFICT satellite; we were close enough to the border to get a clean signal. Chill's mother was still a Free Québec citizen and she got the rolling access code legally, "at her own risk." Of course it was illegal to use it in the Heartlands, but that never stopped the Darks.

Chill had to pull my hands away to close the lid. I'd been trying to catch another report from a story I'd been following, something about a group of autistics at the University Hospital being taken to safety across the border by some very rich woman politician.

He blew me a kiss as he went to open the door. "We try to not make it too hard for Tom, OK? He has to pretend not to see enough around here as it is."

When I saw Tom in the doorway, I clamped a hug on him that left him winded. Tom's expression when he stepped back to look at my face crushed me until I remembered I had heavy purpling bruises around my neck, my temple was swollen and discolored, and my eyes were still red with broken blood vessels.

Tom rested his hands lightly on my shoulders. "My god, Dax, you're lucky to be alive. I've seen..." He cleared his throat but the words still didn't come out all the way. "...seen those kind of marks... when... didn't survive..."

Tom looked at Chill and me standing there together, reading what he saw. He sighed heavily and sat down at the dinette.

Chill pulled the other dinette chair out for me and stayed standing behind me. "So what's the story, boss?"

Tom looked at me. "Have you paid the taxes on the house for the quarter, Dax?"

I said I didn't know, that the Mistake took care of it and he never told me about it. Tom took out his Sheriff's Department phone, fiddled with it, and said they weren't paid yet.

He did his old thing of tapping his finger on the bridge of his nose that meant for his offbeat kids to look at his face and pay attention. "Dax, Gabe here may not look like it, but he's a damned good accountant. Have him help you get this paid from your personal account before this asshole pays them in his own name. If you made a joint account with the jerk, have Gabe help you clear it out and start your own. It looks like he's been holding out on the power bill like everyone else around here to protest the poor service. Have Gabe pay that in your name."

Chill nodded and scribbled something on a notepad.

Tom gestured at his face to get me to look at him while he was talking. "Gabe said you had issues with the Martels over what happened last night—his mother's going to clear that up. Make sure to thank Luce, preferably not with booze or cigarettes, but do whatever it takes to stay on her good side. You need to have a job on record even if you don't go to it. Last thing you need right now is Workfare problems.

"After I leave here I'm going to put on my body armor and go post a notice to vacate on the front door. Now, in six weeks we can go in there and clear him out for squatting. Got that?"

I closed my eyes and tried to process all the words. Chill wrapped his arms around my shoulders and leaned over me. It felt safe, and I leaned back into the embrace.

Tom asked if what he was seeing meant I wanted to stay there with Chill rather than coming back with him to the farm. I nodded.

Tom frowned. "OK, I suppose this has a kind of backhanded inevitability to it. I hope you get it out of your system, Dax. Pete's working in the city now—she left the Union with me before they closed the border. She still asks about you, and I hope to hell I told her right that you weren't romantically involved with anyone anymore."

I said I didn't know how the hell I felt about much of anything right then. I looked at the side of Chill's face; his jaw was flushed almost the way it used to when he was young.

Tom set his chin forward. "Gabe, I covered your back while you and your uncle committed an act of justifiable double homicide for your sister and this woman—and yes, I acknowledge that she is a woman now—but you turned her over to me when she was still a girl, and you asked me to protect her and raise her as my own. I did that, and then I left her in what I thought were good hands when I did what I thought was right for the rest of my family. That family is dissolved now because I couldn't stop thinking about what I left behind. I'm not going to abandon my duties any more. So, what do you have to say for yourself?"

Chill's eyes were moist against my messed-up neck. "I'm here for her from now on... however she decides she feels."

Tom stood up to leave. "Damned well better be."

...

Merlin Martel stumble-walked down the steep hill from Chill's parent's house, his footsteps spraying fresh gravel. Luce called out something after him in profane joual about not being a stranger. He responded in the same key without turning around as he walked the more level ground toward his truck in the central lot. As he dusted his pant-legs, he saw me at Chill's window and waved me out. Chill had been watching from behind me; he stepped and opened the door.

Merlin took up most of the doorway with his substantial body and peeked around Chill. "Ah, the Man of the House, very good. I wished to extend an apology to the Pixie for lumping her in with her... whatever he was. One can find oneself in an impossible situation. One tries to help and is made to pay for it when the victim returns for more abuse. I'm glad to see she's made the sensible choice. Do let her know that I hadn't realized she was Sheriff Webster's daughter, and that I'll be assisting him in removing her unwanted tenant as soon as the legal niceties are complete."

Chill nodded. Merlin put his hands in his pockets and began speaking in a more businesslike French than he'd used with Luce, too fast for me to follow. Chill nodded again and asked Merlin in.

The laptop came out, and Chill pulled up what looked like financial transaction screens. I motioned that I was going to go sit on the patio out back. Chill gave a thumbs-up.

I took Chill's sweater off the hook by the kitchen door and stood outside on the neat square of bricks. I looked up the hill to see Luce leaning on her deck rail watching me. She gave a shrug that might have meant to come up. I gestured that I didn't understand. She responded with a wide wheelhouse wave to get myself up the hill.

...

Luce had set out a couple of shot glasses on the round metal table and put the bottle between us. "Don't want the relatives thinking we're acting like Indians, sitting in the cold, drinking straight from the bottle outside under the morning sky." She looked at me sideways.

I pulled Chill's sweater around myself. The breeze was sharp, and the deck cut into it like the prow of a boat. The warmth of the whiskey was pleasant in the clear, cool sun, even though it stung my bitten tongue. I felt my eyes close like a contented cat.

Luce's voice had a kinder tone to it than I'd heard before. "Those are some marks you got there around your neck, girl... what was it Gabriel decided to call you?"

"Dakini."

Luce chuckled. "Yep. Dykie. Thought so. You probably don't have too high of an opinion of anything with a dick right now, Dykie, and I wouldn't blame you."

I shrugged. Luce noted that the view was nicer than it had been the last time we chatted on that hill, and I nodded. The compound spread out in an organic pattern of neat houses and utility buildings gathered around the central lot and extending along a gravel road that skirted the base of the hill. It looked even tidier than it had before.

Luce lit a cigarette and took a deep drag. "Be good to my kid, OK? Don't let him know I said that, because we generally stay out of each other's business."

I turned to look at her.

She offered the pack, and when I said I didn't smoke, she nodded. "For the best. Anyway, Merlin's sending him back to the city for a few weeks. Stay here 'til he gets back. It'll be safer, and if you decide you're going to go, at least give him a chance to talk it out with you. He's got unfinished business about you he needs to settle in himself.

"He still kicks himself for not coming back from Mexico for you before you hooked up with the piece of shit that did that to your neck. If he had, his brain might not be fried as it is. He never took a bullet while he was gone, but he came home with phantoms twittering around in his skull he doesn't talk to anyone about.

"Have to say, too: don't let Angie mess with your head or his, however you work it out. I think she's drawing a bead on him since he's dared to maybe be happy."

...

I came awake sharp to headlights coming in Chill's window and drunk white men bellowing. I pulled on a sweatshirt and reached for the rifle Chill had told me to use; it was a hell of a lot better made than mine. I slapped the loaded clip into it, threw Chill's black shadow-camo night-poaching coat and a balaclava on, and went out to face whatever it was.

One of the Dark cousins was walking around the end of the hill, and about five more scattered up into the woods below Luce's house, disappearing into the shadows. The lead cousin saw me come out of the house, started to wave me back in, and then changed his mind. He put his finger to his lip, gesturing me to walk up alongside the drive on the far side and stay low. Sam Champetty's truck was stopped partway up the hill, the headlights and a roof-mounted poacher spotlight glaring at Luce's front door. He and Bill Martel were kicking at it. Sam was yowling something about knowing Angela was in there.

Michel Dark stood on the unlit deck watching them from around the end of his house. I could make out, low and loose in his hands, the ancient AK Luce kept by the bedroom door.

He cleared his throat loudly and raised the automatic when there was a break in the noise. "Gentlemen—gentlemen... My daughter is a very long way from here. She's living with her uncle, and where that is exactly I wouldn't tell, even if I knew."

Bill Martel stepped back from the door to get a look at the deck.

He flinched when the sound of a bullet being cocked manually into a rifle chamber echoed from the darkness, but covered the fumble. "Allo, Mikey... what a surprise to find you here. Anyplace but your wife's house. You too old now to have those baby blues work on anyone else?"

Mike shrugged but kept the AK at a businesslike level. "Nah, they don't work on anyone anymore. Best take boyfriend home an' tuck him in. If he keeps that tantrum going he'll wake Luce— and she's likely to call your brother if she gets disturbed from her beauty sleep."

Sam had stopped kicking the door; he moved along the house away from the spotlight. I pulled the balaclava up over my face, stepped behind a tree, and got him in my scope. I realized I'd been sent to cover that side of the drive because I was the only gun with a clean shot at the area beyond the door. Sam looked up at Mike bantering with Bill, and reached inside his coat.

I tapped the barrel of Chill's rifle against the tree and dropped my voice as low and hoarse as I could get it. "Je ne ferais pas ça à votre place..."

Bill whirled around. Sam stayed frozen in confusion for long enough for a grinning Mike to adjust his position so he could spray along the side of his house with the assault weapon. Sam lifted his hand back out of his coat, keeping it in sight as he backed toward the truck.

Mike motioned for the two of them to keep everything where he could see and to get back in the truck. "Like my cousin says, don't do anything stupid. Go on home to bed now."

As their truck wallowed and fishtailed back down the loose gravel, Mike cupped his hands and made a soft owl-hoot. Rifle barrels emerged from the woods across the drive in an irregular honor guard that tracked the departing truck until it was out of the compound.

...

Chill fumbled with something in the pitch darkness. He'd said he'd been shopping while he was away. He laughed softly at himself and rubbed his face against my stomach. I felt something familiar cinch around my waist and the tops of my legs. I knew he'd talked to the Sterling Island barracuda boys, but I hadn't thought about how much of my secrecy he might have breached.

He let out a chuckling sigh. "Little help, Babe? Pretty clear I don't know what I'm doing. Sorry."

I stroked his hair. "Goes like this..."

I guided his hands on the harness adjustments, then he guided mine over what he'd put into it, as though he was making it a part of me. Once it was in place, my body felt sentient with it the way he handled me, slicking the now firmly-in-place toy with lubricant as if I could feel the way his hands caressed it. If I listened with something in me he was reaching, I did feel it.

He pulled me close and rolled onto his stomach. "C'mon in. Gotta warn you, sometimes if it's too good, I... well... I've got kind of a hair-trigger, if you get my meaning."

I started the toy a little way into him. He cooed and adjusted himself.

I put his hands on my hips to guide me the way he wanted. "You say that like it's a bad thing."

CHAPTER TWENTY-TWO

Ladies and Gentlemen, I speak before you today only because of a series of unlikely events. It was far more likely I would have died prior to the moment Dame Boadicea Sinclair, the woman next to me holding my speech-synthesizing equipment, bought me and thirty-four of my fellow experimentals like cut-rate chattel on the open market. The transaction was negotiated after the University of the Northern Heartland Medical Center determined we surviving autism-utilization test subjects of the original forty had been too contaminated by shoddy protocol maintenance and control management to warrant the burden of our continued existence. I have learned that the most expensive element of the bargain driven by Dame Boadicea was for the motorized wheelchairs used by some of us with significant physical affect—she could have purchased the lot of us strapped to gurneys for less than half the final price.

I am told by those confined in the same secret ward of a Laithbourn facility the lone person who fought for my life while I was in a neglect-induced diabetic coma was a female minimum-wage caregiver, a "Miss Webster," also autistic, who went up against the supervising physician and a phalanx of orderlies and held them off from "euthanizing" me until Miss Evangelina Ellway, the University Hospital representative in immediate charge of the experiment, returned and put a stop to it pending authorization from the UNHMC study leader, which was not given. The caregiver was taken away, and I've been unable to find out what became of her.

Now I understand that the sole reason this incident is being investigated by the Northern Heartland government is that the death of Miss Ellway at some point during Laithbourn's evacuation of the facility has been found suspicious—not that some fifty other disabled residents of that facility who were not a part of the University experiment have simply vanished.

Classified testimony of Miss Amelia P. before closed-door
session of NATO/OTAN Commission on Human Rights,
Disability Subcommittee, January 15, 2044

LUCE SAT WITH ME in the late-morning sun on Chill's patio. She kept looking around the end of the house toward the entrance to the compound. The steady pounding of a seismic frac-testing truck searching for deep gas deposits by hammering the ground like a vertical battering ram bounced off the hillside as sound and came up through the brick pavers as jolts through our bodies. Gabriel folded his arms as he leaned against the back wall of the house; his hair was tied back like Chill's now, and silvery white. He'd brought Angela home for a visit with her son, with Michel Dark hosting as Proud Gran'pa. Sam Champetty's truck was parked at the foot of the steep driveway. Luce avoided looking at it.

She gritted her large, straight teeth and nodded toward the source of the banging noise. "I swear I will kill someone if that keeps up. Must be what your world feels like every day, Dykie—no wonder autistics get violent. Teach me some of whatever it is you use to keep yourself non-homicidal sometime. If Chill was here he'd accidentally put a bullet in the hydraulics—never mind it's a Martel project. This property won't pass quake specs, so it's no money in my pocket. My foundation's cracked—won't take much before the retaining wall goes. Didn't think there was anywhere drillable along here. Can't legally keep them off, but if they had to worry about replacing a cylinder they might show more respect."

Michel Dark appeared on the deck above us, partly screened by spring growth in the trees, and whistled sharply. "Hey! Gabe! Brother-mine, come up and see your damned grand-nephew!"

Gabriel sighed and peeled himself off the wall. I thanked him for the first decent haircut I'd had in too many years, and he smiled. Luce told him she'd be up soon because the infernal pounding was worse than being around the vicious little gargoyle. I invited her inside.

She shook her head. "Nah, thanks. That vile kid's going to burn my house down if no one's watching him, and chances are no one is. No grandson of mine—not planning on embracing Sammy and his spawn into my family. Angie's bad enough. Gabe would stay here if he didn't have to keep her away from her nominal husband and her kid. Poor Gabe, he's a better mommy than any of us. Anyway—if Chill catches me in his house he's not likely to forgive it for a while." She put her hand up at my objection. "If he hears about it, he's going to be sure I worked on you."

She sighed and put the cap on her bottle. I walked her to the base of her driveway.

There was a sudden grinding crash from the testing truck, followed by a brief shearing whistle, and then silence. Luce grinned and headed up the hill. A white Martel pickup pulled into the lot with someone in the passenger's seat talking on the two-way radio. Merlin rolled the driver's window down as the Dark cousins gathered around. The senior one climbed down from the roof of the tiny wind/solar off-grid power plant and cursed fluently about the damage the ground shocks had done to the turbine generator. Merlin said something soothing to him, accompanied by a packet of cash. The seismic truck limped into the lot, bleeding a viscous fluid, and the cousins swarmed over it with their tools like hyenas around a dying water buffalo.

Luce looked down her precipitous driveway; she stood a few seconds and went in her house.

I started back to Chill's house, but Merlin called to me. "I must see the new coiffure. It suits you perfectly, Pixie—may I get a closer look?"

He strode over with his hands in his pockets. "Pixie, before you go in..." His voice dropped below the volume of the mechanics' discussion. "...I want to tell you... that, ahh, Tom Webster had me handle... it became difficult to execute the eviction by officially prescribed procedures. I must return to the mother country. The family wants my brother Bill to take over here, and he's... not the right party for the job, so things had to be... expedited. Mikey Dark had mentioned privately that his impression was you were open to a permanent solution. Well, let us just say that your unwelcome tenant won't be reappearing."

I felt something dropping inside my chest and stomach like a chunk of iron. Merlin's tree trunk of an arm blocked me from tilting over.

He guided me to sit on the edge of the rail-tie planter next to the door. "Pixie? Pretend I never said... Let me rephrase—I completed the sheriff—your father's wishes, and I shielded him from any need for impropriety on his part, as a professional courtesy that entails no obligations. Got that, dear?"

I nodded. Something made me take his massive hand with both of mine, and I realized my eyes were getting wet.

Merlin looked down, his expression no easier to read than it ever had been. "Yes, dear, you are free. Now, with encouragement from your father, I have brought in an old friend of yours to work on our current project. She found something this morning I think she'd like to show you."

...

When Chill drove up, I was being covered in puppy-breath scented kisses. Petra had been watching me feed the emaciated, squirming waif chicken-and-gravy baby food off my fingers, but the little guy couldn't stop licking just because the food was already sucked off my hand. He couldn't take his blue-clouded eyes off Petra; if she got out of his sight he'd start his tiny howl and flail his huge paddle-like feet. She'd been checking property lines before they started the seismic survey when she found the puppy huddled in a clump of dry grass for warmth. She'd named him Timothy for the nest of hay that had kept him warm enough to survive. The rest of the litter nearby hadn't been that lucky. He was black with touches of tan on his paws, eyebrows, and muzzle that suggested he was mostly Rottweiler. From his massively bony skull and the size of those paws, he'd probably top a hundred pounds before he grew into himself.

Petra was smiling at me. The dental work she'd had done was nearly invisible, even though I knew where to look for it. She'd just moved in with Tom, taking Liam's old room and mine next to it as an apartment.

Chill slammed his truck door and stalked to his front door. "Hey, Pete—wasn't expecting you. That's an original gambit: puppy. Don't bring it in my house, if you don't mind."

Merlin got up from his seat on the planter. "Easy, Gabriel. We found it this morning. Miss Sexton rescued him, and she'll be taking him home. You don't happen to have a suitable box?"

Chill muttered that he'd find something and disappeared into the house.

Merlin gestured to Petra. "Dear, since Mr. Timothy has thoroughly decorated the inside of my truck, would you be kind enough to drive it back to the office and give it a wipe-up? I'll ride back with the crew once we're temporarily patched together."

I returned the wriggly handful to Petra. He expressed his joy with a fusillade of yelps, yodels, and squirms. She gave him her pinkie to suck and said she'd have to work something out with one of the neighbor's kids to see he was fed during the day. She grinned at me out of Chill's sight-line as he walked over with a box from a fancy pair of boots.

Petra thanked him, joking that the size marked on it was smaller than the ones she wore.

Chill said, "Yep."

...

As I watched Merlin leave, shreds of guilty fear and exhilaration swam around in me, surrounded by something too raw to name. Chill picked up on it and danced me to the sunlit bedroom; he'd always wanted the cover of night before. He'd brought back restraints from his trip and wanted me to try to force him into them. He dangled them from his long finger, his face glittering with the game. He provoked me enough to bring out the snarling animal in me and fought just enough that I had to fight as hard as I could. By the time he was in them, that was where I damned well wanted him, and when I harnessed myself up to deal with him, I dealt with him.

When I let him free, he lay prone on the towel instead of cleaning himself up immediately. There were chafes on his wrists and he'd bitten his lip hard enough to leave a red raw spot. My ferocious was spent. I stroked the ligature mark crossing the snake tattoo around his left hand.

He stretched and purred. "That. Was. Amazing."

The strafing afternoon sun caught a double row of raised dot-scars running down his back that the ink of his wings had obscured; they looked like ceremonial braille.

As my fingertips read the pattern, it slowly came to me. "Hook suspension?"

Chill made an "mmm-hmmm" noise in his throat, spreading his arms, his long fingers curved back like a soaring hawk. I lay on him in a sphinx crouch. He twisted underneath me, dabbed himself with the towel, and tossed it on the floor. I took the equipment off myself and set it on top.

He touched the abraded harness-imprints on my hips. "Yep, a few of them. I don't got enough card-carrying Injun in me for a rightful Sundance. I do my flesh-dancing in the shadows. There was a club—true-religion, no-mercy sado-fetish. I sent a picture from it once, from the bar—not the room where they did the rigging. Long, long time ago..."

He looked up with the same things happening on his face that made me feel unsafe when I was in the bath that first night we were together. My body ached for completion even though my brain was satiated. His limp little natural equipment would take time to recover, if it ever did in that harsh light with him staring at my pathetic femaleness. Other forms of satisfaction involving digital or facial proximity to each other's unappealing plumbing were out by mutual agreement. I pulled the black sheet around myself.

He sighed, turned away and then looked at me sidelong with a jolt of that back-of-the-neck-prickling expression. "I brought you something else."

He reached into his travel bag and pulled out what looked like a small, oblong case covered in enamel-work in an Asian design of a red dragon on a black field. I hardly needed to tell him it was gorgeous; he read it on my face. He spun a story about how it came to be at the weapons dealer from a collection that went back to a WWII-era American soldier serving in the Philippines.

Then he pressed it carefully into my grasp and made a sharp twist that whipped my wrist to flick open what I was holding. "This is how it works."

The switchblade glinted wickedly.

Chill pulled me closer by my hand around the knife, opened his legs, and raised one knee. "This is yours, always yours..."

He guided my hand to draw a fine, red, dripping line down the inside of his thigh. I pulled back and shook my head, sliding out of his grip, wiping the knife on the towel and closing it before forcing him to take it back. It had had its effect, though; Chill's equipment was flying at full staff. He murmured "always yours" again, coiling himself around me with a grip that made clear what a joke it was to think I'd ever forced him into anything. He pushed me open, slithering over and into me, reaching inside my head for an animal I didn't know I had in there—an animal that screamed for him. That was an animal I didn't want to be.

···

The shower hadn't left me feeling cleaner. I went back to the empty bedroom and put on what I'd been wearing the night I'd arrived. I didn't want to be in any borrowed clothes.

When I came out, he was leaning on the back of a chair at the dinette, grinning. "So that's the key to ya??"

I skewered my glare into his eyes. Another animal came fully awake inside me, one I did want. I sent a straight-up right hook to that vile grin. I'd never hit anyone that hard when I wasn't defending myself or someone else in a fight. It came from my hips and my shoulder and the hard roar in my stone heart—respectable even by male standards, if not outstanding by the measure of someone who'd been fag-bashed a few times.

He slid into the chair and opened his mouth to speak. Blood rose in the ridges between his big teeth, smearing his tongue from the gash his jaws had cut inside his cheek. He closed his mouth again, the words unsaid. He leaned forward on the table and covered his head with his samurai-chrysanthemum tattooed arms as if from an attacking bird.

I put my punch-bruised hand on the doorknob. "I need to go walk—"

Chill didn't look up. "Yep."

···

I'd wound past Gabriel's house and up the path to the decrepit trailer Angela used to stay in. The door was open, and I could hear her singing inside. Her voice was a deep, clear-running river. I listened a while and then headed farther up the hill to where I could feel the wind.

I lay down on a piece of ledge rock, closed my eyes, and let the air clean me.

A familiar chuckle jolted me out of it. "Hey, Runt-ette! I heard you on the path—thought you were stopping in to see me. Whatcha doing up here?"

I made some kind of face, but no words came out of my mouth.

Angela sat next to me and gave me a nudge. "Don't suppose you want to play, then? Sorry—you look kind of rough. That wasn't funny, I guess."

I could never tell when Angela was being a mean-girl or when something had really touched her, or if there was ever a difference. I shifted away from the warmth of her body.

She looked down. "I never should've let Runt sic me on you and Pete back at the beginning. I'm sorry..." She lifted my chin to look at me straight on. "I mean it—really. I've learned a few things—not much, maybe, but something. I'm sorry."

She got up and headed back to the trailer. I pulled out my phone.

...

I sat on Chill's step in the dusk half-light, gearing myself up for going inside. The table was set for dinner. He was putting something from the oven on a serving platter when I came in.

His bruised mouth caught the glare from the overhead fluorescent when he smiled. "Didn't know if you were coming back."

"I'm not."

His expression fell apart.

I hadn't expected that reaction, but I squared myself up to it. "I just needed to tell it to you to your face. I owe you that much."

I pulled my rifle from the rack in the gunroom. I had things to talk to him about, but not just then. The headlights from a sheriff's department all-terrain SUV came in the window, saving me from having to wait outside on the step.

...

An involuntary noise came out of my mouth when I saw the Mistake's old camo-painted truck parked by my front door.

Tom turned to me. "Guess that's yours by forfeiture now. You sure you don't want me to stay over, just until you get yourself settled back in?"

I nodded and hugged him before jumping out. He waited until I was inside and had a battery-powered light on before he honked the horn, waved, and headed down. I stood in the doorway until his bouncing headlights disappeared around the curve and left my cold house the brightest thing in sight.

The Mistake's keys—to the truck, the front and back doors and the padlock he kept on his room—lay on the table, along with a small stack of Federal cash. There was a Martel International business card next to that, with the name Mathieu Martel on it. The "Mathieu" was crossed out and "Merlin" written in tight, precise engineer's printing. The Mistake's coat hung neatly on the rack by the door. His leather work gloves curled with the gesture of his hands on the hall table next to it. The dishes were washed; the floor wasn't sticky.

I put my head down on the table and let out a sub-human howl.

CHAPTER TWENTY-THREE

Dear listeners, I need to report a rape—a rape of my personal air-waves. WWBF's frequency has been hijacked by a pirate radio station emanating southward from the Great White Wasteland, run by none other than the Bodilicious Dame herself. I will personally, and with particular pleasure, make her pay for every hour she over-rides the signals of this station with an hour of an intimately personal, individualized hell I shall devise for her...

<u>*"O'Brien on the Brink" attempted broadcast, digital archive*</u>
<u>*January 25th, 2044*</u>

C HILL SENT ME A TEXT. *"Won't do much good to say I'm sorry, but I am—puking-my-guts-out sorry."*
   I said, *"Ok.'"*
   Chill responded fast. *"Thought I'd help you forget some stuff— thinking like an idiot. Only been with a woman couple of times— not under best circumstances. I'm clueless. Read too many advice blogs by wrong people. I have to say this—should've said it when I had the chance—I love you."*
   I wrote back. *"I hope you mean that like friends"*
   "I don't know how the hell I mean it, babe."
   I took a few minutes to answer. *"Then I guess I love you too. Doesn't change things. I don't have the spare brain cells to think about it anymore."*

...

Petra was working on the Mistake's beer supply. I'd packed up what belongings of his he might have taken with him if he'd left for good on his own and hidden them in the basement before she got there. Tom had said he didn't want her knowing anything, and it was time for me to learn how to keep secrets. I told her the Mistake had left me the truck because he got a better one, and she'd sniggered. Her beautiful new Maple Leaf Motors ride next to it in the drive made it look even shabbier. She watched me trying to get my recharged phone battery seated. The power light came on briefly and then stubbornly disappeared. No matter how I jiggled and teased, it stayed off.

Petra muttered into her beer. "Chill-fucking-Dark... He knew when he set you up with that goddamned Canadian newsfeed on that dinky thing that you'd wear it out."

I said it wasn't Chill's fault for offering me access to the Darks' mesh network through the phone. He'd warned me it'd take a lot of juice and he'd score me another backup battery. He hadn't found one yet, but I'd still spent four or five hours a day watching hi-def satellite download on a communication device intended to be fully powered a few minutes at a time.

Chill was still doing my financial chores and generally helping me hold my life together without having said another word about where we were emotionally. He'd promised Tom he'd be there for me however it worked out, and he was.

Petra didn't care for that. "Don't like you having the Darks handling your money that way. No one's checking on what they might be pulling off your account for the cost of their services."

I told Petra to let it alone. She'd set the ground rules for no commitments a long time back. I didn't want to rely on her, and she was pushing me near the point I'd have to say so.

As usual, she read my face. "OK... I won't pick the scab, but we gotta go if we're gonna go. Are you *absolutely* sure you want on a Champetty job? Bill Martel said you'd be with new workers, but it's still Sam's house—Merlin gave me veto proxy if his brother put you on a bad crew. He thinks Bill might play you, just for jollies."

She looked around at the kitchen, stripped of the Mistake's existence. "You ran your ex off so far Sam can't find him. They were getting to be drinking hubbies since you left, and Sam's missing the commiseration. Angie just told him she's filing for divorce at long last—so goes the grapevine, anyway. She's given up being kind to him by cutting his tail off an inch at a time. No more date nights and flowers from the baby-daddy when she's bored and there's no one else around to torture. I don't want you to be part of a 'Let's cheer up Sammy' show his friends put on."

I pulled my fleur-de-lis and hammer Martel International work jacket off the hook. "Not going to let myself get played."

...

Sam Champetty had been renovating a farmhouse for himself and his son. Bill Martel was donating my trim carpentry as a company favor. The taste of that wasn't good, but I needed work, and Bill had promised Petra Sam wouldn't be around. She drove her new truck, which let me keep my head in what I needed to do. It was a midwinter day; the sun would set with a clang at around three o'clock. The slant light had cast hard shadows at high noon, and the daylight was going when she and I pulled up. There were two Martel International vehicles parked in front of the house.

Petra said, "Fuck."

Sam Champetty waved from the recently painted porch.

Petra put the truck in reverse. "Son of a bitch! I knew something stank about this..."

I needed the job to meet Combating Autism Act Workfare requirements. Bill Martel wasn't going to cover for me the way Merlin had. I said I might as well get it over with. Champetty would be involved in any Martel work anyway. I reached for the hand brake. Petra started arguing. I got out and walked toward the house, and she followed fast.

Sam ushered us in, making a point to lay his hand on my back. "So are we a girl or a boy now, or what? I thought you liked to be a ladies' man, but since you've been consorting with my faggot excuse for a brother-in-law, maybe I should grab your backside to make you happy."

I sidled away from his touch. "Just because he hammered your ass at deer hunting doesn't mean that's what I let him do."

Sam grinned and pushed us toward the living room. "Let's take this from the top. I know you do good work, Scope." He winked. "Dax, rather—no need to get prickly. Don't want you tattling to Big Brother Merlin that you're spitting the job out because the boys didn't play nice. We shall be gentlemen and comport ourselves in proper Martel businesslike fashion. Please meet my son, since you didn't come up when we visited Grandpa Dark."

The kid was barely into adolescence. He had Angela's full-lipped, sensual pout, Sam's light, coarse hair, and Chill's pale gray eyes, which were more in keeping with his fair coloring. He appeared to have a prosthetic foot. He limped over and collected our coats without acknowledging us. Petra glanced into the dining room where two Métis-featured Québécois sat at a plywood-and-sawhorses table strewn with evidence of heavy alcohol consumption.

Sam said "Ahh... Forgive me, these are the new crew members," and tossed out a couple of French names I instantly forgot.

The kid clomped upstairs with our coats. There was a bulge in his hip pocket that could have been a weapon. Sam started pouring drinks, and Petra accepted one.

Sam was saying that they'd be putting in central heat since the kid's amputation made it hard for him to be cold, but it must have been eighty degrees in that house. The fumes from several cheap kerosene heaters sank thick on the first floor. It felt like I had a diesel slick in my throat.

One of the Québécois headed up to show the work. As I came to the upper hall, I stopped at the bathroom. A lot of things looked wrong. The bedroom doors were hollow-core plywood, but the bathroom door, usually the cheapest one, was solid six-panel pine. There was a heavy duty slide-bolt on the outside, and the catch had big steel screws sunk into the framing.

I pretended I needed to use the toilet and closed the door. There wasn't another bolt on the inside, just a knob-lock; the passage key for it hung on a hook out in the hall. There was an exhaust fan in a rectangle of fresh drywall where there should have been a window. There was a big closet, fresh-painted, with no shelves.

When I came out, Sam caught me looking at the door. "Well, she has good taste in building materials, anyway."

He said the Québécois upstairs got it on special sale because it was already cut for another customer who measured wrong, and look—it just fits perfectly even though the knob doesn't work right. "Dax is good with fixing things like that, eh? It will be much prettier than our clumsy make-do. Right, girl?"

This time I kept my mouth shut, but a lot of things ran through my head very fast.

I pulled Petra aside and took the drink out of her hand. "The fumes from those North Korean heaters are getting to you. We need to get our coats and go."

I waved vaguely at the men, got her jacket off the bed, wrapped it around her, and shoveled her out the door. "I'm not telling you what I've figured out. You've been too good for me for that. I love you, and I want you to tell Chill I love him, too. *Do not* say anything over the damned CB or I'm going to be a dead freak the next time you hear anything about me."

I drove her back to my house, picked up some tools, got the Mistake's pistol and his truck, drove back short of the farmhouse, and parked in the woods. I watched the house. The pistol felt awkward in my jacket. Sam and his son were at the door, then Sam left. The Québécois men yelled about something in the back. I slipped in the front door, up the stairs, and eased myself silently into the bathroom closet.

Nothing had changed. I was just thinking how I was going to get out again when there were heavy sounds on the stairs. First I heard the kid clump into the bathroom, then water running in the tub, some thumps, and whimpering like someone with their mouth taped. There was a big splash and thrashing. The kid laughed that high, ugly laugh his father had. Then there was the sound of the tape being ripped off and a woman gasping.

The woman's voice came hard and clear. "You should've died in that fucking trap instead of just leaving your foot to rot in it. Wish I'd aborted you—" The voice was cut off with a hard slap and another dunking.

Angela didn't give them the satisfaction of one more sound except more gasping. They tired themselves out holding her under water, and then she wasn't fighting anymore. They sounded worried they might have drowned her. One of the men talked in joual about keeping the fun in check until they'd had their family chat. I heard the kid say she had a pulse; he must have checked her eyes, because he said they were rolled back so she wasn't playing fox about having passed out. Someone took a piss and didn't flush. The Québécois slapped each other on the back talking about what they could do next. They laughed but the kid didn't, so I guessed he didn't speak French. The door opened and closed, the bolt slid, and they all stumbled downstairs.

I opened the closet door about an inch an hour and saw Angela lying in the full bathtub with her head back, looking like I did after the Mistake was done with me the last time. She blinked; I put my finger to my lips and shook my head. Her hands and legs were taped, and the water was bloody pink. I cut her free, got out my pliers and screwdriver, and started working the hinge-pins out of the door; my hands were sweating and the urine smell was making me sick, but I couldn't flush the damned filthy toilet to make any noise.

I'd never had to use more strength in my life than I used to ease that door off the hinges and the bolt free of the slide and the jamb with no leverage—without making a sound. Angela hobbled over and helped me get that last eighth-inch of lift. It looked like her ankle might be broken. I made a sign for her to wait as I peeked downstairs. The two men were passed out drunk.

I started counting the heaters; there were five in the one room. The kid came in from the kitchen with a kerosene can in his hand. I thought at first that he'd been refilling the heaters, but he methodically tipped each one over and watched the fuel spill out onto the floor. They were labeled as safety heaters; the flame was supposed go out as soon as they tilted, and they seemed, remarkably enough, not to be defective. The kid worked his way toward the door, laying out kero as he went. I grabbed Angela and signed for her to get ready.

The kid got out a lighter. I yelled, and Angela and I came thundering down the stairs and outside with me half carrying her. Her son stood in the doorway with the house on fire behind him, still holding the kero can. I saw headlights at the foot of the drive, flaring in the softly falling snow, and I thought, *O holy hell Sam's back,* but it wasn't Sam. It was Uncle Gabriel, Mike Dark, and Chill. Mike was driving. I could make out Chill in the dome light as the doors opened, and Gabriel crouching in the truck bed.

Mike screamed, "Get down!"

Angela and I fell into a snowbank. Chill set up his rifle in the rolled-down window of the open door and took aim at his nephew, who was reaching for his hip. Chill brushed a tendril of dampened hair away from his face and squinted into the reticle. The muzzle flared, and the harsh crack sent a snow-muffled echo across the hill.

The brothers lifted Angela soaking and shivering into the open back. Her lips were turning blue. Mike climbed in with his daughter, wrapping himself around her, and Gabriel got behind the wheel. Chill yanked me in. My arm was out the window he'd just shot through. Chill leaned out of it behind me, breathing hard.

He swallowed and then held me in so tight my ribs hurt. "Pete came to the house—said you were pulling something. We saw Angie was gone. This is family shit, babe, don't get—"

Gabriel said, "Shut up, Gabie."

We took off toward the settlement.

Gabriel was saying, "You decided to spend the night with Chill. If there's a question about anything, that's what you were hiding. Angela was with us, and she fell on the ice. When Tom gets here, he's going to see a dead kid burned to a crisp with a kero can in his hand, and hopefully he won't want to look in that mess for any bullets..."

Chill looked over. "One bullet."

Then he looked sick. We had to stop short of his house so he could throw up. After, he took a handful of snow in his mouth, spat, and got out his flask. I opened it for him because his fingers were shaking. Gabriel left us there so they could get Angela warm.

...

When we got in, Chill turned on the light, slumped into his big chair, and pulled me onto his lap. "You are never so attractive to me as when you've been fighting for your life."

"You never look so good as when you're saving my ass."

I wasn't going to leave him alone with the images that had made him vomit. I still had things to discuss with him, but they didn't feel that important. I told him I'd give him what he'd wanted, and to talk me through it.

He nodded toward his bedroom door. "We'll need to push aside your rivals."

On my side of the bed were his ancient laptop plugged into a FedWeb hack-jack, several detective novels, a well-thumbed gun catalog, a couple of fancy heavyweight paper year-end automotive magazines, something called a Zen Reader, an open bookkeeper's ledger, and a couple of spiral bound notebooks. "As you can see, I've been living quite the wild life."

I looped his belt around his wrists and pulled him back with me. He told me to restrain him like I meant it, and I did. He was breathing through his mouth, and his eyes were black and hungry. I'd looked at him then, with that beautiful expression on his face, and I wanted to get to his skinny little body so bad I tore his shirt opening it up. When he asked me to get out the knife he'd given me it seemed beautiful at that moment, as if he was offering everything of himself, and I'd been too rigid to accept it before.

...

I had the taste of the knife tip in my mouth—iron, salt, and steel—from when Chill had asked to see me lick his blood off it. Raw chafe marks showed around the leather restraint cuffs on his wrists stretched over his head. A facial tissue was stuck to a stubbornly bleeding cut on his shoulder. The pale skin on his neck and chest was blotched and angry from a storm of thin little test slices, but I'd given him what he'd asked for—a scar to remember. He'd told me to twist the blade tip and drag it crossways to leave a wider mark that would raise as it healed. The reddened tissues I'd laid carefully over the inverted triangle I'd left on his lower belly had been disrupted by what I'd done afterward when I'd let myself be moved by the thing we were both feeling. He hadn't lasted a full minute, and he apologized one more time for not being able to give me satisfaction.

I put my hand over his mouth. "I don't know what to do with your freaky body, but you are the most beautiful piece of twisted fuck-up I have ever seen..."

He wrapped his legs around me. "Same to you, Lady. There are worse things to base a relationship on, no?"

I kissed his forehead and undid the restraints.

He licked and blew on an abrasion on his wrist. "What do you want? You tell me. That goes for now and for wherever we go from here. You're the driver."

I said I wanted to make love to him.

He understood what I meant. "Sure, but I need to clear the back gate, if you get me…"

He was a while in the bathroom. When he came out he wasn't bleeding anymore, but his face was drawn like his nerves had caught up with him.

He lay on his back and stared at the ceiling. "There's more than one kind of shit in me I might sometimes need to deal with. I'll take care of it, never let it touch you. Same for you, whatever you need, you do it. Up to you whether you tell me about it."

I shrugged as I buckled myself into the harness.

He held my face with simple tenderness. "Who the hell am I fooling? I've got no standing to hold you to anything if I wanted to. Had a moment between the acne and the crow's feet when I looked the part enough to pull off the diva bullshit. Lost whatever beauty I had getting in the middle of too many fights with no right side, aiming a gun at people no worse than I was. Adds a lot more years than the calendar. That's all a long time gone. As for the freaky old body, it's all yours, whatever you're inspired to do with it. I'm glad you want it."

He rolled over and presented himself, exhaling a soft, welcoming sigh as I lubed him. He pulled my hand to his mouth, his tongue flicking over my fingers.

He murmured as I set myself firmly inside him. "You wrote me something in a text a few days ago. Tell it to me out loud so I can keep your voice in my head— the part before 'Doesn't change things…'"

"I guess I love you."

"Yeah, that's it."

It took a long time because he was so spent down. At first he lay quietly. He told me with soft grumbling coos when I'd found the resonance. His face flushed a little, letting me know I was getting somewhere. He crouched on his elbows, and I reached forward and grabbed his forearms to keep myself in the saddle. I felt the jolt of arousal run through him. He moved into the most submissive position he'd ever offered me, urging me to take what I owned, raising his skinny bum with his inked arms stretched back so I could grip his wrists. I felt something in my heart weld to him in a way I knew was going to be there until the day I died.

He clenched his fists and then slowly opened them. The backs of his thighs began trembling. The flush spread down his cheek and then his jaw shuddered as he let out a harsh, chattering gasp. I couldn't feel that beautiful twitch inside him, but I knew it was there. I felt like the lord of the whole damned universe.

CHAPTER TWENTY-FOUR

Ladies and gentlemen of the Wyandot Sub-Region, if you can hear me, this is Boadicea Sinclair. This is my third and final transmission notifying you that I will be leading an international team to investigate the disappearance of some fifty disabled citizens during the evacuation of the CareWell facility. I'm broadcasting on this frequency because some of your radios may be tuned to it, and it's my best hope of reaching you. After this I will no longer interfere with your standard programming. We have made arrangements with Martel International to be sure we observe the appropriate legalities while we are in your territory. If you have any information regarding this incident, please contact my delegation or the NATO Human Rights Commission Disability Subcommittee...

<u>Unidentified Broadcast over AM frequency 58.1,</u>
<u>January 26th, 2044</u>

C HILL AND I WOKE to a pounding on the front door. He had my pistol in his hand before he pulled his pants on. He checked the security camera feed. It was Tom Webster knocking, not in uniform and not in a sheriff's department vehicle. Chill's shirt wasn't hiding much of what I'd given him. The big tear along the button placket gaped to show a driving storm of thin red cuts above his waistband. He passed the gun to me. I pocketed it and stood behind him.

He answered the door, still buttoning. "Hey, Massa Webstah. What I can do for you this fine mornin'? I sees you still can talk yourself past a gatekeeper. Need to have a chat with the Cousins about that."

Tom sighed hard. I realized my hands were resting possessively on Chill's hips.

Tom muttered "fucking Darks" and made a stern come-on gesture at me. "Dax, looks like you've decided which side you're on. We need to talk—*Now*. Put your damned sweater back on right side out. I'm taking you by your house to pick up what you need—you can't stay there alone and you can't be out wandering around like an amnesiac in a minefield. You're in deep shit, and at least this place is guarded, even if I shouldn't have been waved through. Then I'm staying out of Martel jurisdictions and you're staying wherever Gabe tells you to—and I *do not* want to know where that is. After this, you're his problem."

Chill blinked like he didn't know what Tom might be talking about.

I ducked into the bedroom to fix my sweater, gave Chill a peck on the cheek, and went out to Tom's truck. Chill patted my hip as I went by to make sure I was still armed.

Tom stepped up into the driver's seat and slammed the door. He had bruise-colored bags under his eyes. He gave off silent currents of disapproval as he drove the unplowed track between the settlement and my house. Ruts of compacted snow were the only sign of where the road crossed the fields. He kept scanning the woods and outcroppings as if we were being watched.

When we rounded a curve to a sheltered spot, he stopped the truck. "Dax, is this something you really feel, emotionally... or sexually, or are you just still exploring?"

That wasn't a conversation we'd had even when I was an adolescent growing up in Tom's house. I pulled out a small, damaged gear shaft bearing that one of the Dark cousins had given me to play with. It had a soothing chatter in its stuttering rotation. Tom scowled at the noise.

As I spun it in spite of the disapproving look, I saw hadn't completely washed Chill's blood from under my nails. "I'm not sure what I feel—something like an ocean that connects. Something resonates... not what I ever expected to feel." A stronger voice came out of me. "I can push him harder than I'd ever push a woman. Most times the rocket doesn't clear the launch pad, but sometimes it's a hell of a ride."

Tom drummed his fingertips on the wheel. "That's honest, anyway."

I spun my bearing race and stared out the fogging window at the granite ledge concealing us.

Tom looked up at the sky. "I'm not going to go into what you should have done. Sometimes I think your ex must've bashed the good sense out of you. I'd give a lot to know what possessed you to hook up with him. Anyone could've told you how it'd end."

I kept looking out the window at the rock.

He slapped the wheel softly. "You were doing so well, Dax. You were beating the autism. You'd picked yourself up from when Pete let you down. Why!?"

I rolled the bearing around on my face to calm myself. "Autism is what I am, Tom—it's not something I can beat any more than I can beat being small. I can compensate, come across as what you want me to be for a little while at a time, but I can't keep it up. I need the help... Petra understands."

"Well—you won't have Pete's help anymore. She was working up the nerve to ask to move in with you, trying to earn your trust back from the last time one of the Darks sabotaged it. You've made your choice—it's going be a different life for you now. OK, said all I'm going to on that.

"I'll tell you this once, and fast—You were reported as an escapee from Thunderbird. Legally, you are a fugitive with a psychiatric designation and a history of violence. Anyone on your trail has no obligation to bring you in alive. You need to bury the name you were born under, along with the bodies, and you need to lie and lie well so it stays there."

He checked my face to make sure I'd taken in what he'd said and that I was still listening. "I dicked your records before I put you in school—a public search should turn you up as my birth daughter with a clean sheet so long as no one knows to look for other threads. Champetty's a problem—you may have to deal with him one day. I will also say once, and once only, that he does a fair amount of poaching, just like everyone at this end of the county. Poaching accidents are not uncommon, and don't generally warrant official investigations...

"As far as Laithbourn Internal Affairs knows, you're one more secret lying shallow under the dirt, and the couple of trusties that never came back to Thunderbird were the only real escapees. Angie was too drugged to remember anything. I took her in front of the magistrate, told him I'd found her in the woods beat up and naked. He made some calls and got her off for time served. You will make sure that story holds together if you are ever asked, and you will not bring it up to anyone."

Tom reached under his seat and opened a small metal box full of contraband electronics parts. "You still have that FedWeb hack, right? Pete said the pack wouldn't take a charge. You'll need reliable communications—see if one of these works in your equipment. Nobody hears I gave you a box full of department-seized hack parts, understand?"

I nodded. I rummaged through the box, pulled out the most likely couple of candidates, and slipped the box back under the seat. I'd held my bearing so tight it'd tattooed my hand with a red mark. I rolled it along my cheek and tried to breathe.

Tom mimed punching the dashboard. "Now I have this disaster. Sam's looking for blood. He kept asking about bodies last night—how many. He didn't want us taking his son's back to the morgue. The fire caved in on itself and Municipal Emergency gave it a hose-down. We haven't pulled the two Martel guys out yet. I'm assuming they're in there."

I nodded.

Tom looked down. "Sam seemed to think Angie might be in there, and maybe you too. The cousins at the gate said she busted her ankle last night. I'm going to assume she's OK."

I started to say something.

Tom cut me off and rubbed his face. "Do Not Tell Me Anything. I'm just warning you of where things are. You're gonna have to be careful of Sam for a lot of reasons. Told the department we wouldn't need autopsies—funds better spent elsewhere, but we still have the kid until I can accidentally lose him. Yes, he has a bullet hole clean through his heart. I'm hoping to Hell I can get him cremated before the coroner decides to come back to work. Huge amount of cash was stashed in that Martel crew truck parked out front of the burn site. Funny how some of the brass knew right where to look for it, while the damned house is still smoldering. Wyandot Jurisdiction confiscated it and closed the file, so you and Gabe should be OK for now.

"If Martel International investigates, they'll have to pay for it. Bill's branch is in too deep to want to change the story—Angie's pyro kid dies snuffing his dad's intoxicated free-lancing drug-distribution business partners for their share of the goods. If the Montréal home office decides to do an internal inquiry, it's gonna come apart like a balloon full of piss when they poke it."

Tom's voice started to break. "If the neanderthal legislature would just give us wireless coverage out here instead of the damned CBs..."

He put his hand on my cheek to get me to look at him. "I understand you couldn't call out on an open band, but you should've sent Pete to me, not Gabe. Doesn't matter she knew better. Pete does whatever you tell her to. She'd follow you off a cliff... while you sit there playing with your face. She's earned better from you, Dax. God *damnit*. Fucking Darks."

...

Chill sat at the dinette with a jeweler's loupe in his eye, holding a pair of slightly trembling tweezers, his desk lamp focused on my phone's dead battery pack, trying to match up the minuscule leads from one of the broken-open packs Tom had given me to the one I'd been using. "You got a good eye there, Smallstuff. Looks like you picked out the only couple of Polaris packs he had—they're getting rare these days, real premium. Trafficking them's a capital offense now—could possibly have something to do with it."

The mention of Polaris gave me a jolt. I asked how badly Tom might be in trouble if anyone in his department found out he'd passed the things to me.

Chill set the loupe down and rubbed his eyes. "Well, if anyone could decipher Tom's fudged records, he could theoretically get the death penalty. Not likely, particularly since you didn't take the whole box. Can't say I'd have had the restraint to give it back since he offered. I doubt anyone in that office would recognize Polaris parts—probably it was just a list of 'miscellaneouses' and some dubious numbers. He loves ya, though... it's a risk that likely costs him sleep."

There was a tap at the kitchen door. Chill tucked the parts and tools back in the box and slipped it into the bookcase behind a pile of millennium-era paperbacks. He handed me one of the Darks' mesh-network handsets to use and said he'd work on my equipment later. In an emergency, the gear could be configured to send an open-airwaves call with a shorter but more reliable range than the CB. He kissed me on the head as he put the lamp back in its usual spot.

I asked if he was going to answer the door. He told me to get it if I felt like it. He left out the front as I stepped out onto the wet patio to offer Luce a cup of coffee.

She rubbed her arms from the raw damp of the freak thaw and came inside, careful to wipe her feet. "Goddamn, girl, I'm glad you came back! He was folding into himself bad there when you left— the ghosts start popping out when he gets that way."

She looked toward the front door. "Mike's taken charge of getting Angie patched up back in the Mother Country. He used a Martel safe passage across the border, and I haven't heard anything since. I suppose he's decided his little girl is where his heart is these days."

I raised an eyebrow.

Luce chuckled into her coffee. "Let me rephrase... When they came tearing back here with fuck knows what after them, I told Mike to get his brat away from the compound before I killed her and left the body outside the gate for Granny Dark's pet windigo. I called ahead to have Merlin wave the two of them through to Québec on family credentials, and I told him to collar her on her way back in and give her instructions on what's expected from her. Goddamned time the Dark brothers quit protecting her from her consequences. You should've just let the kid..." She checked my face and looked away. "...but he needed to go. The boys were ready when you sent Pete over."

I didn't say Petra had taken that on herself, just as I hadn't told Tom when he'd made that assumption. Tom couldn't have gotten there in time, and drunk as she was, Petra had been thinking more clearly than I'd been. I'd only wanted her to make sure Chill knew how I felt about him. I'd figured she'd just drive home and sleep, and if I didn't make it out alive, she'd let him know one day.

I offered Luce a shot of Chill's Spicebox Canadian in her coffee.

She nodded. "That was a decent slug you gave him—and he had it coming, as I told him when he explained why he looked like he'd had a disagreement with the front of a truck. He's way out of his depth, and, in ways you probably understand too well, he's post-traumatic as hell and it can make him act like an idiot. He trusts you. Says... I want to get this right... paraphrasing— 'your mind is a deep river he can drown in without dying.' When you ditched him, it left a mark on more than his face. He doesn't exactly have a wealth of resources to call on for intimate advice on females of the hard-ass persuasion, so he was stuck with me. I'm glad if anything I said helped."

I raised my coffee cup in a toast, and she clinked it with hers. We drank quietly until we heard the Gabriels trudging in the sloppy, thaw-heaved gravel, chatting about poaching while they had the weather. Luce started to get up.

The blast of a truck horn came from outside the gate, followed by joual bellowing in a voice I felt like I should recognize but I wasn't placing it.

Luce pulled on her coat. "I need to get down there, Dykie—this ain't good."

Chill pushed the kitchen door open and gave his mother a vile enough expression that I started to get up to say something.

Luce's small, steely hand clamped down on my shoulder. "This is his castle, by treaty. Don't get in the middle of us and the way we work things. You try to make us hold hands and sing kumbaya and I will slap your hard little dyke ass even if he won't. Now, Bill Martel's got a Workfare officer with him, and they've already been by your house—I guess you didn't get that or you'd be hiding under the bed where you belong. Chill—cover my back if you'd be so kind."

Chill opened the front door for his mother and grabbed his best sniper rifle on his way out.

...

Chill and I walked together, and Gabriel trekked ahead of us. He kept looking back, annoyed whenever our voices rose above a whisper. He and Chill held tight to their rifles. Bill Martel hadn't backed down for Luce, and it had taken another display of Dark firepower to get him and the Workfare officer to leave without me. They'd promised they'd be back with more authority.

We were headed to my house to see what had been done there. The Gabriels would scout deer at the same time since it'd been warm enough the last few days that vegetation was budding out and the herd would be stuffing itself. We wore red bandana do-rags as a slight nod to gun safety. I insisted on wearing my Martel field coat with its reflective safety strips; it was loud enough to warn off anyone more or less innocently looking to cheat the lone Wyandot game warden. I didn't say it, but if someone was gunning not so innocently, I'd hopefully draw them off.

Chill kept vaulting fallen logs just to show off that his mid-thirties legs still could do it.

He offered his hand as I scrambled after him. "I'm a male, you're not. We could get married..."

I took a gentle swing at the spot on his grin I knew was still tender. "Va te faire foutre, as your dad would say. Whatever makes you want me?"

Chill chuckled. "You're the finest little intergalactic vortex I've ever met. First conversation we had, I had to take your word on the Nietzsche quote—looked it up and you were right. You'd read at fifteen what I was pretending to have read at seven years older: Foucault and Fanon. You'd blow another dimension in my brain and then close your eyes, wrap your arms around your knees, and rock me out of your mind when you'd had enough of me. Then you showed me that eeee-vuhl phone—told me how you got it, domming for the Sterling Island Billionaire Boys Club..."

We'd come to my house up through the woods; Gabriel was reading a notice posted on the door claiming the property as forfeiture to the Northern Heartland Department of Workfare for the owner's failure to report to an approved jobsite for three consecutive days.

When I got out my key, he shook his head. "The place is wired, Dax—it'll blow. But take a look inside."

I peered through the blinds on the fortified window. All the boxes of the Mistake's stuff I'd hidden in the basement lay open.

His coat, his gloves, his old interactive porn console and games... all his mended, badly folded clothes were strewn across the floor.

...

We'd trudged on silently to the amputated mountaintop wasteland of the Darks' exhausted strip-mine. Scrub trees poked through the coal waste, and the deer had devoured their sickly leaves as soon as they'd appeared in the brief gust of warmth. The Darks had set up the blackened bowl as a deathtrap. They kept a feed-station with a saltlick and a clean rainwater collection trough; a tree-stand along the perimeter overlooked it. Gabriel didn't like the way things felt. Chill joked grimly it was the windigo that his grandmother used to trade soul-eater recipes with sometimes. She'd told him it was set free when the top of the mountain was blown off to get at the coal, and it had shut off their water in revenge so they had to drill deeper wells, but of course that was because of the curse, not because the blasting had damaged the upper aquifer.

He snickered softly. "Nana used to warn me I should leave the heart from anything I killed on the mountain as an offering to keep the peace. Didn't do that when I took that buck I have on my wall. Nana probably heard about it—right, Uncle G? Your mother never liked skeptics, but you chat with her sometimes when the moon's in the right alignment, so put in a good word for me. I've heard you, so don't look like you don't know what I'm talking about."

Gabriel gave him a complicated and not overly pleasant look before gliding off and vanishing into the scrub. He reappeared on the other side of an outcropping, climbed onto it, and sighted over to the tree-stand. He slid down and tested the shaky climbing cleats up to the platform. Chill climbed the outcropping, looked to Gabriel in the stand, and nodded that something seemed odd. He gestured that the saltlick had been moved. Chill was standing about eight feet above me near the edge of the granite, and Gabriel was another eight feet above that on the rotting tree-stand.

Gabriel's head snapped over to look behind me. A roar came out of his mouth that blew me backward as something hot sang over me, cracked, and sprayed fine granite shrapnel. My face and hands stung, and I had rips in my jacket. Chill was vaulting down when there was another crack. He twisted and snapped in the air like a rag doll, and red bloomed on the inside of his left leg.

Gabriel dropped from the stand, boards cracking and breaking as he fell. A piece of jagged wood stuck out from under his shoulder blade, and red bloomed around that. He tried to reach around to his back as he stumbled toward Chill. I pulled him down as another hot thing sang and sprayed shards. I wrenched the board out of him and we dove for Chill.

I screamed as loud as my body could, "I'm hit bad! Oh my god, Gabriel—he's dead! Gabriel! Gabriel!?? Oh my god!"

I yanked the bandana off Chill's head, tied it with the one I had, and tied that around his leg where the black-red bloom was growing in pulses. He looked at me, and his eyes rolled back.

I kept whispering, "Make a liar out of me... make a liar out of me... make a liar out of me..."

Gabriel crawled, keeping low and trying to drag Chill behind the rock. I lifted his bloody legs, and we got him there. Gabriel took Chill's head in his lap and slapped his face. I grabbed his snake hand and rubbed it, but his lips and nails were turning blue.

I was saying, "Stay with me, sissyboy. Do not let go, you little son-of-a-bitch—" I felt him grab my arm hard with his other hand, and I said "Hold on—Leave some bruises, babe—leave me black and blue—just hold on—"

I felt Chill's fingers deep in the muscle of my arm, and it was a precious ache. He slipped in and out and in again. His blood dried on my hands. Gabriel shivered. My eyes burned. The rotten eggs smell of freshly exposed granite lingered. The vision in my left eye wasn't clearing, but I knew I shouldn't rub it. Gabriel said I looked like I'd taken a face full of birdshot. I wasn't sure if he'd been hit, but he said he'd just missed his footing on a rotted cleat. He'd seen someone wearing white gloves raising a gun.

I pulled the mesh-network handset out. It was totally unsecured, but it was all I had. Anyone listening in would know I was still alive. I opened it up to every frequency in reach and started screaming. Gabriel waved at me to stop, but then slumped back against the rock and closed his eyes.

A horrendous roar came through the handset, along with a deep male shouting. "Pixie? Pixie? Is that you? Merlin Martel here—I'm on my way to... office... helicopter—sorry for the engine loudness—it's very hard to hear... I have you on locator... I believe we can land there... Do you need us, Pixie?"

CHAPTER TWENTY-FIVE

As of this date the border between the Sovereign Province of New Albion and the Northern Heartland Region of the former United States is closed indefinitely due to the seizure of a lawful and unarmed NATO Human Rights delegation at that border by an armed Heartland Nationalist group. The mercenary security service that was to accompany the delegation into the Wyandot Sub-region was inadequate to deal with the level of the attack, therefore we must consider the border to be inadequately supervised and defended for the safety of New Albion citizens...

Statement from the New Albion Office of Information,
March 23rd, 2044

A MAN IN A MARTEL INTERNATIONAL JACKET gave first aid to Chill and Gabriel as I shivered under Merlin's arm. The helicopter engine was so loud it felt like it would break my bones. I told Merlin what I could about what had happened. He asked the man giving first aid to get a look at my left eye. I said I couldn't go to the Laithbourn Healthcare urgent care center.

Merlin rubbed my shoulder. "No, no, Pixie—you shall be our first patients. I have called ahead for the red carpet." He jostled me against him and pointed out the window.

Below, the CareWell building rose up toward us; the faded helipad red cross on the roof had been repainted with a fleur-de-lis and war hammers.

...

We weren't the first patients at the new International Cooperative Healthcare Center. A contract worker at the building materials reclamation plant had been turned away from Laithbourn UrgentCare for inability to pay, and had been delivered to the Martel facility in the back of a pickup. He'd been cutting up old lumber with "repurposed" sawmill equipment and had lost his hand and most of his forearm. His coworkers had tourniqueted him as well as they could, but he was close to bleeding out. He was blessedly unconscious. I heard French medical talk about transfusion supplies as three Québécois doctors worked on him.

A triage nurse finished cutting away Chill's jeans and waved over an orderly to clean Gabriel's back. No curtains were up in the triage area. It had the feel of a battlefield hospital.

Merlin sighed. "Our first four patients, and none are paying customers. At least you're under Martel insurance and we'll eventually be reimbursed by the indemnity company."

I murmured that I thought Bill Martel had terminated my employment. Merlin asked what made me think that; I said I suspected it when Bill had shown up at the Dark compound with a writ to take me in for indigence and my house was posted for seizure by Workfare with a Regional permit allowing it to be rigged for deadly force.

Merlin gave me a sharp look and told me to hold the thought as he stepped over to the injured millworker and questioned the doctors, gesturing for two of them to attend to the Gabriels. He apologized for my having to wait for treatment.

I shook my head and asked if the millworker would survive. I swore under my breath that he'd no doubt had to sign away his right to sue in order to get the job.

Merlin edged himself so I couldn't see the man's wound cauterized, but I could smell it. He asked about the reclamation plant. I'd dealt with it when I was in trade school; this wasn't the only accident I'd seen come out of there. He listened until the triage nurse asked to look at my eye. She pointed her light into it and pulled the lower lid down, and the room started spinning.

...

As I blinked and tried to get Merlin in focus, he smiled. "You fainted as the nurse checked your eye. There were particles of grit needing to be removed with tweezers, and the doctor suggested you might benefit from an analgesic injection which might also make you quite drowsy. We thought you'd find it less traumatic if we simply went ahead..."

Merlin didn't give me much time to think about that. He said the doctors had removed the debris from Gabriel's back and stitched him up, and he'd be discharged soon. He wouldn't have much use of the upper arm and shoulder for a while, but eventually it should be functional. Chill's wound was more complicated; the bullet had torn through the interior stabilizer muscles of his thigh, damaged a major nerve, and lacerated an artery before flattening out against his pelvic bone. He'd be vulnerable to re-injuring himself, but should be healed enough to return home in a couple of weeks.

I asked how the millworker was doing.

Merlin rubbed his face. "Pixie, he'd lost a great deal of blood, a blood-type hard to match—requiring an O-negative emergency transfusion. The younger Gabriel is type O-negative—we couldn't give him the Rh positive we have—both needed the same thing. We have a painfully limited supply. Gabriel had a much greater probability of survival. We had to put what we had on the bet with the best chance of living to benefit."

I stared at the stained ceiling tiles. "Fuck this... just fuck this world..."

Merlin let out a tight sigh. "We tried to purchase several units from Laithbourn—their response was that they were not in the business of helping their competitors, and if we should succeed in driving them out of business they would be sure to dump whatever remaining blood supplies they had on the ground outside our front gate."

He stood and took my hand. "My dear, I must ask you to tell me exactly what happened between you and my brother. You said Bill had your house seized? I trust you had pocketed my business card, that it wasn't lying around with those keys..."

I nodded, but when I told him what I'd seen spread out on the floor when I'd looked in my window, his face took on a shade of tension that made my stomach knot.

He reached in his jacket. "Ah. I see. I believe I need to give you something, especially as you have such limited emergency communication equipment. This is my business phone—you may want to familiarize yourself with it as you wait for your friend to come out of surgery.

"It is possible I might have left the old server chip from the security system for this building in it—if so, I have forgotten. Fortunately for you, Bill is unaware that the monitor network had a secondary internal backup. I only shared with him the portion of the recording prior to shutdown. As I've said before, I have plans for my Pixie.

"There's also a GPS-active recording of an overflight we did of a hunter's campsite hidden in the woods shortly before I heard your distress call. It belongs to someone very much invested in remaining unseen. If you look closely you may find some white gloves. If you should go in search of the owner of those gloves, you would be wise to take an extended vacation immediately afterward somewhere outside Bill's north Wyandot jurisdiction."

...

The motion-activated backup-powered video surveillance equipment tracked me, flicking on as I entered each empty corridor, the rifle on my back. The system had watched me read the LWAG's suicide note, listen for her death rattle, tease the note from under her arm, and tuck it in my pocket. I backed the recording to the last minutes of the LWAG's conscious life. She screamed soundlessly into an office phone; the system ID'd the incoming number as from the University Hospital. Tears flooded her bruised face. Still farther into the past, the outside cameras were still functioning. Two buses with blacked-out windows were loading clients from the secret wards. I saw one horribly sick-looking figure that made my heart jump. I gasped, "Amelia!" The doctor who'd been ready to euthanize her was dragged between a pair of University Hospital ops, his battered face barely recognizable.

I steeled myself for the preceding hours. At the beginning of that stream, the lights were bright and there was audio. I watched a Laithbourn technician tinker with the upstairs computers. The system announced the connection to Central Command was being disconnected. The ranking officer came on the PA to warn that the building would be shut down in thirty minutes.

The lights dimmed and the sound died. I watched the LWAG being questioned, and the stream of elevator runs from the public wards to the basement. I saw the injections—the terrified death grimaces—the drugs inducing tight, suppressed convulsions in people I'd cared for. I checked the cameras covering the furnace to confirm what the Mistake had said, and shut the phone off.

...

I curled next to Chill on his hospital bed. He cupped his hand around my head and kissed my hair. He'd told me to go away, and I'd told him to forget that. He'd grinned, sighed, and held me weakly with one arm. I didn't think I'd given anyone that much comfort before in my life.

He twisted a wisp of my hair gently in his fingers. "This could be a bumpy ride, babe. You're already showing a bit of silver in here. You're as crazy as I am if you decide to stick with me."

I made comforting noises. When he murmured that he didn't think there'd be much he could do for me for a long time, I said he made me feel like I owned the world a couple of times and that would do me for a while. Then he noticed Merlin's phone in my jeans pocket.

He flicked the brushed steel case with its embossed Martel logo out like a professional pickpocket and navigated to the user ID screen. "What we got here? You do get around with the big boys and their high-end communications devices, Smallstuff. 'Mathieu' Martel's personal piece? Damn."

I said I supposed "Merlin" was a nickname. Chill said, "Yep." He tinkered with the passcode and muttered it didn't go very far into the system and to be damned careful to pull the battery when I didn't want the company knowing where I was.

When I told him about the transfusion, he clicked his teeth together. "Yep. That's mommy's side of the family—the unusual blood type. Martels are almost all O-neg, but I'll wager you didn't see Master of Illusion Merlin rolling his sleeve up to donate."

...

Luce looked at her son and swore in an ornate Algonquian French that was half profane incantation. Gabriel huddled inside his oversized hospital robe in the worn vinyl chair by the bed.

She stared hard at Gabriel. "Angie's running the shipment—period. The family is giving her a little stay at one of our safe-houses until the border settles down, and then she's taking over the regular route. Nobody knows where Mike is, or if they do, they aren't saying. The Home Office isn't dawdling anymore. Chill's not an option." Her voice rose enough to be heard by Merlin in the hall. She repeated herself slowly. "Chill. Is. Not. An. Option. Angie can fucking well do something for the family instead of the other way around for once."

She sat on the edge of Chill's bed and took his hand. "Aww, Hell! I don't wanna have this pissing session now. You lived this long without taking a fucking bullet—jeezus—baby…"

Chill smiled and told her if she didn't stop using such vulgar language he was going to have me throw her out of his room.

...

The GPS in Merlin's phone had kept us on track. The logging road had petered out miles back, and the trek had been an ordeal compounded by knowing someone might be lining us up in his sights as Chill hobbled with his arm over my shoulder. Sam's encampment was so deep in the tangled woods on the far side of the windigo's mountain that even if he'd been using a rifle to keep his smoker stocked, no human would necessarily have heard it. The camp backed against a south-facing ledge. It was hard to get a good vantage on it without being exposed ourselves, but Gabriel found a stakeout spot where we could see coming and going, if not the actual campsite. Chill took Merlin's phone and disconnected the power source.

There were a couple of bear heads on pikes with the skins stretched and scraped as a warning to others to stay away, so Sam had probably used firearms at least twice since he'd been there. Two rifles nested in their cases, so wherever he was hunting, he was doing it more quietly. Merlin had said to watch out for the crossbow, that Sam was a wicked shot with it. The smoker was full of rabbit and a fat quail, which seemed to prove his point. The smoker used a tiny bit of wood and didn't generate a visible plume like an open fire. There was a fishing rod and a small white-gas lantern in the tent along with a few cans of fatback beans and a bottle of vitamins on a little shelf. A coverall, long johns, and socks were drying on a line. A box of disposable white cotton gloves, a big bottle half-full of rubbing alcohol, a can of fuel and a can of water, a shaving kit, a first-aid kit, and a carefully rolled alpine sleeping bag were stashed neatly in a corner. That was it.

We'd been huddled together about three hours when Sam appeared, carrying a couple of rabbits looped in a snare line, a plump groundhog toted over his shoulder by the twenty-inch aluminum crossbow bolt skewering it. He looked harder and more efficient than I'd ever seen him. He'd been a Marine, and it showed. He gutted his take away from the campsite and buried the offal. He came back, and the scent of rubbing alcohol rose. We heard the smoker open and Sam whistling softly. The tune was a popular stalker-type love song, but Sam gave it a jaunty edge. Chill shuddered. He used his hands to adjust his bad leg where it'd gotten stiff against the rock.

Everything was quiet for a couple of hours, then Sam came out to the open area. He stood eating smoked rabbit, washing it down from a military canteen. He stretched, walked a little way into the trees, and pissed. He gave one of the bear heads a mocking French kiss and disappeared into the part of the camp concealed by the ledge. Eventually he snored; that let us know we could one at a time take an exceedingly quiet leg-stretch around one in the morning. By sunrise, Chill looked like an old man. Gabriel whispered did he want us to go take care of it. Chill shot ice out of his eyes as an answer. Gabriel gave him a wry look.

We heard sounds from inside the tent. Sam emerged in his long johns, stretched, and repeated the routine from the night before, including kissing the bear. He pissed in a couple of different spots along the perimeter, disappeared back into the camp and came out in the coveralls, the crossbow and a quiver of bolts on his back. We gave him a ten-minute head start, and then Gabriel manifested his magic. He dashed and zigzagged in total silence across the area where Sam had headed... almost a negative sound. He motioned to us, and as much as we'd practiced—on dry leaves and twigs, on pea gravel, on crisp pine needles—we sounded like an earthquake as we caught up. He gave us a vicious scowl and Chill took it.

We kept that up for a couple of miles. Chill started to loosen up and become quieter, and Gabriel looked less annoyed. He suddenly scooted ahead of us, motioning us to stay where we were, and damned quietly. He was gone about five minutes, reappearing from a different angle. He got on Chill's right, and we moved together as a hush guided by Gabriel's soft, magic feet. We sifted through the trees as a single being. A mist of wet snow filtered onto our faces, cooling Chill's sweaty forehead and letting him breathe a little easier.

We stopped, turned our head with Gabriel's eyes, and became Chill.

Sam stood on a small boulder staring down into a ravine where a gorgeous buck browsed. We were looking slightly up at Sam from behind and a little to the side, from about a hundred yards away, as he sighted his cocked crossbow, the bolt draw locked and ready. Gabriel and I got into the brace positions we'd drilled until we could do it in our sleep. Chill set up on our living tripod.

He aimed lower than I'd expected and started counting under his breath. "Lumbar five, four, three, two...," moving the rifle up the height of a vertebra with each number.

We exhaled, and squeezed out the small concussion of the shot. Sam toppled into the ravine. The buck leapt and swerved away. The crossbow clattered down the rocks, harmlessly releasing its bolt with a shuddering hiss. We approached. Sam looked up at us, mouthing something. A red-black blot widened from a tiny round tear in the coveralls on his lower back. Chill stood over him and grinned, licking the hot muzzle of his rifle suggestively. Sam tried to pull himself up, but his legs were useless meat. Another, colorless, stain spread from the front of the coveralls.

Gabriel quietly knelt next to him. "You're paralyzed, aren't you, Sam?"

Sam's eyes were completely black. He didn't say anything.

Gabriel touched Sam's forehead. "That would be a terrible way to die, wouldn't it... to be out here alone, waiting..."

Sam's eyes started to roll.

Gabriel opened his canteen and poured water on Sam's face. "You needed to die in that fall, didn't you? Wouldn't that be a better, more merciful thing?"

Sam focused on Gabriel and put everything he had left into forming the word "Yes."

Gabriel adjusted his position. "Just relax, then..."

Almost tenderly, he smoothed Sam's coarse red-blond hair back until his hand rested at the back of his crown. He nestled the other palm carefully under his jaw, breathed evenly... and made a sharp, twisting snap, the sound of which I will carry to my grave.

...

Gabriel got up slowly. He turned away, closed his eyes, sighed in deep a couple of times and stood. Chill leaned on a rock to lower himself next to the crook-necked body, took out his knife and slashed the start of a rip in the chest of its coveralls and undershirt. He kept pulling on the tough fabric until the ragged hole exposed the pale, freckled skin over Sam's silent heart.

He looked up at the leaden sky. "Peace, Nana D'Arc. He's all yours. Call in your scavengers. No more Champettys left alive to infect your empire. You can rest easy—no more sick ghostfaces colonizing your bloodline. We're done. We can all go to bed now... Tell your coyotes and maggots to come wash us clean so we can sleep good and deep in the healing dirt."

He cut a small "x" in the flesh at the center of the torn opening and murmured it was a shame it was too cold for flies. He wafted his hand over the cooling red trickle pooling in the cut to spread the scent. He put his fingers in his mouth and whistled like he was calling something, and then made a quiet, high-pitched, tight laugh that made my back prickle. Gabriel said it was time to go. Chill looked blankly at him with a half-grin fading from his face.

Gabriel tucked himself under Chill's right arm and helped him to his feet. Chill slung his rifle around onto his back, took a last look down into the ravine, and then squared up between us for the hike to the logging road. My feet felt like they belonged to someone else, someone very old. Chill needed me to be his left leg, so I had to get over it. We could've gone the way we'd come; it would've been more level, but longer. Chill was struggling. The snow came heavier, and our feet slipped on the steep spots. Gabriel kept us in the right direction even with the heavy overcast. I had an idea of where to head, but even with GPS I wouldn't have been able to bring us out right by his truck the way he did, and Chill had insisted we keep it shut off. The icy wind whipped up. Powder-dry squalls were catching the slope of the ridge and roiling around.

Gabriel scooped up snow and wiped his hands together. "Hope to hell Sam washed his hands after skinning those rabbits."

Chill told him to cup his palms. He took his flask out of his jacket and poured in a splash. Gabriel wiped his hands down with the whiskey.

Chill patted Gabriel's back. "Sam wouldn't be stupid about something like that—he had rubbing alcohol and soap."

He leaned into the passenger's side of Gabriel's truck, put his rifle in the rack and tried to haul himself onto the bench seat. Gabriel pushed him farther in and then winced, held his still-healing shoulder, and asked me to drive. Chill dragged himself to the middle.

I got us turned around toward the low noonday sun, a paler spot in the gray sky. The road was a rutted track with young trees coming up in it. The snow was starting to build. The suspension creaked and the steering groaned. Chill got thrown into me or Gabriel every few yards. His leg was shaking but I didn't slow down; the road was slick enough I couldn't afford to lose momentum.

Chill grabbed at his tongue. "Why I did that, Ladyfriend-perthon?"

"Gun barrel was still pretty warm, huh?"

"Yep."

Gabriel looked over and said we needed to get back to the compound, pack up and make our goodbyes so we could get the hell out of Wyandot. I told him I was doing my best.

Chill lisped that we were making our elders uncomfortable.

I kept my eyes on my driving. "You are a sick fuck, Chill—but that was the most perverted thing I've ever seen, even from you."

"Then it wath worth it." He put his burned tongue out as if he wanted me to kiss it.

Gabriel said "Shut up, please—I need to locate my humanity before we get home."

Chill quit lisping. "Sorry—sniper's high. Haven't smooched the Devil's ring in a long time. Hits like a new drug—still hopped up on adrenaline and endorphins. If I rein it in you're gonna have to carry me."

He turned to me. "Apologizing in advance. When I come down I ain't gonna be pretty. Probably best if you let me keep my mouth shut."

I said no problem.

Gabriel asked how I was doing.

My hands were clamped to the wheel. "Numb, and trying to keep us from getting stuck out here for the windigo to find."

We got quiet. With the snow thick in the air it was plenty dark enough, and I was glad as hell it was the middle of the day.

•

ACKNOWLEDGEMENTS

It's rare that a publisher gives an author virtually complete artistic control over the presentation of the work, and for that gift of trust I am profoundly grateful to Corbett OToole of Reclamation Press, and to my editor there, Ibby Grace.

I want to thank the shifting membership of the East End Writer's group for their endless patience in the ongoing process of nurturing this book series to completion, particularly Paula Martinac and Lucy Turner, who between them have put in countless hours honing the edges of this work to whatever polish they have, and Kristie Linden, who has never failed to be supportive.

Lastly, I wouldn't be here to write these words if Grandfather Duncan Sings-Alone hadn't helped me across some deep water, and my spouse Suzanne hadn't pulled me out when I reached the other side.

Selene dePackh
www.neuropunk.xyz

Reclamation Press gives a platform to disabled writers.

This book is set in the serif font developed for Librerías Gandhi.
The Tipografia Gandhi project was initiated to design a family of fonts
specifically for ease of comprehension by a wide range of readers,
even if printed or displayed with less-than-optimal equipment.
It is available free at
www.tipografiagandhi.com.

Typesetting and design for cover and interior
are by the author under her working name
Asp in the Garden.
Interior illustrations utilize graphic elements from
Garry Killian's *Big Data* series.
Cover utilizes graphic elements from CruzineDesign and Go Media.
Ubuntu Monospace is the primary display font.
Additional fonts used:
Entra by WildType.design
Architect by Inspirationfeed
Radios in Motion by Typodermic

Made in the USA
Middletown, DE
18 November 2018